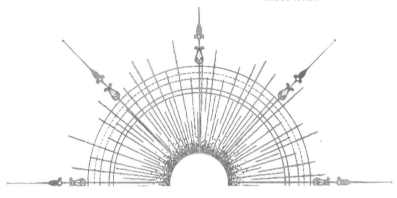

# OF WOLVES AND WARDENS

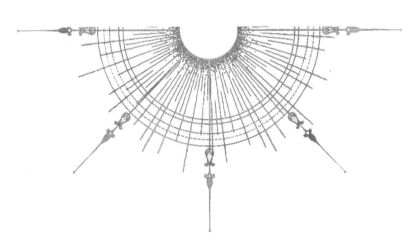

# OF WOLVES AND WARDENS

© 2021 by Sylvia Mercedes
Published by FireWyrm Books
www.SylviaMercedesBooks.com

All rights reserved. No part of this publication may be reproduced, stored in a retrieval system, or transmitted in any form or by any means—for example, electronic, photocopy, recording—without the prior, written permission of the publisher. The only exception is brief quotations in printed reviews.

This volume contains a work of fiction. Names, characters, incidents, and dialogues are products of the author's imagination and are not to be construed as real. Any resemblance to actual events or persons, living or dead, is entirely coincidental.

Cover design by Saint Jupiter

## ALSO BY SYLVIA MERCEDES

### Bride of the Shadow King
*Bride of the Shadow King*
*Vow of the Shadow King*
*Heart of the Shadow King*

### Of Candlelight and Shadows
*The Moonfire Bride*
*The Sunfire King*
*Of Wolves and Wardens*

### Prince of the Doomed City
*Entranced*
*Entangled*
*Ensorcelled*
*Enslaved*
*Enthralled*

### The Scarred Mage of Roseward
*Thief*
*Prisoner*
*Wraith*

### The Venatrix Chronicles
*Daughter of Shades*
*Visions of Fate*
*Paths of Malice*
*Dance of Souls*
*Tears of Dust*
*Queen of Poison*
*Crown of Nightmares*
*Song of Shadows*

See all books and learn more at
www.SylviaMercedesBooks.com

*This book is dedicated to Annika,
with many thanks for being our family's
personal angel during this crazy summer!*

# 1

## BRIELLE

I place my feet carefully, making certain to disturb neither leaf nor twig as I progress through the humming stillness of the forest. All around me I feel tension—in the air, in the ground, in the leaves interlaced over my head. It's as though the trees themselves are holding their breaths, waiting for me to pass by.

Trees are no fools, after all. They know a predator when it walks through their midst. They don't want to draw my attention or interfere with my hunt.

A smile curves my lips, small, bitter. Even a little cruel. No, who am I fooling? There was a time when I could have denied my natural bent for cruelty. But it's always been there. Deep inside me. Pulsing through my soul like poison in the veins.

And now—now that everything I ever loved is taken from me, gone—why shouldn't I indulge the truth of my nature?

I'm following a trail. Not a particularly difficult one. My quarry is either unaware of or simply unconcerned by my pursuit. It leaves clear indications of its progress everywhere it goes. It seems unsteady on its feet, bashing up against tree trunks and shrubs, leaving large tufts of reddish fur in its wake. Occasionally I spy an enormous pawprint with deep indentations where the claws dig into the soil. Almost like it left them on purpose. Just for me. Showing me the way.

I adjust the strap of my quiver across my breast. I've faced my fair share of foes over the last few years. Killed a couple of them too. I'm not afraid of a fight, not afraid of a little slavering, some claws, some teeth. I've spent my whole life in the company of monsters of one kind or another, and it's hardened me to my core.

But I've never been sent out to track, stalk, and kill a creature quite like this before. The thought makes my stomach knot uncomfortably.

With a growl, I shake my head and force that knotty feeling down deep where I can't feel it. It's not as though I have any choice, after all.

"Seven years," I whisper.

I don't belong to myself. Not anymore. I belong to Granny Dorrel, the ward witch of Virra County. For Granny saved my life . . . but only at a price. And that price was me. My obedience. My skills. All at her disposal. For seven long years.

I was unconscious at the time the bargain was made. Otherwise, I would have put up a fuss. Still, can I honestly say I would rather be dead now than indentured into my own grandmother's service? I'm not entirely sure . . .

My ears prick. There's a strange sound up ahead, a sound I can't quite place. Kind of like a growl, kind of like a high-pitched whine. But also distinctly—and horribly—like a woman's sob.

I shudder. I'm close now, though. Soon this whole sorry business will be behind me. My first hunt at Granny's command. There will be more hunts, of course. That's why Granny wanted me, after all—for my woodcraft and my archery skills. And Granny has more than a few problems in her life that could be simply solved by a well-placed arrow.

But this first hunt is the worst. Surely. Nothing can be quite so bad after this one.

I slip an arrow from my quiver and nock it in place. One eye on the ground to make certain I won't step wrong and give away my position, I creep through a stand of young fir trees and peer through interwoven branches into a clearing down at the bottom of a small incline. A quiet, peaceful scene appears before my vision, gently lit by dappled sunlight, and graced with a pool of crystalline water in the center of a swath of emerald-green grass. The pool reflects a clear patch of sky overhead. It's all just a little too perfect, a little too pure to be believed . . . but that's the sort of thing one finds in Whispering Wood. As long as you're not fool enough to actually *drink* from a pool like that, you should be fine.

A figure sits hunched over that water. Large, ungainly, covered all over in red and black fur. At first glance, I might easily mistake it for a wolverine. A second glance would quickly change my mind. No wolverine could possibly grow to such a size—at least as big as a small bear. Nor could it crouch like that with its overlong hind legs bent at a pair of knobby knees. Its forearms are too long as well, covered in fur, muscular, but relatively slender.

Its shaggy head with a long muzzle leans over the water, almost as if it peers at its own reflection. The still surface of the pool ripples with little drops. I realize with a sudden, sickening lurch in my gut that those drops are tears.

*Tears.*

Oh, gods on high, the creature is *crying*. Weeping as though its heart will break.

The sickness in my gut coils a little tighter, like a poisonous snake. It's for the best, I tell myself, and step softly out from among the firs. I take a stance, raising my arms, my bow. It's for the best that I put this beast out of its misery. Werebeasts are abominations. Unsightly, ungodly, never meant to walk in this world or any other. However it came by this curse (if it is a curse; I'm still not entirely certain on that score) the monster certainly will be better off dead.

It's a mercy, what I'm doing.

Not murder.

Mercy.

I draw my arrow, my right arm strong, my left wrist straight, my gaze focused true. Slowly I let out my breath, counting down from five. I take aim for the back of the skull.

And I stand there. Frozen.

*Come on.*

*Come on, do it.*

*Do it.*

My arm begins to shake.

Suddenly, the monster's head comes up. A loud, snuffling growl erupts from its nose and throat, as though it chokes on a sob. The bristles on the back of its neck rise.

Then it turns. Looks directly at me.

*Do it.*

I stare into those red eyes. Eyes glowing with a light of pure madness.

*Do it!*

But I can't loose my arrow.

With a roar, the monster lunges into motion. Its overlong forelimbs tear into the ground, propelling its strange, hunched-over body up the incline and straight at me. I have a split second in which to decide.

Biting out a curse, I drop my arrow, turn, and flee into the trees.

What a fool! What a fool, what a fool, what a thrice-cursed fool! The ground behind me reverberates with the pounding stride of that creature racing just at my heels. I can feel its hot breath panting through ravening teeth. Any moment, those teeth will close on the back of my neck, snap my spine, and shake my body until I'm nothing but a broken, lifeless pulp.

So much for my first hunt.

Instinct tells me the monster is leaping. I can almost feel its feet leaving the ground. Instinct also tells me to stretch out my right arm, to grab hold of the trunk of a nearby tree. To swing myself around it like a pole. My own momentum nearly yanks my arm from its socket, but the abruptness of the maneuver is just quick enough.

The werebeast surges past me into a thicket of gorse, spraying yellow petals and dark pricklers every which way as its claws tear into the dense growth.

I have time enough to gasp a huge breath.

Then I turn and run again. Maybe I can get enough distance between myself and the werebeast before it quite works itself free. Maybe I can still take a solid stance, slap another arrow into place, aim. I'm good under pressure. I can hit that monster square in the eye if I need to. I can still recover from this, I can—

"*Oof!*"

All the breath bursts from my lungs as I fall headlong and slam into the dirt. Gods blight it! Did that tree just stick a root up and trip me? Never trust the trees of Whispering Wood. Only the oaks are friendly to humans. All the rest? They're just looking out for themselves. If they see you as a threat, they'll take any and every opportunity to bring you down.

I scramble to right myself, my boots scrabbling in the dirt. My bow? Where is my bow? I must have flung it when I fell and now . . . there! Several feet away, caught in the branches of the same cursed tree that tripped me. Even now I see the branches lifting my weapon higher out of reach.

Behind me, the air fills with the *puff, puff, puff* of hot breath as the werebeast lurches after me. Cursing through my teeth, I reach for my boot and draw a knife. I roll, catch on my own quiver, and struggle to get into a seated position, knife upraised.

Then the werebeast is bearing down on me. I stare into those mad red eyes. Full of hatred. Full of bloodthirst. Full of revenge. A huge arm draws back, claws gleaming. I brace myself, try to angle my knife for defense, knowing all the while how futile it is.

That arm swings.

There's a dull thud of heavy bodies.

A blur of gray fur against red. A flash of teeth.

I sit back, blinking, my knife still upraised, my heart pounding. At first I can't make sense of what I'm seeing. Slowly my vision clarifies, and I see . . . *two* monsters. Gods above! *Two* of those awful horrors, locked in a vicious brawl. They tear with their teeth and swipe with their claws. Worse still, they rise up on their hind legs and swing at each other with movements that are altogether too human for comfort.

Parting, they circle each other like wrestlers, then lunge again, all teeth and fur and grasping arms. The red werebeast is nowhere near as large as the gray, its body not so muscular, its shoulders not so broad. It isn't long before the gray beast knocks the red off its feet, pinning it to the ground beneath its huge bulk.

I watch in open-mouthed horror as the gray werebeast roars

straight into the red monster's face. I half expect to see it tear into the fallen creature's jugular and rip it out.

Instead, the gray backs up. Still on all fours, it retreats, lifting its weight off the red werebeast's body. The red scrambles up into a crouch, panting and foaming, eyes rolling with dread. The gray, its haunches tensed for another spring, holds its gaze with steady ferocity. Then it opens his mouth and roars again.

A little whimper escapes the red werebeast's throat. It turns and, with a last glance my way, lopes off into the trees. Soon the ruddy fur vanishes among the green foliage.

Still panting, its ribcage expanding with each labored breath, the gray werebeast turns its wolfish head and looks directly at me. For an instant—an instant so brief, I almost miss it—I see that same flicker of hatred in his eyes that burned so bright in the red werebeast's gaze.

Then he speaks in a low, rumbling growl: "Are you all right?"

## 2

## DIRE

I'm a monster.

Lost in a tangle of flashing teeth, slashing claws, fur and sweat and always—*always*—blood.

The pulse of blood rushing in my veins.

The delicious stink of blood staining my opponent's fur.

The need for blood, thick and sweet on my tongue.

I pound the snarling red face in front of me, the force of my huge paw knocking the red werebeast off balance. *Dreg.* Her name is Dreg. I've known her for years. We aren't friends but have been fellow prisoners. Up until this morning.

This morning, when she was set free.

She staggers, regains her footing, and lunges at me. Though

she's smaller than me by nearly a head, her desperation propels her with tremendous force, slamming into my body. Her long arms wrap around me, claws tearing into the fur on my back. She tries to get her head under my chin, tries to get her jaws locked on my throat.

I throw her off. Her tail lashes wildly as she tries to catch her balance, but I'm too quick. I leap, catch her by the shoulders, and drive her into the dirt. She's pinned beneath me, her eyes hopeless and pulsing with red curse-glow.

*Dire!*

She doesn't speak with human words. She doesn't have to. She speaks in the language of beasts, a growling, guttural language spoken as much with the flick of an ear as with any sound.

*Dire, please!*

I stare down at her. At this creature who is like me. Cursed. Forsaken by the gods. A fellow monster. My breath comes in hot, panting gusts. Foam drips from my lips, my teeth, spattering in her fur.

Then, for an instant, her face seems to transform. As though peering through a hazy veil of reality, I see the truth of what she is beneath the curse. Not Dreg anymore. Just a young woman. A frightened young woman. Who never deserved any of this.

*Please, Dire!* she begs. *Let me kill her!*

Snarling, I back up, lifting my weight from Dreg's body. She scrambles into a crouch, and I flash my teeth in warning. Her gaze is so wild, so vicious, I can no longer discern any trace of her former humanity.

*Get out of here,* I growl. *You're free now. You no longer serve the witch. Get out of here while you can.*

She shakes her head, spraying droplets of blood and foam. Her eyes spark with madness, and . . . and are those tears? I hope not. Gods on high, how I hope not!

*You know it's a lie,* she says. *There is no freedom for us. She will send that one.* Dreg swings her head toward the young huntress lying beneath the hickory tree. *It's all the same for us in the end.*

She's right, of course. I know it as well as she does.

But I also know that killing this huntress will do no good. If she's dead, the witch will simply send another in her place. She always will.

*Go,* I repeat. *You don't have much time. Find a way to live away from here. Away from all this.*

She holds my gaze for a long, terrible moment. In her eyes, I see myself reflected—the great, gray bulk of me. Massive and hideous and terrible.

A whimper vibrating in her throat, Dreg rises and flees into the forest, hunched over on all fours. I watch her go until the red gleam of her coat disappears into the shadows. Someday, sooner rather than later, I will be fleeing too. And who will be sent to hunt me down then?

I swing my head around, focusing my gaze on the girl beneath the tree. She's propped on her elbows, staring at me, her mouth hanging open. There's a small cut on her cheek, a line of fresh red blood. My nostrils flare, breathing in the smell. Urgent instinct churns in my gut.

But I'm under orders. Orders I cannot help but obey.

"Are you all right?" I ask. The words are strange coming through my muzzle and teeth. But the day has progressed far enough that I can make myself understood with only some difficulty. A few hours earlier, only a series of growls would have emerged.

The girl blinks. Her teeth flash in a grimace. "You let it get away!"

I don't answer. Why should I? I sit heavily on my haunches and watch her pick herself up. She tosses a snarl of hair out of her flushed face, her fingers brushing the line of blood into an ugly smear across her cheek. She's a slender, angular thing, too thin for her frame. But every move she makes hints at hidden strength. A graceful strength not unlike that of a caged wildcat. And the glare she fixes on me is downright ferocious.

Not ferocious enough, however, to disguise her fear. That, she cannot hide. Fear rolls off her in a stink that my sensitive nose cannot mistake. She may posture all she likes, but her scent betrays her every time.

"You let it get away!" she snarls again, squaring off in front of me. Her fists clench as though ready to do battle. Foolish creature. Doesn't she know I could break her in half with a single swipe of my arm? "What were you *thinking?* You had it *right there.*"

My lip curls. "Dreg's murder is your task, little huntress, not mine. I'm merely charged with seeing that you don't die in the process."

Another burst of strong scent erupts from her, a stench of anger almost strong enough to overwhelm her fear. There are no words in human tongue to clearly describe the way that scent affects me. Humans simply don't deal in scented emotion, so they've never developed the language with which to express it. To me, it's almost as though the girl is suddenly surrounded in a raw, red aura.

"My dying or not is *my* business," she says. Though her smell is hot, her voice has gone cold, dark. "And I'll thank you to stay out of it next time."

I huff a stream of air through my nostrils. "Sorry to contradict you, Miss Dorrel, but your life isn't *your* business anymore. You swore your service to Granny Dorrel. Thus, your life is *her* business."

I watch the angry flush drain from her face, leaving behind a sickly pallor. Her eyes seem suddenly lost in dark hollows.

"Miss Normas," she says.

I flick an ear at her. "Pardon?"

"Miss *Normas*. Not *Dorrel*."

"You are Granny's granddaughter."

"Yeah, well, I might share her blood. Doesn't mean I have to share her name."

With that, the girl turns from me and stomps over to the old hickory tree under which she fell while fleeing Dreg. She viciously kicks the base of the trunk and, hands still clenched in fists, stares into the branches overhead. "How'd you like *that?*" she shouts. "Tripping a person midflight. Nasty trick to play, and what did I ever do to you? Now give me back my bow!"

I watch her, wondering. I've never known a human to be so

strangely comfortable within the bounds of Whispering Wood. I've lived in the shadows of the Wood for nearly twenty years now. But even I, beast that I am, infused with enough rotten magic to make even the fae wary of me, wouldn't dare speak to any of the forest trees with such audacity.

But the girl goes on bullying and haranguing that poor hickory until finally its branches rustle, and something drops at her feet. It's her bow. A sturdy recurve bow with a red grip.

When she picks it up, it falls into two pieces in her hands. The string hangs in limp strands.

"Thanks for nothing," the girl snaps and kicks the tree once more for good measure. Though her booted foot couldn't have done any real damage, the tree shudders, the roots just beneath the soil rippling uncomfortably. It seems to utter a faint sigh of relief when she turns and stomps away from it. I even see it draw one branch back as though to hit her . . . but decides better and settles down into stillness.

The girl inspects her broken weapon, pretending to ignore my presence. A foolish pretense. I can clearly smell her every sense prickling with awareness of me.

"You'll have to give up this hunt," I say. "You cannot bring down a werebeast without a weapon."

"You think?" She shoots me another one of those vicious glares. Then she heaves a frustrated sigh and bundles the broken ends of the bow together, leaning them across her shoulder. "Looks like it's back to Granny's for me. You can make yourself scarce. I'm not likely to need any more of your *protection.*" She spits the last word out bitterly.

I shrug. It's an odd movement in this bestial body of mine. But as the day progresses toward dusk, more and more of my human shape is returning, and with it, those unconscious human gestures. "My assignment is to watch over you."

Her lip curls. Many times in the past few weeks since she came to stay at the ward witch's house, I've thought she would make a fine wolf. A better wolf than me, in fact. Though, after nearly twenty years, I scarcely remember a time when I wasn't the beast I am now. Perhaps those long-ago hazy days were nothing more than a dream.

"Do as you please then," the girl says and, with a firm set to her jaw, stalks off into the forest.

"My *pleasure* has nothing to do with it," I mutter, falling into step behind her. I'm not entirely certain where she's going. The ward witch's house lies in the opposite direction of her current route. Then again, the girl never seems to move through Whispering Wood in the most straightforward manner but somehow always manages to arrive at her destination. It's strange how naturally she fits into this world, human though she is.

But then, she is Elorata Dorrel's granddaughter. A creature of magic and malice by nature.

Bile rises in my throat as I pad through the underbrush after the girl. Despite my best efforts, base animal instincts churn in my blood—instincts that tell me *prey* walks before me, her back to me. She ought to flee . . . and I ought to chase. It's the way things are, the way things will always be. I can almost feel the delight of my own massive feet tearing into the soil when I break into swift pursuit. I can feel the joy of the moment I knock her to the ground, pinning her beneath me, the warm sweetness of her blood on my tongue as I sink my teeth into the soft flesh of her neck. The crack of bone, the tear of muscle beneath my jaws.

It's what I'm meant for. It's what I was created to be. A beast of bloodlust.

But it wasn't always this way. And deep down—down where a man's heart still beats—I find the will to resist.

I shake my heavy head, forcing my wolf's gaze into submission and my human gaze to take dominance. Swimming into clarity before me comes a fresh image—the same girl, but as seen by a man, not a beast. A tall, slender, strong girl, undeniably womanly despite the aggression seething through every pore of her body. Her hair has fallen loose from the tight knot in which she habitually keeps it and tumbles in tangled waves down her back. Ribbons of bright red, like an autumnal forest.

My heart gives a strange thud in my breast.

But I know what this feeling is: hatred. Pure hatred. Hatred of this girl, this huntress. This witch's spawn.

My enemy.

# 3

## BRIELLE

The shortest way to Granny's house is by the Holly Path.

It's difficult to explain the paths of Whispering Wood to those who are unfamiliar with the rhythms of this place. They aren't *paths* in the normal sense of the term. They don't even lead through the forest. Not exactly. It's more like they *bypass* the forest. Allowing one to step just beyond the trees and move through a world of shadow and light, covering miles in mere moments.

They're extremely dangerous. But I don't mind that.

I marked a holly bush not far from where I found the red werebeast, knowing I would need it for my return journey. I retrace my steps that way now, perhaps not as quickly as I should. I don't relish the idea of facing Granny without her trophy in hand.

This is the first assignment she's given me since my term of service began. Failure will require a price. I don't know what price exactly. Possibly an extra day added to my seven years. Possibly something else entirely. But I will have to pay, of that I have no doubt.

Granny is not the forgiving sort.

Dire stalks behind me. He doesn't speak, thank the gods. I'm not sure I'll ever get used to the sound of a man's voice—however garbled and growling—emerging from that wolfish snout. Everything about him is unnatural and unsettling. The fact that he's been sent to watch over me doesn't make his presence any more welcome.

After all, he's tried to kill me twice already. One of those times just two weeks ago, when Valera and I came looking to Granny for help.

Valera...

The image of my sister's face as I last saw it fills the dark spaces of my mind. She bent over me where I lay prostrate in bed, nearly dead of a terrible curse, her face drawn with worry, scarred with heartache. Heartache that I had orchestrated. All with the best of intentions, of course. But with disastrous consequences.

Valera...

Where is she now? She left soon after bargaining with Granny to spare my life. That bargain was the only thing she could do to keep me alive. I know this. I do. And I'm determined not to resent her for it. But sometimes...

Well, she's gone now. Gone deeper into Whispering Wood and on to the strange worlds of Faerieland. She might be dead. Seven gods know she isn't prepared for everything the Wood and the fae will throw at her!

Either way, she's lost to me. Forever.

I grit my teeth, my grip on my broken bow tightening. I won't think about it. I won't think about her. I have my own life, my own troubles. I've got seven years of service to a witch ahead of me.

A witch who's determined to turn me into her personal executioner.

A flash of red berries through the greenery attracts my eye. The holly bush. Its shiny, pointed leaves and brilliantly colored fruit stand out in the shadows of this secluded glade. I cast a glance over my shoulder. Dire is still close, but I can't spy even a glimpse of gray fur. For so huge a beast, he can move with surprising stealth.

"Too bad it wasn't *his* head Granny sent me to fetch," I mutter, adjusting the set of my broken bow against my shoulder. If I ever get a clear shot at him, I don't think I'll hesitate.

I circle the holly bush three times. There's an art to opening the gates to the Hinter Realm. I'm not particularly accomplished at the skill, for I possess only the barest traces of magic. As Granny Dorrel's granddaughter, I was bound to have at least a small amount. Nothing like Valera's, but enough to feel the simmering magical energy in the atmosphere around me. Enough to reach out to it, to pull and manipulate it until the boundaries between realities open to me.

On my third turn around the holly bush, its shadow suddenly lengthens, shooting out in a dark line into the forest. The trees on either side of that shadow retreat, their roots rippling under the soil, creating a straight path through the growth. A path that will lead eventually to Granny's front gate. My ordinary sight still sees it as nothing more than a shadow. But a small piece of me sees something more—something sharp and solid. Something dense enough to walk upon.

I pause and cast a last glance over my shoulder. There's still no obvious sign of the werewolf. But I know he's there. Watching me.

"Are you coming?" I call. "The gate won't stay open long."

No response. Well, that's not a surprise. I don't think Dire likes to use the Hinter Paths, preferring instead to make his own way through the depths of Whispering Wood, following trails he sniffs out as he goes. It's not as fast or efficient, but he makes it work. He's never far behind me, that's for sure.

"Suit yourself," I shrug, and step onto the path.

I've used the Hinter Paths for years now. I first learned the secret almost accidentally as a child, not long after the wicked fae came and stole Valera away from me. I've always been drawn to Whispering Wood, but after that terrible night, I plunged into its depths with wild abandon, desperate to find and rescue her. It wasn't long before I stumbled on my first path and experienced the terror of the Hinter Realm firsthand.

It's not a terror one gets over. No matter how many times one experiences it.

I feel it there now, raw, eager to take hold of me. But I ignore the sensation and stride on down that shadow-path. All around me, the world feels, on the surface at least, very much like the forest I just left behind. Green growth and flashes of golden sunlight illuminate a leaf-strewn floor. But that's not what's real.

What's real is the space just beyond that immediate impression. The huge, rolling, vast space extending on all sides to an endless horizon, all lit by an eerie silver glow. There are things in that space. Huge things, lumbering things. Things that don't bear describing. Things that should never be looked at directly.

That realm—the Hinter, in all its vast, unknowable enigma—is far more real than the forest. But I cling to my false impressions with everything I have. They are the only shield between me and madness. Best to keep my eyes focused straight forward, fixed on the goal ahead.

Finally, the shadow-path ends in a great tangle of holly bushes. I breathe out a sigh of relief. I'm close to Granny's house now. At that thought, however, my relief melts away, leaving behind a twisting unease in my gut. Seven gods above, I'd almost rather run stark raving mad into the Hinter than face that woman and admit my failure!

But she saved my life. I owe her my service. I can't disobey her no matter how I might wish to.

I get down on my hands and knees and crawl through the tangle of holly. The sharp leaves scrape at every bit of exposed skin, and the branches catch at my quiver and my broken bow. I push on through and tumble out into proper forest, leaving behind the strangeness of the Hinter. It's hard to measure time in a place like Whispering Wood, but when I glance at the sky just visible through the branches overhead, I estimate that my return journey took less than an hour.

Brushing myself off, I march through a final stand of trees and arrive at a stone wall, twelve feet high and covered all over with dark green moss, as though it's become a natural part of the landscape. Indeed, it's so well camouflaged, one might almost miss it entirely were it not for the huge iron gate. Iron does not belong in a place like Whispering Wood. It's abhorrent to the fae folk and the denizens of Faerieland. Only a witch as powerful as Granny Dorrel would dare bring so much iron this far into the boundaries of the Wood.

But Granny has made numerous enemies over the years. She needs a little extra protection. And what with the iron gates and the many curses and enchantments lacing each stone of the wall, she's made a veritable fortress for herself. I can't imagine anyone, fae, monster, or human, being foolish enough to attack it.

I step up to the gate and rattle the end of my broken bow against the bars. They sing out a sour sort of tune, and I add my voice to the dissonance. "Granny! Granny Dorrel! It's me!"

No answer.

I wait, the last echo of iron ringing in my ears. After a minute, I step closer and peer through the bars, trying to make sense of the landscape on the other side. I've lived in Granny's house for two weeks now, recovering from the injury that first put me at the old witch's mercy. During that time, I've yet to get a solid impression of anything beyond the gate. Granny layers everything in coats of glamour and enchantment, but her magic only goes so far. Generally the glamours are only vivid in the space Granny herself occupies. The rest is left a formless sort of nothingness. If you try to focus a little harder, try to see the reality underneath, you'll only end up with a pounding headache.

I feel a headache coming on now. Growling, I turn my back on the gate, lean my shoulders against the bars, and stare off into the surrounding forest. Its greenery is a relief to my strained eyes, and slowly the tension in my head reduces.

Suddenly, I become aware of another presence nearby. *Dire.*

He may not have used the Hinter Path, but he's not been slow navigating the Wood. I don't know how he does it. I consider myself something of an expert tracker, but if I tried to make my way on my own through those green depths, I would soon be hopelessly lost. Whispering Wood is not friendly to humans. Apparently, it doesn't try its tricks on a werewolf.

"Where is it?"

I start at the sound of that voice and whirl about. Granny stands just on the other side of the gate.

I'm not sure I'll ever truly adjust to the sight of my own grandmother. She goes by her witch's title, *Granny,* because of her age and experience, her place of standing among the other ward witches of the kingdom. Unless I'm much mistaken, she's over a hundred years old by now.

But no one looking at her would ever think so. Not when faced with that tall, upright, statuesque figure, that perfectly regal face with its chiseled cheekbones and exquisite jaw set atop a long, swanlike neck. There isn't a trace of gray in the bounty of her glorious red hair, which she keeps piled atop her head in an elaborate arrangement of curls, fixed with gold combs that give the impression of a crown.

Indeed, at first glance, she doesn't look any older than my nineteen years. With our similarly colored hair one might almost mistake us for sisters. But in truth, the hair is where the similarities end. Where she is pristine and delicate, her complexion a perfect cream, I am rough, tanned, and freckled. My features favor my father, who is handsome enough in his way, but doesn't hold a candle to my grandmother's ethereal beauty.

Whether or not that beauty has any truth to it however . . . that I cannot say. Granny is always swathed in so many glamours, who knows what the truth underneath might be?

"Well, girl?" Her clear blue eyes run slowly up and down my body, noting all the stains and tears in my clothes, the scratches on every bit of exposed skin. They come to rest on my broken bow for some moments before finally returning to my face. "The head. Where is the werebeast's head?"

"I don't have it."

Granny's full lips curl in a beautiful sneer. "I was clear in my instructions, was I not? *Bring me its head,* I said. I could not have spoken more plainly."

I clear my throat, adjusting my stance slightly. "I ran into problems. We had a bit of a . . . a chase. And I fell on the wrong side of a hickory tree." I hold up my broken bow as evidence of my words. "Since I can't very well take down a monster without a weapon, I'll have to go out again tomor—"

The growl in Granny's throat sounds frighteningly like a werebeast's. She steps back, utters a sharp word of command in a language I do not know, and gestures with one arm. The gate shivers and responds, swinging open with an ear-splitting creak. Before I can do more than take a backward step, Granny reaches out, catches me by the wrist, and drags me through. "Get inside," she says, pushing me several paces into the nothingness of her little domain. "I should have known better than to bargain with that fool sister of yours! Your father's blood is too thick in your veins. He was just as useless as you."

Her words sting more than I like to admit. Worse still, they call vividly to mind another face from my past—a face I don't like to remember. *Father.* Far away, beyond the reach of Whispering Wood. He'll be alone now in the little cottage I rented for the two of us these last few years. How will he make the rent now that I'm not there to provide for him? He won't. That's the truth of it. He'll be kicked out, left to rot in a ditch somewhere, stinking of drink and bitterness. With both daughters gone, there's no one left to pick him up and nurse him along.

Not that it will make much difference. Granny placed a powerful curse on him for stealing away and marrying her only daughter, a curse that includes long life so that he will suffer for many, many more years. He'll survive. Somehow. Alone and miserable in his fetid existence.

I shudder. Funny—if anyone asked, I would insist I have no love for my father left in me. I would say he beat it out of me ages ago. But the truth is, my heart hurts at the thought of him. Of the ongoing misery he will endure.

Seven gods, I'm getting as soft as Valera!

Granny secures the iron gate with another word of command, then takes a moment to step up to the bars. "Dire!" she calls out, her erstwhile lovely, moderate tones unexpectedly shrill. "I know you're out there. Clean yourself up and report back here in an hour. I've a guest tonight, and I require you to serve at dinner."

I raise an eyebrow. Granny wants a werewolf to play butler this evening? And who is she hosting? Granny is not exactly a social creature. Perhaps one of the other ward witches is coming to call. Someone who won't be offended by a werewolf waiter, anyway.

I pull my expression back into studied indifference as my grandmother turns to me. Her mouth is pursed in disgust, yet somehow she still manages to look beautiful. "Get inside," she says. "I'll put out something decent for you to wear. Wash your face and present yourself in the dining room. You're *my* granddaughter, remember, whatever else you might be. Try not to disgrace me."

It's as good as a command. I turn, for once eager to obey, and hasten across the murky landscape hidden behind Granny's stone wall. The door to her house manifests as though out of thin air and opens as I approach it, revealing a small, cramped hallway. The last time I passed this way, it was a large, grand foyer . . . but that was in company with Granny, which makes all the difference.

My bedroom, at least, holds onto some of its glamours even without Granny's presence. Not that I find it particularly comforting. Everything about this room is simply *wrong* for me, from the rose-colored counterpane to the ornate scrollwork furnishings to the huge, gold-framed mirror dominating one wall. If I didn't know any better, I'd think Granny glamorized it on purpose to make me as uncomfortable as possible.

Actually, I take it back. I'm quite sure that's *exactly* what she did.

The real question is *how?* How does Granny manage such elaborate glamours, layer upon layer? Both on herself and on her home? That kind of magic requires a source of power. Granny isn't fae, after all; no natural magic flows in her veins. The power must *come* from somewhere, some source that continues to feed her.

And if there's a source, that might also mean . . . a weakness . . .

With a growl, I toss my broken bow into a corner of the room and slam the bedroom door behind me. There's no point indulging thoughts like this. My service is sworn to Granny Dorrel. I must honor that vow, like it or not.

I stride across the room to the delicate cherrywood washstand, pour water from the pitcher into the matching porcelain basin painted with a series of vapid, dancing maidens. I set to work, scrubbing my face and hair with a bar of lilac-scented soap, and when I'm through, reach for a fluffy towel, turning as I mop off my face.

My eyebrows rise in surprise. Somehow, a gown has magically

manifested on the bed behind me. It certainly wasn't there before. I would have noticed something quite so . . . so very *purple*.

It's not that it's an ugly gown. In fact, the cut and style are simple enough, I might not put up much fuss being asked to wear it under ordinary circumstances. The bodice is billowy and loose and looks comfortable, and there's a brown outer vest that cinches the waist and keeps the gown from being too blousy. The fabric, when I slide it through my fingers, isn't one of Granny's glamorized silks or satins; it's a simple muslin with a strong weave. It might even be real.

Who did a gown like this once belong to? My mother, from back when she used to live here? Or . . .

A frown knots my brow as I pick the gown up and hold it close to my nose. There's a scent here that I almost recognize. A faint scent, barely a memory of perfume. But definitely familiar. Now, who does it make me think of? Not Mother, for sure. Not Valera either.

I pull the dress back and glare down at it in my hands. "You've got to be kidding me," I whisper. Because it smells something like the red werebeast I hunted today. The werebeast who had, presumably, once been human.

Did this gown belong to her?

I close my eyes and see again the image of that monster crouched over the pool. Weeping. Tears falling from its face.

*"Bring me its head,"* Granny had said.

I failed my mission today. Tomorrow, I'll have to try again. And again. The terms of my service mean I'll have to keep trying until

I succeed. Or until the werebeast kills me. Whichever comes first.

Knees trembling, I sink onto the edge of the bed, letting the dress fall from my fingers to the floor. I bury my face in my hands. But I won't cry. I won't! I'm not one of those silly damsels, all fair and feeble and fainting. This is my life and, like it or not, I'll manage. Just like I've always managed in the past. But if it were up to me . . .

I lift my head and stare up at the ceiling, breathing out a long sigh. If it were up to me, I'd simply walk out of here, find that red werebeast, hold out my arms . . . and let her savage teeth and claws do their worst.

# 4

## DIRE

I stand before the witch's iron gate wearing nothing but a bit of rag about my loins. As twilight deepens, the gray fur that usually covers my limbs has retreated to almost nothing. Tufts cling to my shoulders, neck, and the backs of my hands, but in another few minutes they will vanish too, and I will, for the next hour at least, look fully human.

But when the hour is up, the beast will start to return. By the stroke of midnight, I will be completely lost in its form. A beast in mind as well as body, with no knowledge of who I am. That too will fade, however, and as the hours creep on toward dawn, the beast will retreat, and the man will reassert itself. Then, in the pink and gold light of the new day, I will once more know my true shape, my true self.

I look down at my body—my real body. The torso, arms, and legs with which I was born. Though I've been under this curse for twenty years, I've not aged significantly since the day the curse first fell. I don't quite understand it. The best explanation I have is that time only affects this body when it is fully human. Which means I only age two hours out of every twenty-four.

Strange, to have lived so much life without ever actually living it.

I sense movement in the murky nothing beyond the gate bars. Quickly, I draw myself to attention, making certain my face is blank, betraying nothing. Not that it will fool my mistress. She knows me too well by now. But it's part of the game I play with myself, the game of trying to hold onto my self-respect, my dignity. The minute I lose that game, I will lose everything. Dawn or dusk will no longer matter—I'll be a beast through and through.

The murkiness parts like a curtain, and the witch manifests before my eyes. She is, as always, a vision—a beautiful temptress clad in forest green that brings out the porcelain of her complexion and the vivid hues of her hair. The gown is wide at the neck and plunging, showing to advantage the perfection of her figure.

Elorata Dorrel is, by far, the most beautiful creature I've ever seen.

She was beautiful the first day I saw her. The day she tempted me into her embrace.

She was beautiful the day I fled her, realizing my error. Too late, too late . . .

And she was beautiful the day she turned on me with vengeance in her heart and curse magic at her fingertips.

She smiles at me now, that same winning smile that turns my blood to ice.

"Well, well, Dire," she says, purring the name she gave me. "You're as handsome as ever, though rather less formal than I require tonight."

Her gaze rakes over my naked body, approving and possessive. It makes my skin crawl. Elorata notices and laughs a single bright, bell-like note. Then she waves her hand, and glamour overwhelms me, wrapping my limbs. I close my eyes until the worst of it is over. When I look down at myself again, I'm clad in an elegant white uniform, complete with gold buttons running up the front of a perfectly fitted jacket.

"There," the witch says, tilting her head a little to one side and giving me another slow once-over. "You'll not disgrace me now, I think. Come! My guest has already arrived, and I hate to keep him waiting."

With another wave of her hand, she opens the iron gate. I have no choice but to step through at her beckoning. Rather than turn at once and lead the way to her house, Elorata stands where she is, waiting for me until I stand less than a foot from her. Then she reaches out and gently touches my cheek.

"Hmmm," she says, her eyes narrowing ever so slightly. "So rough. So unkempt. And yet, I find it suits you well. But tonight!"

She gently trails her fingers over my face. I feel the bushy growth of beard melting away until there's nothing but neat, trim hair left behind, smooth as though freshly oiled.

"Yes," Elorata says, running her fingers lightly over my lips. "Yes, I like that. It reminds me of when first we met."

There's enchantment in her voice. A lure, like a siren's song. It prickles my senses, and I feel the profound pull of it.

It doesn't matter. She's a powerful witch, undoubtedly; but no power of hers could ever force its way through the many layers of hatred I feel for this woman. I give my head the barest shake. All the enchantment vanishes, leaving behind a sour stink in the air. I meet her gaze, watch how her lovely face hardens.

She removes her hand and takes a step back. "You always were a dashing one, my Dire," she says, her eyes lidded. "Too bad the paths of our lives took the turns they did. But come! Let us not dwell upon the past. You have work to do tonight. Inside with you!"

She turns in a sweep of green velvet and sets off through her indistinct garden. I have no choice but to follow in her wake. Soon I find myself stepping into her house—this space that never feels quite real, quite fully formed. I hate it. I hate the stink of magic, which assaults even my dull human senses and makes my gut churn. I hate the glimpses of fabricated beauty in between the stretches of nothingness and blur.

There's only one room in this house that always feels solid. One room that I believe is real, truly real, not a figment of glamour and guise.

The Hall of Heads.

They line the walls on either side, their glass eyes gleaming, not quite lifelike. Many of them have been stuffed with their mouths open, displaying great white fangs. All are animal, and yet, not quite. Strange combinations—wolves, bears, wildcats, and deer blended with distinctly human qualities, making for a nightmarish whole. Some of them I recognize. Too many, in fact. Not friends, exactly. Fellow sufferers. Fellow slaves.

There's an empty plaque at the end of the left wall. A place for Dreg's head. She's escaped this gruesome fate today. But how long before she joins the others?

How long before I join them as well?

"Dire!"

Elorata's sharp voice brings me back to myself. I see her standing at the far end of the hall, holding a door open. She motions sharply with one arm, the long sleeve of her gown fluttering delicately. "Make haste."

I bow my head, trying not to look at the faces above me, but feeling their glass eyes following me as I shuffle by. It's a relief to step through the door into the chamber beyond.

Here I find the reason why most of the house is lost in murk and gloom. The vast majority of Granny Dorrel's powers are concentrated here, creating a grand, sumptuous space. The ceiling is high and set with an ostentatious chandelier, white wax candles dripping on a table long enough to seat at least twenty guests. The backs of the chairs are tall and ornately carved, the upholstered silk gleaming with shiny embroidery threads. Each place at the table is set with full sets of silver cutlery, gold-edged dinnerware, and crystal goblets. It's so much, so over the top. And yet somehow, utterly convincing.

Only one person sits at that great expanse of table. I cast him first one swift glance then another, longer look. The man couldn't be more unsuited to this setting if he tried. A great bulk of a fellow—not fat, but extremely broad and muscular. He wears leather armor that exposes bare arms boasting enormous, corded muscles and intricate tattoos from wrist to shoulder. His hair is long, black, and loose, and his beard is equally thick and dark. One eye gleams bright and quick with a savage sort of intelligence. The other is gone, the empty socket hidden behind a patch that does not fully cover the scar across his cheek and forehead.

I've never seen this man before. Never smelled him either, but something about him—something that my repressed wolfish senses detect, perhaps—feels *wrong*. Dangerous and wrong. Looking at him, meeting that one-eyed gaze, I can't help feeling as though I'm facing down an apex predator, more dangerous even than I.

A low growl rumbles in my throat.

"Dire!" Elorata's voice startles me, making me jump and look sideways at her. "Enough of that," she says and motions me to go stand by the wall, out of the way. I obey, glad the big man's attention has shifted from me to the witch. I take my place, glowering from beneath my knitted brow, and watch as the stranger rises and offers a stiff but courteous bow. More than I would have expected from a brute like him.

"Conrad! My dear, dear Conrad!" Elorata smiles brilliantly and holds out a hand to her guest, like a queen expecting to have her ring kissed.

He looks at it uneasily, takes and presses her fingers, then quickly lets go and puts both his hands behind his back. "At your service, ma'am," he says simply. His voice is tinged with an accent I don't recognize. Something thick and dark like the man himself.

Elorata offers a gracious, "Please, be seated," but the man has the good manners to wait until she has taken her own seat at the head of the table, draping her long green sleeves over the arms of a throne-like chair. "My granddaughter will be joining us soon," she says, with a twinkling smile that positively begs the man to question how one so young, so beautiful as she is could possibly have a granddaughter.

If he is surprised by this revelation, the hulking Conrad offers no comment. His face is impossible to read behind the beard and eyepatch. He merely inclines his head a fraction and sits back in his seat, one fist resting on the table. Resting nearest to the silver knife, I note with interest. Is it intentional, or simply an unconscious choice born of a predator's instinct?

Elorata's smile falters somewhat before her guest's stony facade. But she rallies quickly and motions for me. "Sherry, Dire," she says briskly.

Glancing around, I discover a little table with a cut-glass decanter and tiny, jewel-twinkling cups just to my left. I'm fairly certain it wasn't there a moment ago. Silently, I sidle over to it.

Magic emanates from the walls and floor all around me—magic Elorata has implanted using secret runes and called to life tonight in order to put on this fine display. I don't pretend to know much about witch's magic, but I do know that such runes can only be used once. After they're gone, they will need to be redrawn if she hopes to recreate this same effect.

I also know that the drawing of such runes requires tremendous strength. Strength of which Elorata seems to have an endless supply.

I pour the amber liquid into the delicate cups while Elorata continues to play the hostess. "How is business, dear Conrad?" she asks warmly. "I'm sure a man of your skill is always in great demand."

"Business is good," the man replies. I can feel his one eye on me as I set the glasses on a little tray. When I turn, I catch his gaze and watch his thick brow lower. I bend slightly at the waist and offer my tray, amused to watch the flash of uncertainty across his face as he takes in the delicate cups. This is a man intended for quaffing large quantities of hearty ale, not sipping at sherry. But he gamely selects a cup and sets it down beside his plate.

"Do you find yourself spending more and more time around these parts?" Elorata presses as I offer the second sherry glass to her. She plucks it from the tray and takes a dainty taste, all without looking at me.

Slowly, the big man shifts his gaze back to her. "More work up north."

"Ah, yes! Always more monsters to be had up in the northern counties, for sure. The wardens there are far too lax, and creatures from Eledria are constantly creeping through the Wood. Why, if I've told Mother Granchen once, I've told her a thousand times, she needs to strengthen her borders! But then, her rune work was always a bit slovenly."

She blinks across the table at Conrad. Realizing she requires an answer from him, he grunts. Which probably passes for eloquence in his part of the world.

My task complete, I return my tray to the little table and stand by the wall again. My heart pounds harder than before, and my blood is beginning to boil. I've realized who and what this man is. Part of me had suspected the instant I set eyes on him, but this conversation has only confirmed it.

He's a Monster Hunter.

Elorata Dorrel has hired a professional Monster Hunter. To hunt down Dreg. She's not going to risk the red werebeast getting away due to her granddaughter's incompetency.

I close my eyes . . . and I see again the moment I glimpsed through the foliage earlier today. The moment when the red-headed girl stepped out from among the firs, drew her bowstring, set her sights on her prey. And hesitated. I watched her face go pale, watched her hands begin to shake. I watched and I silently urged her, *Don't. Don't do it, girl. Don't.*

Like a miracle, she almost seemed to hear me . . .

The door opens. I turn sharply, my lips drawing back to show my teeth, an unconsciously feral gesture. Into the room steps a figure I don't know at first. I take a second glance, then a third, and only then do I recognize the girl. The huntress. Clad, not in her green tunic and trousers and tall boots as I've always seen her before.

She's wearing a gown. An actual gown. Not particularly well fitted, but distinctly feminine. She's a slight, bony thing, but this garment gives her shape that I'd scarcely realized was there before. The outer leather vest nips her trim waist, but the laces pull open slightly across her bosom, emphasizing her curves. The under blouse is too big, the wide neck tending to slip and fall off one shoulder. She pushes it roughly back into place, but it slips again, exposing a startling amount of pale skin.

I realize I'm staring. Hastily, I tear my gaze away, concentrating on my own two feet. Feet that, within the hour, will start to warp and enlarge, sprouting hair and claws until even magicked boots won't be able to contain them anymore. Not long now.

I feel eyes on me. Her eyes. The girl's.

I'm sure she recognizes me—we've met once or twice while I wore my human shape. What she makes of me clad in this elegant uniform I can't begin to guess.

I certainly don't look up.

"Ah, Brielle!" Elorata trills, extending a gracious hand her granddaughter's way. The girl makes no move to take it but stands there just inside the doorway. "Do come in, darling," her grandmother continues, motioning to a chair opposite the Monster Hunter, who rises and offers a stiff bow. "This is Conrad Torosson, a well-respected man in his field. He honors us tonight with his presence. Do show him a curtsy, there's a dear."

"I'm not curtsying, Granny," the girl growls.

Elorata's gaze sharpens, and her smile turns deadly. "I said *curtsy*, my dear."

From the tail of my eye, I watch the girl fight the command. Her fists clench, her back straightens, and I hear her suddenly labored breathing. But it's a useless battle.

She gives in at last and bobs at the knees, her hands holding out the folds of her skirt in an awkward flare. She's as badly suited to these kinds of social graces as the Monster Hunter. Maybe more so.

"Thank you," Elorata purrs, sitting back in her own seat, her smile easy and gracious. She points to the empty chair across from the Hunter. Her granddaughter obeys the unspoken command without protest, sinking into the seat and staring hard down at the empty bowl in front of her. "Now," the ward witch says, "let us eat! You've kept our guest waiting overlong, my sweetness, and I'm sure he is quite ravenous."

That's my cue.

I lurch into motion. A soup trolly has miraculously appeared where the sherry stand stood but a few moments ago. I push the trolly to the table and begin ladling soup into gilt-edged bowls painted with garlands of exotic flowers. This creamy, saffron-spiced soup is, in reality, nothing more than boiled turnip gruel. The bowls are made of wood, crudely shaped, and splintered on the edges. But Elorata's glamours are so strong, it's impossible to stop my mouth from watering. I'm not even sure my wolf nose would smell through magic this potent.

The witch and her two guests are totally silent as I make my way around the table. Brielle subtly leans away from me when I extend my arm to ladle her soup. As I bend, I catch a whiff of soap from her hair—a surprising sweetness that momentarily dislodges the enchanted spices in my nostrils.

Probably just another glamour. I give my head a quick shake and move on.

When I've served Elorata's bowl last of all, she waves me aside without a look. I hurry back to my place by the wall, trying to blend into the moldings. I may only have an hour in this form before the wolfishness returns, but seven gods spare me, it already feels like three! After this interminable stint as butler, it'll be a relief to flee back to the forest and patrol the perimeters of the witch's house until dawn.

"Do eat," Elorata says, smiling at her guests, who both study the numerous spoon options spread before them. Conrad finally selects the correct spoon, holding it all wrong as he struggles to get any soup into his mouth without dripping on the tablecloth. Brielle chooses a too-small dessert spoon but manages it with a little more dexterity. All the while, Elorata keeps up a steady stream of polite conversation that would not be out of place at any gentleman's manor house back in my old life. The whole scene is so incongruous, I almost find it amusing.

Suddenly, the ward witch sets down her spoon and delicately

dabs a napkin to her full red lips. Then she leans an elbow on the table and inclines her head toward the Monster Hunter, her eyelashes fluttering softly. "I'm sure you're wondering why I invited you here, dear Conrad."

He grunts and attempts another bite of soup.

"It's my granddaughter," Elorata continues. She cups her pretty chin in the palm of one hand. "She has the makings of a proper Monster Hunter in her, I do believe. But the actual . . . how shall I put this? The *brutality* of the task seems to be more than her maidenly sensibilities can stand."

"*What?*" Brielle drops her spoon with a clatter and glares at her grandmother. "Maidenly sensibilities be damned!"

"Watch your tongue, dear," her grandmother purrs, but there's an edge to her voice. I feel the spell going out from her, clamping the girl's jaw tightly shut.

Elorata turns back to Conrad, tilting one eyebrow fetchingly. "I've heard such wonderful things about your skills across the wardships. Mother Granchen spoke highly of you at the last coven. She claims you brought down a griffin that had gotten all the way through the barrier and was picking off cows and children from one of her villages. Such a noble endeavor! Worthy of heroes!"

Conrad makes no answer. He gives up on his spoon, reaches across the table to a basket of crusty bread, pulls off a chunk, and begins dipping it in the remnants of his soup, popping bites in his mouth.

The witch relentlessly pursues her course. "I wonder if I could convince you to give my granddaughter a little training."

Conrad swallows and wipes his mouth with the back of his hand. "For a price."

"Granny, I don't need training—"

Elorata flicks a hand, and the girl's jaw once more shuts fast. Her eyes blaze, and she digs the prettily scrolled handle of her spoon into the tabletop like a knife.

"What is your going rate for a werebeast head?" Elorata asks smoothly.

The Monster Hunter pauses, a bite of soggy bread partway to his mouth. "Werebeast?" One bushy eyebrow rises slightly. "Don't usually hunt werebeasts."

"Oh, come now, I don't believe that! A big strapping fellow like you? And what's a werebeast compared to a griffin? Quite a little bit of a nothing, I should imagine."

Conrad takes his bite, chews, swallows, then reaches for another.

Elorata puts out her hand and rests it feather-light on top of his. A gentle, ladylike gesture, but once again I sense the power in it even from where I stand by the wall. The formidable Conrad flashes her a wary look with his one good eye. His left hand twitches as though he's only just keeping from reaching for the knife at his belt.

"Will you make a deal?" says the witch.

Conrad glances Brielle's way, his gaze traveling over her. Her blouse has partially slipped from one shoulder again. Her face is a mask of fury. The Monster Hunter withdraws his hand from Elorata's grasp and clenches both fists on either side of his soup bowl. "You want me to train the girl?"

"Yes. Take her with you, let her see how it's done. And bring back the werebeast's head." Elorata smiles sweetly. "You'll find I'm more than generous."

Conrad nods slowly. Then he picks up the last of his bread, dunks it in his soup. "We eat. Then we talk," he says.

Sitting back in her chair, queenly and regal, the witch smiles beneficently. "An excellent plan. Dire! Serve the next course if you please."

I close my eyes, draw a long breath. I cannot resist her command for more than a second or two. But in that second, in that quiet space of darkness behind my eyelids, I see again Dreg's face. Covered in foam and blood. Her eyes wild with curse magic and desperation. A monster. Like me.

*Let me kill her, Dire!* she'd begged.

I open my eyes again, my gaze inexorably drawn to the girl at the table, sitting there with her eyes downcast. Her mouth is twisted in an expression I cannot quite name.

Should I have done it? Should I have let Dreg tear her apart? Could I have resisted the witch's command long enough to let it happen?

"Dire!" Elorata repeats sharply.

I lurch into motion, obeying my mistress's command.

# 5

## BRIELLE

I keep my eyes downcast, allowing the back-and-forth between Granny and her guest to carry on over my head. I don't really hear them. There's too much throbbing pain in my head. I know there isn't any point in pushing against Granny's hold over me; the binding of the service oath is too strong. And Granny is a canny old witch—she wouldn't allow for any loopholes in our agreement.

But I can't seem to help myself. I must push. I have to try. No matter how useless it is.

*Oh, Valera! What have you done to me?*

Hastily I suppress this thought. It's not my sister's fault. It's not! She was only trying to help, only trying to save me. But sometimes . . . oh, sometimes, I wish she'd just let me die!

The meal drags toward its end. Granny orders Dire to serve us all hot Vaalyun coffee out of little white-and-blue cups scarcely larger than bird's eggs, then dismisses him from the room. That's a relief at least. Though I took care not to look at him, I felt his eyes on me through most of this evening. He hates me. I'm sure of it. Hates me for what I'm being forced to do.

For what I will someday be forced to do to him.

I stare down at the steaming dark liquid in front of me, trying to make my eyes see through the glamour. I can almost, *almost* discern a plain wooden cup full of dark well water—but the effort makes me sick. I blink and let it go. The image reverts to the coffee, and my nostrils inhale its delectable aroma.

I won't drink it. I grip the arms of my chair hard, my knuckles turning white with effort.

"So, it's settled then," Granny says at last, setting her own coffee cup aside in its saucer and rising. She holds out a lily-white hand, her long velvet sleeve fluttering from her elbow. "You will take my granddaughter with you tomorrow. And you will bring me the werebeast's head."

The Monster Hunter stands. Watching him from beneath my eyelids, I see how he hesitates for half a breath before accepting my grandmother's hand. He's got some sense in him, at least. Sense enough to hesitate over shaking hands with a witch. But he doesn't want to offend her either, so he barely touches her fingertips before retracting his hand and taking a step back from the table.

Granny smiles. She knows exactly how nervous she makes the

powerful hunter. "Will you sleep here tonight, dear Conrad?" she asks, her voice rich and syrupy sweet. "We have plenty of room, and I'm sure I can make you . . . comfortable."

There's something in the way she speaks that last word that makes my skin crawl. For all I call her *Granny*, for all she is my mother's mother, her self-worn glamours are as powerful as any fae's. She is, in a word, stunning. Seductive. A true vision of both beauty and power, with all the allure of a siren's song.

How does this allure affect the big man in front of her? I watch his cheeks go pale beneath his black beard, and if I didn't know any better, I'd say there was a flash of fear in his one good eye. "I'll thank you, but no, ma'am." He takes another half step back. "I'd best be on my way. I'll report to your gates at dawn."

"Until dawn then," Granny says, and her expression is pleased, almost smug. She sweeps an arm toward the door. "Allow me to see you out."

I don't rise. My fingers tighten on the arms of my chair, as though I can somehow prevent Granny from speaking a command my way. Maybe it works. She doesn't acknowledge me at all but leaves me where I am as she guides Conrad from the room. The door shuts behind them.

I close my eyes and breathe out a long, long breath. "Oh gods!" I gasp, the words bursting from my lips as I lean forward, planting my elbows on the table and resting my head in my hands.

It was bad enough going on that hunt today. But I'd always known, or at least suspected, that I would find some way to *not* complete the task assigned me. This time, Granny has guaranteed success. One look at the mountainous Conrad, and I know he won't hesitate in the moment before the strike. The red werebeast may be a monster, but she's nothing, absolutely nothing, compared to that giant of a man with his tattoos and his scars and his massive presence.

And I'll be right there. Right in the center of the blood, the carnage.

Is this what I'm going to become over the next seven years? A mindless killing machine? Will I eventually grow hardened to it, no longer feel this sick churning in my gut at the prospect of the next day's hunt? And when the seven years are up . . . what will be left of *me*? Of my soul? Will there still be any trace of the Brielle I used to be? The Brielle my sister knew and loved?

I see it all before me, a dark, shadowy future. A future that extends far beyond seven measly years. When my term of service comes to an end, I won't be free. No one is ever truly free of Granny's service.

With a growl, I push back my chair and rise. The room has shifted around me since Granny left. Murky nothingness creeps in around the edges, though the glamour clings in places. The chandelier still hangs over the table, its candles sunk to mere nubs and trailing long tails of wax, but the cup of coffee is now definitely nothing more than a cup of water.

I pick it up and down the whole cup in a few gulps. What a relief to have something real to ingest! The liquid cools my thick throat, but pools uncomfortably in my gut. Somewhat nauseated, I toss the cup to the floor and make for the door. Best to return to my own rooms while I can. Granny rarely troubles me there, and more than anything, I need sleep.

I open the door, step out into the passage beyond. And stop.

Dire is there.

He still mostly wears a man's shape. Some of his uniform—no doubt a glamorized gift from Granny—has melted away, and fur pokes through at the elbows and shoulders. But he stands upright, a long, lean figure, not bulky, but obviously strong. His hair hangs to his shoulders, and it's as gray as his wolf's coat, though his face hardly looks over twenty-four or twenty-five. An unexpectedly neat beard frames his jaw and makes his cheekbones stand out more sharply above hollow cheeks. There's something undeniably feral about him. Feral and lethal and . . . and . . . attractive.

I shake that thought away and very nearly step back into the dining room and draw the door shut behind me. But what is the good in that? Besides, while he hasn't turned to look at me, I'm quite sure he's aware of my presence. I can't let him know how he unnerves me.

He's staring at something on the wall, his attention apparently riveted. I look to see what it is: a monster head. One of the many horrible trophies Granny likes to keep lining this particular hall. Not glamours, I've learned over time, but one of the few truly real things in this whole wretched house.

This particular head is perhaps a little less monstrous than the others. While most of them are hideous conglomerates of humans and predators—bear, wolves, weasels, and the like—this one is gentler. A weredeer, with soft brown eyes. Her features are mostly those of a deer, but with just a hint of humanity in them. One can see in a glance that, whoever she once was, she was a timid, shy, delicate thing.

I turn my gaze from her back to the monster below her. The way he looks at her . . . did he know her? Was she a slave here during his term of service? If so, it was before my time, for I have certainly never glimpsed her. Something about the look in his eye tells me she was more to him than just a fellow slave. She was important.

Why does that thought make my stomach knot a little tighter?

Seven gods save me, I don't like seeing him like this. I've only encountered him in this human form a few times, but somehow the sight always puts me ill at ease. I prefer him as a monster. At least then I know how I should feel in his presence: revulsion.

But seeing him like this, even with the wolf beginning to take over his shape, he seems so strangely *normal*. A *real* person deserving of my pity. Even compassion.

A shudder ripples down my spine. I've never seen the red werebeast in a state like this, but presumably she sometimes takes human form as well. And tomorrow, I'll have to . . .

*They're monsters!* I clench my jaw, close my eyes, and force my thoughts into proper alignment. *They're monsters. They might look human sometimes. But it doesn't matter. They shouldn't be, they shouldn't exist.*

Why can't I make myself fully believe it?

I've lingered too long, letting the moments get away from me. Dire still hasn't turned or acknowledged me, but he's more than aware of my presence, I'm sure. And he's standing between me and my room.

Best to brazen it out.

I tug my loose blouse sleeve back up onto my shoulder and start down the hall at an easy saunter. He doesn't turn, doesn't look, and I could probably go on by him without saying a word if I wanted. But something in me—some cursedly stupid part of me—makes me say with callus sarcasm, "Friend of yours?"

He turns.

The motion is so sudden, it's almost a blur. I don't have time to catch a breath, to put up my arms in defense before he's on me. Long fingers grip me by the shoulders, push me back five paces, and slam my back against the far wall. When he opens his mouth in a snarl, I see the flash of long, sharp canines.

But when I look into his eyes, I discover they are gray. Gray and ringed by long, dark lashes. Painfully human. Shimmering with tears.

I should fling off his hands. He's strong, but in this shape, he's not too strong for me. I could get my guard up, break his hold, shove him with everything I've got, creating enough distance between us to hurl a solid punch at his jaw.

Instead, I stand there. Staring into those eyes.

"Don't," he says in a human voice, even as a growl vibrates in his throat, "speak of her. Don't . . . don't . . ."

I become aware of his hands, trembling as he grips my shoulder.

My sleeve has slipped again, and the fingers of his right hand dig into bare flesh. Is that a hint of claws beginning to tear into me? I want to writhe, to squirm in his grasp. But I won't give him that satisfaction. And I won't break his gaze.

"Her name," he says, the words panting through his gritted teeth, "is . . . was . . . Misery. *No!*" He snarls, a purely animal sound. His shoulders hunch and his head bows, as though suddenly heavy on his neck. His hands squeeze even tighter, and now his arms are shaking. "Her name was . . . was . . . Misery. Misery. No, *no!* Her name! Her name . . ."

Quite suddenly he lets go and sinks to his knees in front of me. His hands hit the floor, his elbows bend, give, and he nearly falls flat on his face. I stare down at him, watching how his arms begin to reshape. I can almost see the bones breaking, warping, reknitting. The uniform has melted away still more, revealing the bare, muscled flesh of his back, and swiftly sprouting fur.

My mouth is dry, my heart throbbing. For some inexplicable reason, I want to reach out, to touch his head. To run my fingers through that long, soft hair of his before it becomes lost in the rough fur coat. I want to say something. Something gentle. Something comforting. Something to ease the pain that wracks him body and soul.

Seven gods, am I really going so soft?

I pull back, pressing my shoulders against the paneled wall. I feel the gaze of the deer-woman across from me. I can't quite tell if her glass eyes are watching me or focused on the broken creature in front of me. I only know that she, at least, wouldn't hesitate to offer this man whatever comfort she could.

I lick my dry lips and let out a shuddering breath. "I . . . Dire . . ."

His face comes up. I choke on a scream, pressing a fist hard into my open mouth. His muzzle has begun to protrude, and saliva drips from white fangs. Fur creeps from his beard up his cheeks to his forehead, and his eyes have transformed from gray to yellow with sharp dark pupils.

He opens his mouth, and an awful, growling voice emerges: *"My name is—"*

Whatever he might have said, it ends with a roar loud enough to shake me to the core. I cower back, my knees buckling, trying to make myself melt into the wall. But he turns from me and lunges with his strong back legs, stretches out his elongated forelimbs, and gallops down the hall. The eyes of the dead werebeasts seem to watch him until he reaches the end and vanishes from sight.

Whatever strength was left in my legs gives out. I sink to the floor and bury my head in my knees, cover my head with my arms. But I don't cry. I won't cry. Never again.

I simply sit there. For a long, long time.

## 6

## DIRE

The next day passes much as any other in the long years of my servitude. I undergo the waxing and waning of my monstrous self, enduring the hours of complete brutishness followed by the slow return of my human awareness.

As the day draws toward close, I stand guard at the witch's front gate. Elorata has acquired a fair number of enemies over the years, and it's not uncommon for one of them to attempt breaking through her defenses. None have ever gotten past me, but I have many a scar to show for the battles I have fought in her service.

Today is calm, however. Whispering Wood stands before me, green and lush, full of secrets, but not so menacing as I have known it to be. The secrets it hints at now are more subtle and sinister than overtly threatening. I have little to do, little to occupy my mind. Nothing to distract me from the unpleasant sensation of my own bones shifting beneath my skin, of fur thinning and giving way to bare flesh.

Some days the return of my human self is a relief. For an hour, at least, I can breathe and pretend at some form of normalcy. Today, however . . . today I wish I could hold onto my wolf self a little longer. I wish I could take refuge deep down beneath the animal, where feelings are dulled by the constant ebb and flow of instinct. It would be easier today.

At least until after the Monster Hunter has returned with his prize.

My nose twitches. Though it has already begun reshaping into a man's nose, it's sensitive enough to pick up the delicate scent of hyacinth approaching from behind me. Elorata. I'd know her perfume anywhere.

My hackles rise, and my clawed hands clench into fists. But I was commanded to stand guard at the gate. I cannot flee, no matter how I might wish to. I must stay put, smelling her approach, feeling the slight tremble in the ground as her soft footsteps make their way through the blurred nothing of her garden. Soon she stands just on the other side of the iron gate.

Her breath is low and soft in my ear.

"Well, my Dire," she says after a long, painful silence. "They should return soon. Another hunt come and gone."

A tremor runs down my spine. If only I could act upon the base impulses of my nature! If only I could turn, lunge against that gate, stretch my overlong arm between the bars, and catch the old witch by her perfect, white, swanlike neck. I could break it with a single twist. But deep sorcery ensnares my very bones, holding me rooted in place.

A featherlight touch runs down my arm. The fur is receding more quickly now, and I feel the delicate tracing of fingertips against my bare flesh. My skin burns in response. That touch moves from my arm to trail a scorching line across the breadth of my shoulders.

"Hmmm." Elorata's low voice is almost a croon. "It's such a shame how things turned out between us . . . Eadmund."

My breath catches. My throat closes up, and darkness briefly swarms the edges of my vision. That name! I know that name, I know it deep in my bones. Is it . . . could it be . . . *mine?*

It's all I can do to brace myself, to keep from sagging back against the iron, sagging into her wandering hand.

"Eadmund," she breathes again, letting the word linger across her tongue. "Eadmund, sweet Eadmund. How much we once meant to one another! How much more we may have been. And may be still, if only . . ."

I can't do much. I can't even take a step without her permission. I can do nothing but growl. Deep down, rumbling in my chest, like a threatening storm.

Elorata's hand, which had begun to travel down my spine, pauses. Then she withdraws, and I hear a soft curse behind me. "I'd rather hoped time would be enough to soften that hard heart of yours," she says. "But alas! Beneath all your sweetness, you are possessed of a powerful stubborn streak." Her footsteps retreat several paces. "Three months, Dire. Three months left until your term of service ends. You have until then to decide."

"I have decided, Mistress," I respond, my voice harsh enough to rend the very flesh from her bones. "I decided a long time ago."

She is silent behind me. I don't know what answer she will give, but I am prepared for it to be swift, cutting. Brutal. She holds all the power here, and she is more than happy to use that power for whatever ends she desires.

Before she decides on what form my punishment will take, however, a sound catches my ear. Footsteps approach through the undergrowth of Whispering Wood.

"They're here," I say.

"Ah!" Elorata breathes. The next moment, in response to some silent command, the gate swings open. She steps up to the gate arch, standing with her feet just on the verge of the boundary line. In the nearly twenty years I've served her, I've never seen the ward witch step outside the gates. I don't know if this is a self-chosen limit or something more.

What I do know is that her reach extends far, far beyond those encircling walls. Through servants and slaves, through whispers and rumors, through enchantments and curses, she manages her wardship like no other witch of her time. Well and truly has she earned the superior title *Granny*.

Another few moments and figures become visible through the trees—two figures, one huge and looming, the other slight. Both silent footed. The Hunter and the girl.

My breath quickens. For the next few moments, I still dare hope. Hope that Dreg somehow managed to elude them. Hope that she fled deep enough into Whispering Wood, possibly even into Faerieland itself, where a mortal like Conrad wouldn't dare to follow.

Then the Monster Hunter steps into the clear space between the forest and the witch's gate. And I see the heavy sack he carries in one hand. Blood seeps through the rough fibers.

*Let me kill her!* Dreg had begged me.

But it wouldn't have made a difference if I had. Elorata won't stand for one of her former slaves to live and potentially carry tales to her enemies . . .

Brielle emerges from the forest shadows in Conrad's wake. Her head is bowed, her hood pulled so low that not even a trace of red hair is visible. Her shoulders are straight, however, and she carries a new, unbroken bow. How much did she participate in the day's hunt? Was it her arrow that brought the red werebeast down? I sniff the air. My wolf nose would be able to detect the sour stink of guilt emanating from her pores. But I'm too close to manhood now. I can't tell for certain.

Conrad strides briskly to the gate and, without ceremony, drops the bloody sack at the witch's feet. "There," he says, the single word accompanied by his usual grunt.

Elorata kneels in a pool of silken skirts. She opens the sack, peers inside. Her full red mouth curves in a brutal smile. Tilting back her head, she lifts shining eyes to Conrad's face. "You are most efficient, dear sir!" She rises and extends her hand, as though yet again expecting the Hunter to take it and offer a salutary kiss.

He, however, takes a quick step back and crosses his arms. It's difficult to read anything of his expression behind that eyepatch and beard, but there's something there . . . something my fading wolf senses can *almost* smell. Something like *disgust*.

Never breaking her gaze with the Hunter, Elorata slips a hand into the depths of one sleeve and withdraws a small pouch heavy with coin. She tosses it in an arc, and the Hunter catches it with one hand. "Our bargain is then complete, Conrad," she says. "I thank the seven gods for your success and hope my granddaughter learned a valuable lesson while hunting at your side."

I glance again at the girl, standing a step or two behind the Hunter. Her head is still bowed, her hood hiding her face.

"Will you stay to supper?" Elorata asks in her perfect hostess voice.

But Conrad answers a little too hastily, "I will go," and turns on his heel. He takes a step, pauses, then tosses back over his shoulder, "Should you need me again, I'm easy enough to summon."

With those words and nothing more, he sidesteps around the girl and strides into Whispering Wood. The green boughs close in around him, and soon I no longer hear his heavy footsteps.

Elorata lets out a breath. I glance her way, surprised. Was she uneasy in Conrad's presence? I've never seen the ward witch uneasy around anyone. Her face betrays nothing, and that smile of hers remains firmly in place. "I trust you had a profitable afternoon, dear," she says, fixing her vivid blue eyes on her granddaughter.

"Yes, Granny," Brielle responds, barely above a whisper.

"Very good. You can tell me all about it at supper. Meanwhile, please take *this*"—the witch nudges the Hunter's sack with one foot—"inside."

A shudder crawls through the girl's body. But she's in motion almost before the witch finishes speaking, obedient to the command she cannot resist. She bends, picks up the sack. Is that a gag I hear from inside the shadow of her hood? She steps through the gate and into the murky space beyond.

"And darling?" Elorata says.

The girl pauses, just within my line of vision.

"I have a little task for you to perform tomorrow. I'm nearly out of my *tarathieli*, an important component of an upcoming spell. I need for you to replenish my supply."

Brielle looks back over her shoulder, and I get my first good glimpse of her face. Her eyes are raw and red, her cheeks deathly pale. But more than that, the look in her eye is enough to make my heart stop: Hatred. Pure hatred. A look that would slay if it could.

"It will mean a journey," Elorata continues, quite unperturbed. "To the Quisandoral's garden. Not a pleasant little jaunt, but I'm sure you're up for it. I'll give you the details at supper tonight."

"Yes, Granny," the girl says softly. She turns and continues into the gloom.

"You'll take Dire with you, of course. For security."

Once again, the girl pauses. Just for an instant. Her body is perfectly still.

Then, without a word, she marches on until she vanishes into the swirling nothingness of Elorata's glamoured garden, beyond my range of sight.

# 7

## BRIELLE

In the darkness I see that moment over and over again.

The Monster Hunter straddling the prone hump of red fur and splayed limbs.

Grasping the fur on top of the skull. Pulling the head back. Exposing the throat.

The plunge of his blade.

It was a quick death. Of that, at least, I have no doubt. Conrad knows his trade. The red werebeast never even knew we were coming.

But no . . . that's not true.

She knew.

She knew the so-called freedom Granny gave her wasn't freedom at all. It was a waiting period. Waiting for the death that was sure to come sooner rather than later.

I let out my breath in a stream of bubbles. Then, surging upward, my head breaks the surface of my bathwater, and I gasp in a lungful of air. With one hand I wipe water and soap from my eyes, blinking at my surroundings.

I'm back in my rose-and-white room. When I entered, I found a large bath basin pulled close to the flickering fire, filled to the brim with steaming water and flower-scented bubbles spilling over the sides. It was, like everything else in this room, a lie, of course. There might actually be a basin of some kind, but the water was probably tepid at best, and those bubbles? Knowing Granny, they were probably just scum and frog eggs, unstrained from the stagnant pond water used to fill the basin.

But I stripped out of my hunting clothes and entered the glamour gratefully. I sank down deep into the suds, letting the imagined heat and the nostril-stinging sweetness purge away the dirt and grime of the day.

Then I sank deeper still, plunging my head. And wished I could let this water cleanse my very soul.

Why am I so bothered about it all? It was just a monster. And I didn't even kill it! I stood by like a lousy lump and watched.

But that's just it.

I *stood by*.

And I *watched*.

Watched while Conrad took the unsuspecting creature down with a single shot straight through the heart. Watched while he strode swiftly forward and made sure of his kill by slitting her throat. Watched while he hacked that misshapen head from those muscular shoulders, watched while he deposited the trophy into his sack.

Only then did he look up and meet my eye.

He never once spoke to me throughout the day. Though he'd agreed to *train* me, apparently, in his mind, training meant allowing me to tag along in his footsteps. To be sure, I could learn a lot by simply observing him. Within five minutes of entering Whispering Wood, I realized he could have easily shaken me off and lost me without a second thought. I'm skilled at navigating the secrets of the Wood and its ways, but this man . . . he's something else entirely. So natural and at home in this perilous environment, one might almost think he was fae.

Maybe he is part fae. It can be difficult to judge sometimes.

While he maintained a stony silence, I directed him to the last place I'd seen the werebeast, all the way to the same hateful hickory tree that tripped me. From there, Conrad took the lead, pursuing the red werebeast's trail. Though several times I'd dared to hope the creature had lost us, the Monster Hunter was never baffled for long.

The end of the hunt had been inevitable.

Without breaking eye-contact with me, Conrad tied the sack fast. "This one's hard," he said.

The sound of his voice after so many long hours of silence startled me. I jumped like a frightened deer and only just stopped myself from scampering into the trees.

"This one . . ." Conrad shook his head slowly, his jaw working behind his beard. "Werebeasts are too close to people. Sometimes . . . sometimes it feels wrong." He finished tying the sack, then straightened and slung it over his shoulder, turning to face me straight on. "But the job's got to be done. By someone."

"Got to be done," I whisper now, my mouth close to the surface of the scented bathwater. My breath blows little flotillas of bubbles in eddies and ripples.

Then I close my eyes and sink back under the water. If only I could stay here in the warmth and the darkness. If only I could let my breath go and not surface for another. If only I could simply . . . cease.

But Granny has already assigned me a task for tomorrow. I must fulfill it. Like it or not.

But who knows? Maybe this Quisandoral—whatever it is—will kill me.

One can always hope.

The following morning, I shoulder my quiver and step out into Granny's murky garden, all blurry and gray in the light of the newly risen sun. I stomp through the indistinctness, making for the iron gate, which swings silently open at my approach.

No sign of Granny. But then, that's not surprising. She gave me all her instructions last night over dinner.

"The Quisandoral," she informed me between bites of illusioned meat pie that was probably just some old, boiled turnips, "is a demon. A First Age demon, so not particularly strong anymore. But full of ancient malice. You must go carefully if you wish to survive."

A demon. Great. I've faced a good number of monsters and menaces over the last eight years of my life as I plunged deeper and deeper into Whispering Wood. But a demon is a new one.

Lucky me.

I listened somewhat absently as Granny continued with a series of directions—how to find the demon, how to navigate its domain. What exactly I'm looking for. I nodded, grunted as necessary, and picked at the food in front of me until the old witch finally came to an end.

"Now you must be prompt," she concluded. "The witches of eight surrounding wardships are due to pay me a call tomorrow evening."

"Really?" This at last piqued my interest. I know that Granny is one of many established ward witches whose task it is to guard ordinary folk from the perils of Whispering Wood. I've met one other ward witch in my day, a grouchy old biddy by the name of Mother Ulla. And, of course, I knew the witches all communed with each other to some degree or another. But Granny Dorrel had always struck me as an independent sort—set apart from others of her kind, aloof as a distant queen. The idea of her playing hostess to the likes of Mother Ulla was . . . intriguing.

I wonder what Mother Ulla would think of my current little

arrangement with my grandmother.

"Listen to me," Granny said sharply, drawing my attention back to her. "You must pay attention. I need you to handle this job and return before sunset. *Before* the witches arrive. Do you understand me?"

She might have ended on a question, but I heard the command in her tone loud and clear. "Yes, Granny," I muttered, and shoveled a bite of meat pie into my mouth.

Granny hasn't bothered to see me off this morning. Which is a relief. It's a relief as well to step through the iron gate and leave the gloomy nothing of a garden behind me in exchange for the solid green and gold shadows of Whispering Wood. I close my eyes for a moment and breathe in deep. The subtle scents of the forest fill my senses—scents of rot and growth, death and renewal, darkness and sudden, bursting light. All underscored by a deeper, stronger, indescribable scent of *mystery*.

I love the Wood. I love it in a way I can't begin to explain. If it were up to me, I'd disappear into its depths right now, this very morning, and never look back, either at my own world or this wretched, tiny world of Granny's in which I've been ensnared. I would run and run and run until I had no breath left in me.

Maybe I would go searching for Valera. Maybe . . .

The sound of approaching footsteps brings me back to myself. I open my eyes in time to see Dire appear through the trees. He's fully human, and he's wearing . . . very little.

A hot flush rises in my cheeks. It shouldn't surprise me, of course. I know perfectly well that his slow transformation from wolf back to man doesn't bring with it accompanying clothing. He's only wearing what somehow managed to survive the night—a bit of cloth that might once have been a pair of trousers hanging loose from his hips. He's like a creature of the wild, his body honed to perfectly defined muscle and sinew, not bulky, but lean and powerful.

I shake my head and yank my gaze up to his face. Also lean and strong, the bones standing out a little too sharply beneath taut skin, his eyes and mouth framed by stern lines. Funny how even in his man's shape, the underlying image of the wolf remains.

"Well." I tilt my head to one side, hoping my tone betrays none of the nervous tension the sight of him sends rippling through my veins. "Are you ready for a little adventuring today?"

He growls. It's an animal sound, but somehow worse coming from a near-human throat. "I trust you know the way to . . . wherever it is we're going."

"I do."

He waits a moment as though to give me a chance to explain. When I offer nothing, however, he simply steps to one side and waves a hand, indicating for me to take the lead. I stride forward, plunging into the forest.

Granny told me last night that the Hinter Path would take us to the Quisandoral's garden. "It can only be reached by traveling the shadow of an owl in flight," she'd said.

Great. Finding an owl at dawn wouldn't be the simplest task. But I do have an idea.

"I don't suppose your sniffer is at top performance this time of day, is it?" I toss over my shoulder.

Dire, walking several paces behind me, grunts. "My . . . sniffer?" I glance back just in time to see his confused expression clear. "Oh, you mean my—no. No, it's not particularly strong at this hour, I'm afraid."

"No matter." I face forward again and push on, ducking beneath boughs and weaving through underbrush. "I know a likely spot."

I don't bother to explain. I don't think he's particularly interested anyway. This isn't his quest, after all. Just like last time, his job is simply to keep me alive. Like a gods-blighted babysitter. Not a job I envy, truth be told. Back in the day, back when Valera and I lived with our drunkard father in the old Normas family home, we had to scrape every spare coin together just to keep ourselves fed and clothed. Valera worked as a stitch-girl at a dressmaker's shop. I, still less fortunate, had the unpleasant task of watching other people's children . . . possibly the worst job any person could ever endure.

Well actually, I take that back. Hunting other people's monsters is infinitely worse.

At least I'm not going after a monster today. Granny needs an apple—one of the golden apples that grows from a tree in the center of the Quisandoral's garden. A *tarathieli* tree, it's called, one from a sacred arbor planted by the Goddess Elawynn back in the dawn of the worlds.

"Be certain it's the topmost apple from the topmost bough of the centermost tree," Granny had said last night. "Anything less, and the magic will be useless to me."

"Yes, Granny," I muttered then.

"Yes, Granny," I mutter again now as I trudge through the trees. I cast a sidelong glance back at the werewolf-man again, unexpectedly meeting his eye. My cheeks heat, and I face forward quickly. Which is stupid, really. Why should I care if he catches me looking at him? It wasn't as though I was *really* looking at him. A glance is hardly a look.

But I wish I could ask him about previous tasks he's performed for Granny. Ask what it's like to be Granny's slave year after year after year. Ask him if there's any hope of holding onto a small piece of personhood, of dignity. Of honor.

But what's the point? Though he might *look* like a person right now, already I can see signs of the change. His limbs are subtly lengthening, his face elongating, fur sprouting along his arms and shoulders.

He's not a person. He's a monster. One doesn't make conversation with a monster.

I press on silently, following an inkling of an idea. I know a place where an old hollow oak tree stands, scarred by the lightning that struck and killed it long ago. I found it back when I was still trying to make my way to Granny's house for the first time, before I'd discovered the secret of the holly path. I still vividly recall the uneasy feeling that had come over me at the sight of that poor dead tree. Oaks are friendly to humans, one of the few trees in Whispering Wood I could count on to not actively seek my harm. Seeing one dead and rotting like this had been a bit of a shock.

But I also remember the hollow opening far up the oak's trunk. It had struck me at the time as an excellent roosting place for an owl.

We arrive at the tree now. It had been a large, grand thing back in its day, the canopy of its branches casting such dark shadows that little undergrowth dared to creep in around its roots. Those shadows were gone now, the dead branches bare of leaves, but still the rest of the forest hasn't dared to encroach. Perhaps out of some sort of respect to the dead.

Shading my eyes, I peer up the side of the trunk to the hollow a good twelve feet up. I frown. There's something a little *odd* about that hole. Something I'd not noticed the last time I passed this way. A faint shimmering of magic, a *warping* of some kind.

Looking at the hollow now, I can't help feeling that it's somehow much bigger than it looks to the naked eye.

"Well," I say, lowering my hand and planting my fist on my hip. "Here we are then."

Dire steps to my side, crossing his arms over his bare chest. If he's curious, he doesn't show it. His expression, glimpsed in profile, is utterly unreadable. He's determined to make it through this day without speaking to me save when absolutely necessary . . . which is fine by me.

"Wait here," I tell him, even as I unsling my quiver and drop both it and my bow in a pile beside the werewolf. "I'll just be a moment."

He regards me from beneath faintly upraised brows. I resist the urge to roll my eyes at him and instead turn to the tree. It doesn't have any conveniently low boughs for me to climb, but the trunk has a gnarled tumor near its base, and the whole tree grows at such a severe tilt, I should be able to scramble up, fitting my fingers into cracks in the bark.

I approach the tree. There are strange things lying all around its base, dark lumps that I at first took for clumps of dirt. On closer inspection, they don't seem to be dirt at all, but clusters of . . . bone. And hair. And other strange things. Owl pellets? The smallest is about the size of a small cat. Which is not very encouraging.

I stop at the base of the trunk, considering. What kind of owl will I find up there? Or is it an owl at all?

I feel Dire's gaze on the back of my head. Not wanting him to see me hesitate, I scramble up the tumorous trunk and swiftly scale the twelve feet to the opening. Here, that sense of warping strangeness intensifies. But it's just a sense and doesn't seem to have any physical effect on me. Sometimes that's how magic is—present but not pertinent, as it were. I push on until I reach the lip of the hollow.

Slowly, cautiously, I raise my head. Peer inside.

There's something in there all right. Something huge.

It's an owl. Or rather . . . *not quite.*

My heart suddenly in my throat, I lower myself slowly. My hands are trembling so hard, I struggle to maintain my hold on the trunk as I inch my way back down. When my feet touch solid ground, it's all I can do not to turn and flee. Instead, I force myself to stand there, drawing deep breaths, taking care that my body language betrays nothing of the adrenaline suddenly coursing through my veins.

That owl . . . I don't know what it is, but it's definitely more than an owl. Will it serve my purpose? Will its shadow open the way to the demon's garden?

If I'm wise, I'll get out of here now. Find a different owl. There's got to be plenty of them in this forest, right? But it might take hours. Even now, I feel the compulsion of Granny's command wrapping around me like a snake. I'm to follow an owl shadow-path to the demon's garden and return by sundown. If I walk away from this opportunity, is that a contradiction of my orders? *Can I even walk away?*

I breathe out a long sigh through blustering lips. After all, if I'm going to die today, does it really matter whether it's by an owl-monster or a demon?

Setting my face into a hard mask, I begin to circle the tree. As I go, I reach out with my senses, grabbing at little pieces of magic in the air and pulling them to me. It's not much of a spell so far as spells go. Not *real* magic, at least not in the way I've always thought of magic with all its potions and runes and sigils and things. Still, I've had years of practice, so it doesn't take me long to gather what I need.

All the while, I feel Dire's cold gaze upon me.

I'm just looping the tree a third time when I happen to look up and catch his narrow-eyed stare. His eyes have turned from gray back to yellow, and his face is covered in a lot more fur than just his trim gray beard.

"What?" I demand.

"You're opening a Hinter Path," he says.

"That's about the shape of things, yes."

"Can we not simply *walk* to our destination?"

I give him a look. "Do you know a shortcut to this demon's garden?"

"The Quisandoral?"

"That's the one."

"No."

"Well, there's your answer then." I keep circling, gathering the motes of magic and stringing them together in a trailing line behind me. At least, that's one way to describe it. It's not like I can actually *feel* or *see* the magic. But I sense the effect. I've got enough gathered now; I could open the path—if the conditions are right.

I glance back at the werewolf again in time to see him shudder. He really hates walking the paths. I'd almost feel sorry for him. You know, if he wasn't a monster.

"You can stay behind if you're afraid," I say with a sneer.

He shoots me a withering stare. We both know perfectly well that Granny's command compels him to follow me, regardless of his feelings. He could be positively fainting with terror, and he would still have to tag along at my heels. My bitter, resentful protector.

I finish the final circle of the tree and come to a stop, gazing up to the hollow. I need to get the owl flying so I can catch the shadow and open the path. But if I climb the tree again while trying to hold onto this delicate bit of magic, it'll break to pieces in my hand.

I turn to Dire. "All right, big fellow. Time to put you to some use."

"I am already of use," he responds stiffly. He's got a tail again now. It lashes irritably behind him. "I'm watching over you. Seeing that no harm comes to you."

"Well, I'm not in any immediate trouble, am I?"

"Not so far as I can detect, but—"

"And I *will* be in trouble if I don't do what Granny asks of me, right?"

He doesn't respond.

"Right." I smile as though I've won a point, though I'm not altogether certain I have. "So, in the spirit of keeping me out of trouble, I need you to climb up there and wake the owl sleeping inside this old tree. Get it to fly out, will you?"

He sniffs the air delicately. He's beginning to form a muzzle, and the distortion of his face is unsettling. His lips curl, revealing a line of sharp teeth. "That's no owl."

"What is it then?"

"An owlkin."

I blink. Then I roll my eyes. "Sounds close enough to me." I pause a moment, however, my brow puckering. "So . . . what exactly *is* an owlkin?"

He looks at me, his yellow eyes glittering strangely. "It's a sort of woodland sprite—but not the good kind. By night, they look somewhat like large, winged men and women, and they prey upon travelers through the Wood. Come dawn, they vomit up the souls of their victims, after which they slowly revert back to a more natural owl state as a sort of disguise while they sleep."

Slowly, my gaze moves from Dire to travel around the clearing beneath the dead oak, looking at each of those awful, overlarge clumps. Pellets. Vomited souls? My stomach turns over. For a moment, I'm afraid I'll lose what little breakfast I managed to eat this morning.

Swallowing with an effort, I turn and face Dire again, offering him a determined smile. "It's daytime now. So presumably the creature sleeping up there *is* an owl, right?"

"It wears an owl form, yes," Dire agrees reluctantly. "But it's still not an *owl*. Not really."

"Close enough." I set my jaw. "And I still need you to make it fly."

He shakes his head heavily. I hear a low growl rumbling in his chest.

"Fine," I say with a shrug. "I'll do it myself then."

With that, I turn for the tree. There's no way I can climb up there, drive the sleeping thing inside into flight, and catch whatever path opens in its wake all while holding onto this handful of magic. But something tells me I won't have to.

I'm not wrong.

Before I've gone two paces, a huge hand lands on my shoulder. I bite back a triumphant grin. I knew his compulsion would force him to protect me, even if that means protecting me from my own rash decisions. Turning, I meet his gaze and raise one eyebrow.

He snarls. "Stand back, girl."

Tilting my head, I step to one side. The werewolf sighs enormously. With a last vicious look my way, he strides between the huge pellets and approaches the tree. I gather my quiver and bow, then stand at the ready on the edge of the clearing, my handful of magic upraised. Whichever way the owl flies, I'll have to dart into its shadow, drawing the gathered magic with me to open the path. I've never opened a path quite like this one. It's going to be tricky.

Dire scales the tree quickly, his enlarged hands, now tipped with claws, tearing into the brittle, dead bark. He reaches the hollow and, ears flattened, peers inside. I watch a shudder ripple down his spine just before he casts a look back at me over his shoulder. He shakes his head, his eyes wide.

"Go on!" I urge, motioning with one hand. "Go on, do it!"

Rolling his eyes heavenward, the werewolf faces the hollow again and leans into the dark opening. He reaches one arm inside.

The next moment, a shriek rips the quiet morning air.

Dire flies back from the opening, falling the whole twelve feet to the hard, root-gnarled ground below. In his human form, a fall like that may have done serious damage, and I'm not sure how much this larger, wolfish form protects him. I scarcely have time for a flash of worry, however, before all my attention is diverted to movement in the hollow.

The owlkin emerges.

Massive black feathers tipped with blue fan out to make the already enormous bird look bigger still. But it's more than a bird—I see that truth at once. Beneath the spread of its wings, two large, humanoid arms appear, gripping the ragged lip of the hole, talon nails tearing deep into the bark. Its four saucer-like eyes, stacked two atop each other, blink blindly out into the morning sun.

Then its flat head angles, catching the sound of the werewolf's labored breathing as Dire struggles to pick himself up. The owlkin crouches. I see those awful hands tense, the wings spreading, gathering for a lunge.

"Watch out!" I scream.

The owlkin descends like a bolt of lightning. Two taloned feet lash out, very nearly catching the werewolf by the chest. Dire rolls, and the talons tear into dirt and roots instead. Vast wings pulse and swoop, even as the unnatural arms reach out, bracing for balance. I catch a glimpse of the owlkin's body beneath the wings, weirdly manlike but covered with feathers.

Part of me wants to raise my bow and shoot an arrow over the creature's head, startling it into flight. But to do that, I'd have to drop the carefully accumulated magic, ending my chance of opening the path. But maybe . . .

*"Hey!"* I wave my free arm. *"Hey! Over here!"*

The owlkin's four blind eyes turn to me, the disk-shaped head swiveling.

I kneel, scoop up a stone, and fling it. My aim is good; the stone strikes the owlkin directly on the beak.

It screeches. Spreads its wings.

The next instant, it's lunging straight at me. And I'm frozen, like a stupid little mouse, watching those talons closing down on me—

Something large and muscular slams into me, knocking the breath from my lungs. I tumble, feel the *whoosh* of feathers and talons sweep over my head. Then I'm crushed beneath a huge body, and for a moment, I think the owlkin has pinned me, is about to tear into me with its razor beak, shredding the flesh from my bones. Instead, the musky scent of man and wolf fills my nostrils. It's not feathers I feel brushing against my cheek, but fur.

Dire pulls back. My spinning vision tries to make sense of his awful face. I see his jaw open, hear him roar, "There it goes!"

My limbs jolt. My path! I can't miss it!

"Get off me," I growl, pushing against his chest. He backs away, and I scramble into a kneeling position. I just see black wings disappearing into the trees, angling somehow so that the enormous body glides soundlessly through a space that should be far too small for it. Its shadow flits across the ground in its wake.

I draw back my arm and hurl the accumulated magic.

For a moment, there's nothing. Then—ah! Seven gods be praised, there it is! The shimmering distortion of reality that precedes the opening of a gate. The owlkin's long shadow spreads, spilling out in a long, narrow path leading into the trees. It won't stay open long.

"After it!" I cry, nearly falling on my face in my haste to get to my feet. Without looking to make certain Dire is with me, I stagger, stumble, catch my stride, and leap for the path. My foot comes down hard on the shadow, and I feel the moment of transition, the moment as I pass over.

Whispering Wood fades around me, and the strangeness of the Hinter closes in.

## 8

## DIRE

For a moment I cannot move.

I crouch in place, watching the girl as she leaps like a rabbit, making for that place where reality ripples just outside the edge of human vision. One moment she's there. The next . . . gone.

I don't want to go. I don't want to use one of those gods-blighted Hinter paths.

But Elorata's compulsion is on me. I *must* protect the girl. Like it or not.

Gnashing my teeth, I bolt forward, propelling myself with my overlong forelimbs. They're still mostly human shaped for now, but big enough to allow me to run swiftly on all fours. I lunge for that thin place between worlds, swirling, narrowing, closing. I leap.

My skin quivers with the sensation of a thousand hairline cuts as I plunge through that opening and come down hard on the shadow-path. I land awkwardly, my forelimbs slipping and splayed. My breath ratchets from my throat. I blink swimming eyes, try to make sense of this new reality.

The vastness of the Hinter overwhelms every thought, every feeling, every sense.

I shouldn't look. I should bury my face in my hands, block out that sight. But I can't help it. I stare out into that bigness that is only just visible on the edges of what otherwise looks simply like more green trees. But we're not in the Wood anymore. Not really. Those trees, they are merely an echo, a faint memory of the place from which we've come. It's that bigness that is real, that sweeping away into Forever. A Forever that calls to me, beckons me to plunge into utter madness.

I whimper like a puppy. And I hate myself for it. But I can't stop.

Cold fingers brush my shoulder, slinking through the thick fur growing there. Those same fingers move, trail up to my face, cover my eyes.

"It's easier if you don't look," Brielle says.

I try to speak. The only sound that emerges is another pathetic whimper.

"Shhhhhh." How strange her voice sounds, low and gentle. I would not have thought it possible coming from such a ferocious creature. "Come on then," she says, keeping her hand over my eyes. "Get up. Just shut your eyes and let me lead you. All right? It's really not so bad as all that, I promise."

Part of me wants to resist. I can hear that faint hint of derision underlying her words. I want to yank away, snarl, gnash my teeth at her. I want to pull myself up tall, looming over her, a figure of strength and might.

Instead, I let her help me to my feet. I sway, my stomach pitching with fear. The shadow on which I stand is so thin, so painfully thin! I feel as though it will melt away any second, leaving me to wander for all eternity in this huge emptiness between worlds.

I'm trembling so hard.

But then her touch moves from my face down to my shoulder and lower still, trailing down my arm until she reaches my hand. It's such a simple gesture . . . but also strange. Because she isn't really holding *my* hand. Not the hand that ought to be mine. What she holds is a monstrous thing, warped and twisted. Half animal, half human.

Her slim, strong fingers grip me fast, without hesitation, without trembling.

I . . . I don't know what to do.

I draw a breath. Then I squeeze her fingers back. Just a little.

"That's right," she says and begins to walk, leading me after her. I follow like a child, my huge, clawed feet uncertain at first, but slowly gaining confidence. The terror of the Hinter still surrounds me, but now I'm able to fix my awareness on a single distracting point—that sensation of her palm against my palm, her fingers twined with mine. It's like a small world. A world full of more courage and belonging than I've known in twenty long years . . .

I grit my teeth and very nearly wrench my hand from her grasp. What am I thinking? I'm not, that's the answer. I'm not thinking at all, I'm simply *feeling*. And that's no good. There's no room within a monstrous hide like mine for feeling. I learned that long ago. Best to suppress all feeling beneath animal instincts, focus on nothing more complex than day-to-day survival. Anything beyond that is useless. And dangerous.

"You know, I've been walking these paths since I was fourteen years old."

I jump slightly at the sound of her voice after what feels like a very long silence. Lifting my gaze from the path before my feet, I glance at the side of her face, that strangely delicate profile. Odd that I'd not noticed how soft her features truly are, the curve of her mouth, the roundness of her chin, the upturned tilt of her nose. Ordinarily, her ferocity masks all of this, giving an impression of hard lines and steel. The steel is still there even now. I'm not sure it could ever fully vanish. But for the first time, I think there might be something more as well.

"I'd heard about path-walking a year or two beforehand," she continues, her tone conversational. "I just wasn't able to figure out how to open one at first."

Is she trying to fill the silence for my sake? To calm my fear? I shake my head and almost tell her not to bother. We may be obliged to travel together, but that doesn't mean we need to chat.

Yet somehow, I hear my own growling voice saying, "What was

a human child like you doing, running around Whispering Wood, trying to open dangerous paths?"

She doesn't answer for a moment. Then, with a little shrug, "I was looking for my sister."

I wait. There's obviously some sort of story here. I can't tell from her tone if it's a story she wants to tell or not. So I simply wait.

"My sister was taken from me," she continues at last. There's an edge to her tone now. "When I was eleven years old. She was more like my mother in many ways, older than me by seven years. The fae came and stole her away to be a fae lord's bride. And I was left alone."

Strange . . . I'd never stopped to wonder about her. About her past. About who she was before she showed up on Elorata's doorstep. I've always assumed she was just another being like her grandmother. Vicious. Power hungry. Out for what she could get.

Her hand trembles in my grasp. I almost offer an encouraging squeeze. But what if she recoils from the gesture, withdraws her hand? So again, I wait.

"I was always intrigued by the Wood," she finally says. "I'd slip away to explore the outermost fringes whenever I had the chance, much to Valera's despair. She was quite certain the fae would come and steal me away one day! Neither of us . . . we never thought . . . we never believed *she* would be the one . . ."

Once more her voice trails away to nothing, and I'm left to wonder if her moment of vulnerability has passed. But then, she goes on.

"I was determined to find her. To rescue her. I spent years venturing deeper and deeper into the Wood, learning what I could, where I could, from whoever would teach me. Our local ward witch told me a little here and there. And I encountered travelers through the Wood who would sometimes bargain with me or play games in exchange for information." She laughs bitterly. "In retrospect, it's a wonder I didn't die a hundred times over, what with some of the risks I took! Maybe the gods were looking out for me."

I cast her another sidelong glance. Back before . . . before *everything*, I wouldn't have ventured into Whispering Wood on my own if my life depended on it. What an odd, madcap little creature she must have been, the despair of any caring sister.

She comes to a sudden stop. "Ah! Here we are." Her voice is brisk and hard edged again. "At least, here we are, *I think.*"

I growl with a questioning lilt.

"Well, I'm assuming this path we opened is the *right* path," she says, looking up at me, her brow slightly puckered. "Granny said the shadow of an owl in flight leads to the Quisandoral's Gate. I mean, it *should* work."

I sigh heavily. "I warned you that owlkins are not owls, necessarily."

"Yes, and I heard you just fine the first time," she answers with a sniff. "But we've come this far now, and I don't know about you, but I'm tired of this path already. We'd better try it than not. You ready?"

"Ready as I can be."

She readjusts her grip on my hand, tightening her fingers. The gesture is still so strange, it startles me, and I look down to see her white fingers enclosed in mine just in the same moment that she takes a lunging step, pulling me after her.

Then I don't have time to think or feel anything except the sensation of falling, plunging, and the enormity of empty space all around. A thrill of panic jolts through my soul. Have we taken the wrong step? Have we used the wrong gate? Are we falling into the vastness of the Hinter, hurtling into the void—

My shoulder hits something solid.

Now I'm rolling, my partially furry hide only just protecting me from the scrapes and tears of stones and jutting roots. The scent of greenery and dirt fills my nostrils. The tumble ends. I lie splayed out on my back, arms and legs outspread, staring up into a green canopy of leaves and dark branches.

We are, for better or worse, back in Whispering Wood.

I draw a long, shuddering breath into my lungs and let it out slowly. The air of this forest is not exactly *normal*; it's tainted with the magic that pervades every rock, tree, and creature. But compared to the Hinter, it tastes fresh and delicious and, most importantly, *real*.

I become aware of labored breathing beside me and turn my head. The girl is there, having landed on her stomach, facedown. She pulls her head up, her face half hidden by her green hood and bits of leaves and bracken clinging to her hair. She puts up a shaking hand, pushes her hood back, and I catch a glimpse of her eyes. Wide. White ringed. Just on the edge of frantic.

Interesting. So she was scared too, was she? I would never have guessed it. She'd set aside her own fears, put everything into making me feel safe on that path. Whatever else she is—huntress, murderess, witch's child—I've got to give her credit for courage.

She catches my eye. Her vulnerability vanishes in a single blink, replaced by the hard lines of the mask she usually wears. She pushes up onto her knees, gets unsteadily to her feet, and brushes off the front of her garments, every movement brisk and precise. She doesn't look at me again, but I can tell she's aware of my gaze. Lifting her chin, she looks around us. Her eyebrows rise slightly.

"Ah! That looks like the gate Granny described. Maybe owlkins and owls are close enough after all."

Groaning, I pull my limbs under me and get into a seated position, then twist my spine to look in the direction the girl is pointing. A ruinous wall rises unexpectedly from the forest floor. I can see places where more wall used to stand, but most of it has been consumed by earth, moss, and decay, the stones crumbled into the dust of ages. But just in front of Brielle is a gate arch, still standing, and the remnants of a gate itself, sagging from ancient hinges. It stands a good twenty feet high and must have been rather magnificent back in ancient days.

I sniff the air, my wolf senses rising swiftly now as the day progresses. There's a strange aroma around that gate, permeating those stones. Not a scent I can easily describe. Like . . . *menace*. Or *malice*. Something old, that's for sure. Old and crooked and *wrong*.

"This is not a good place," I say, getting to my feet. My forelimbs are long enough that with little bending I can plant my knuckles on the ground, but I stand up as straight as possible, holding onto what I can of my dignity.

"Yeah, well." Brielle shrugs. "It *is* the entrance to a demon's garden." She strings her bow, her fingers swift, her arms strong with practice, then slips an arrow from her quiver and nocks it at the ready. She casts me a swift glance. "Ready?"

I growl. I'm definitely *not* ready. Not for any of this. But my compulsion gives me no choice.

"Ready," I answer.

With a nod, the girl sets off, striding right up to the gate and stepping through the arch without an instant of hesitation. I hasten at her heels but can't help stopping for half a second to breathe in that strange scent. My skin crawls and my hackles rise.

Then, steeling my resolve, I lunge through the arch.

Immediately my nose is assaulted by hundreds, maybe thousands of scents. Layer upon layer, blocking out every other sensation. My eyes water, and a whimper ekes from my throat. Some of these scents are sweet, some spicy, some hot and intense. Some are nothing I have vocabulary to describe, and these are the strongest, the most intoxicating.

They are all of them deadly.

I stop short in my tracks, swaying heavily, blinded by the aromas. Gone is the freshness and earthiness of Whispering Wood. I'm lost in this labyrinth of smells, enough to drive me mad.

Then I catch a whiff of something grounding—a scent of pine

and leather and honey that I recognize. "Hey?" Brielle's voice finds its way through the throbbing in my head. I feel the brush of her hand through the fur of my shoulder. "Are you all right?"

I lean into that voice, that touch, that smell. My vision slowly begins to clarify, and the world around me swims into view. A world I had already inhaled with vivid detail—lush gardens, extending before me under moonlight so bright, so clear, it illuminates all in vivid detail. I can see the color of each individual flower, all the different hues of the rainbow and beyond, none of which should be visible by night. Flowering trees and shrubs and beds of low-creeping vines undulate across a gently rolling landscape. Dozens of walkways wind around pools, under arbors, into secret, sculpted hedgerows.

And everything, absolutely everything, is poisonous.

I take an involuntary step back, sucking in a sharp breath. Desperately I clap a hand to my nose, trying to block out the perfume, the stench.

"What is it?" Brielle turns from me out to the garden, her gaze quick and sharp. Dropping her hand from my shoulder, she raises her bow, as though expecting a demon to leap out slavering at us from behind a bush.

"It's . . . this place!" I gasp. My wolf-self surges inside me, wanting to take over, to dominate. It's a form of self-protection, for the animal me is better equipped to survive such a world. But I grasp hold of my humanity and hold on fast, struggling to make myself heard through growls and snarls. "Don't . . . touch . . . *anything.*"

Brielle gives me a look. "Why not?"

"Poison!" I gasp. "Everything is . . . *poison*."

Her lip curls and her eyes narrow as she takes in the placid loveliness spread before us. I can't tell if she believes me. Finally, she nods.

Suddenly exhausted, I sag, resting my weight on my hands. Hands that don't look much like hands anymore. "We shouldn't . . . be here," I manage through my strange, long jaw and rows of sharp teeth.

Brielle merely shrugs. "Granny needs that apple." She takes a step, pauses, then puts her shoulders back. "You coming or what?"

I shake my head. But when she continues, I have no choice but to follow her.

Three paths present themselves before us. One leads off toward a pond-side trail, one into an orchard of flowering fruit trees. The center path leads into a shrub-lined walkway that looks suspiciously like the entrance to a maze.

Brielle looks to the orchard, her brow puckered, considering. But she shakes her head. "Granny said the tree we need is at the center of the garden. And this way"—she nods to the shrub path—"looks most likely to lead us to the center."

It looks most likely to get us twisted around and lost forever. But she's not looking for confirmation from me. I merely grunt and repeat, "Don't touch anything." I can almost *see* a rippling aura of poison emanating from those shrubs. They look harmless enough to the naked eye, but the mere brush of a leaf against bare skin could have devastating effects.

Brielle nods. "Got it. Shall we then?" Without waiting for an answer, she sets off with her usual brisk stride, and I'm left to lumber at her heels. She enters the shrubbery, which, sure enough, within ten paces, takes a sudden turn to the left. Then another turn, then a branch of turns. She pauses, looking from one branch to the other, shrugs, and takes the right one.

Soon we're so lost in a labyrinth of greenery, I'm quite sure we'll never get through, much less reach the middle of the garden. Brielle mutters to herself up ahead of me. Regretting her choice, I suspect. I don't bother trying to understand her. The smells are so strong in here, I can't think of anything but trying to stumble my way through the haze.

Suddenly, a slight, subtle sound catches my ear. How it manages to draw my attention away from the aromas, I don't know, but something about it makes me turn my head sharply, ears pricking, eyes staring.

A vine has crept out from the shrub. It wraps around Brielle's boot.

I open my mouth to bark a warning. In the same instant, she looks down, her eyes widening.

She just has time to mutter, "Gods damn it!"

The next instant, it pulls her off her feet, dragging her straight toward the shrub wall and all those sharp, poisonous leaves. The greenery opens like a dark mouth full of branchy teeth.

I'm already in motion.

I land hard on the shrub vine, pinning it with my powerful forelimbs. Then I take it into my jaw, savaging it, tearing. I expect to taste poison on my tongue, but the vine has no leaves on it, just twisting dark stem. Maybe I won't die from this wild rescue attempt? It hardly matters. The instinct to tear and rend is temporarily stronger than the instinct for survival.

The vine lets go of its intended victim and lashes at my face. Whip-like cuts open across my muzzle, but the dense fur around my head protects most of my skin. I clamp my jaw down harder, ripping, pulling. The vine breaks, and I feel a shudder like flitting life going out from it, and a sad, pitchy shriek slices at the very edge of my hearing.

Spitting out the vine, I whirl to face the shrub wall, fur bristling, teeth bared, saliva dripping from my jowls. But the hole has already closed, leaving nothing but dense, well-trimmed greenery before me. All is still save for the faintest shush and slither of retreating vines.

Puffing out a snorting breath, I turn my heavy head around. "Are you all right?" I ask, the words spitting out through foam.

There is no answer.

She's gone.

Nothing but a wall of green shrubbery stands before me, blocking me off from where she had been just moments before.

## 9

## BRIELLE

I land hard on the gravel path, and pain radiates through my hip. Grimacing and cursing, I pull myself up and press one hand against my sore hipbone even as I whirl to face the wall of shrubbery. I'm just fast enough to see a glimpse of gray fur and sparking yellow eyes, savage under moonlight.

Then the wall closes. Right in front of me. Vines and leaves intertwining, faster than clasping hands.

I gasp, take a step, then stop. Dire's warning rings in my ear—*It's all poison.* I dare not touch that wall, dare not try to fight my way through. Even if those serrated green leaves aren't truly deadly, I can't risk it.

I let out a frustrated puff of air. "Dire?" I call. I can still hear the savage sounds of the werewolf battling vines on the other side.

But it seems distant, as though more than a mere wall of leaves separates the two of us. "Dire, are you there?"

The sounds of battle fade away to nothing. I'm left standing alone in the moonlight. In a demon's garden.

"Seven gods!" I breathe and turn slowly in place. At least the shrubbery hasn't walled me up entirely; there's still an open path, leading straight through the tall bushes. Too straight. I'm not stupid—I know perfectly well that this whole gods-damned maze is reshaping itself to take me exactly where it wants me to go. And wherever that is can't possibly be good.

I rub my sore hip again, then check my bowstring and pick up the arrow I'd dropped in the brief struggle. Casting a last glance back at the newly grown shrub wall, I debate the value of trying to get some sort of message through to the werewolf. Maybe I could . . . I don't know. Attach a scrap of fabric to my arrow and shoot it over the wall? What good would that do? I don't have anything to write with, and even if I did, I couldn't very well give him directions.

It just feels wrong to leave him behind . . .

Which is stupid. He's a monster. One of Granny's creatures. Sure, he helped with the owlkin, and he threw himself right at that vine to save me. But none of that was for *my* sake.

"It's just the compulsion," I whisper firmly. "It's just Granny's power over him. He's not your friend. He's not your ally."

Why can't I *quite* make myself believe it?

I slide a thumb under the strap of my quiver, adjusting the

set across my shoulder. Putting my back firmly to the shrubbery wall, I face the open path. No point dithering. If this garden is setting a trap for me, I'm better off marching to meet it and facing the consequences.

I stride forward, stepping through patches of shadow and moonlight. It's rather lovely in its way. *Romantic*, one might say . . . save that the sharp edges of those shadows fill my heart with subtle dread. Many strange scents tickle my nose, and I try not to breathe any of them too deeply, remembering Dire's warning about the poison.

Reaching the end of the shrubbery, I peer out into the new stretch of garden spread before me. There's a great swell of ground here, and built directly into that swell is a stone atrium. Flowering vines climb in profusion up the curved far wall, the colors so vivid under moonlight, it looks almost like hung tapestries or elaborate murals. In the forefront of the atrium stands a long, stone table, stretching from one side to the other. It's crowded with dishes, footed platters, covered trays, and bowls brimming bounteously with strange fruits I've never seen before. All poisonous, no doubt.

Beyond that table, growing up from the center of the atrium, sheltered by the curving hill, stands a tree. The *tarathieli*—it must be. Great, golden leafed, it shimmers as though generating its own soft daylight here in this world of night. Even from this distance, I can see the profusion of plump, ripe apples with gleaming skins tucked in among the leaves.

And right at the very top . . . a single apple bobs from the highest branch.

I peer around the surrounding garden, searching in the shadows. The demon must be close. But I can't see it, and I don't have Dire's wolfish senses to sniff it out either.

All is still. Tranquil.

Too good to be true.

I can't stand here forever. At some point, I need to move. Get this apple for Granny and get out of here. If the demon's going to leap out at me from behind bush or tree . . . fine.

I take a step. That's the hardest one, that first step out of the relative safety of the shrubbery. The next step is easier, and the next after that. My skin prickles with awareness: of flowers nodding from their long stems, their petals opened wide to emit their noxious perfumes; of the breeze wafting from flowerhead to flowerhead, no doubt carrying poison in its wake; of the still, crystalline pool off to my right; of the maze at my back; of the endlessly rolling hills and valleys of this garden world. Everything feels so calm.

It's wrong. I know it's wrong.

But the tree is close. And I just need that one apple. Then back to the gate, back to the path, out of this place as fast as I can. As for Dire . . . he'll just have to make his own way out. Or not. It's no business of mine either way.

I take another step. My foot crosses from the garden lawn onto the first paving stones of the atrium.

In that same moment, the singing starts.

It's not a song I hear with my ears. Not really. It's more like I'm *breathing* in the sound. Drawing it into my lungs, into my body. Letting it creep through every sense, every vein. It's a song that smells like jasmine at night. A song that tastes like pomegranate wine. A song that feels like velvet on the skin.

It's poison.

Isn't that what Dire said? *Everything* in this place is poison. Including this song. It's as poisonous as everything else. More so, probably. And it will kill me. But for the moment I just don't care.

I blink slowly. As my eyelids rise, I become aware of a presence standing on my right.

The demon is there.

Seven feet tall, shaped like a thin woman clad in white, wafting garments. Its hair is white and wafting as well, and its skin is a deep, deep blue, as blue as the night sky overhead. The tips of its fingers end in eight-inch black claws that curl ever so slightly and glint red when the moonlight hits them just so.

It gazes down at me through two eyes deep as wells of sin. But in the center of its forehead, a third eye, blood red, glitters like a faceted gemstone.

I stare into that eye. I can't look away.

Some distant part of me realizes that the demon has no mouth. Yet the song I hear is definitely coming from inside it. Sung in a language so ancient, so deadly, it would kill me to try to understand it.

The demon holds out one hand.

I shouldn't touch it. I know better. Dire warned me, didn't he?

*Everything is poison.*

But then again, why shouldn't I take it? I'm poisoned already, aren't I? Why try to fight it?

A vague smile pulling at my lips, I place my fingers in the demon's palm. Long black claws curl over my hand but do not scratch. There's firmness in that grip, nothing more. There's no need for more. The song is now pulsing through every part of my being. I'm lost to it.

Eyes half closed, I fall into step beside the demon. My arrow clatters to the paving stones, and I only just manage to keep my fingers curled around my bow, dragging it along behind me. The demon leads me to the table, draws back a chair, and graciously assists me as I sit. When it lets go of my hand, I feel a prick of pain at losing that connection. But the song continues to warm me, even as I know—deep down inside, down where a trace of stubborn will still fights—it's killing me.

I watch the demon almost hungrily as it moves to its place at the head of the table and sits. Its glittering third eye stares at me, and I feel the song pouring out from that eye, swelling around me, under me, through me.

The demon inclines its head and indicates the bountiful spread with a slow sweep of its arm. Reluctantly, I tear my gaze from its strange, three-eyed face and look at the table, the platters and bowls and plates, all piled high with luscious fruits. Some of them I recognize—apples, plums, pears. Others are entirely foreign to me, but no less delectable to my eye. My mouth waters.

Then I blink.

For half an instant, a change comes over the table. Instead of jewel-edged bowls, I see large white skulls, like those of great and strange beasts. And instead of fruits, those skulls are piled to the brim with numerous shriveled, severed heads.

My stomach plunges. I recoil in my seat, blinking fast. With every rise and fall of my lashes, the image fades, fades . . . vanishes. I'm once more looking at a bounteous feast, the produce of this very garden. Rich, vibrant, the colors faintly pulsing beneath the glow of moonlight. The bowls are again silver and gold, edged in delicately cut gems. It's all so succulent and tempting.

*It'll kill you, idiot!*

Is that my own voice, clawing at the back of my mind? I shrug and shake my head.

*Just one bite will kill you! Don't be a fool!*

I draw a long breath, breathing in that perfume, breathing in the song of the Quisandoral. Why should I be afraid? Why should I heed that nagging, pathetic little voice? All of us die sometime, don't we? It's only a matter of time. So why not indulge while I can, why not enjoy myself?

It's funny. Funny how I can sit here in company with a demon, knowing that I'm dying, and feel nothing. No fear. No anger. Nothing but hunger. Hunger for that fruit. Hunger for the escape that death will mean.

The escape from enslavement, from seven years in Granny's clutches . . .

Death by demon poison is as good a death as any, isn't it?

I glance the demon's way. It blinks slowly, three eyelids closing. The two eyelids over the dark hollows remain closed, but the third opens again, revealing once more the gemstone eye. Something hot roils in its center, and the song intensifies.

I stretch out my hand. My fingers hesitate only for a moment over a round, soft-skinned peach. For a single heartbeat, it looks like the severed head of a young woman, her eyes closed, her mouth opened in a silent, eternal scream. But by the second heartbeat, it's nothing but a peach again. I pluck it up, bring it toward my open mouth.

"Stop!"

The air around me fractures then breaks. Shatters in a million sharp fragments that feel so real, I could almost swear I feel them slicing into my skin. For a moment, I'm frozen where I sit, staring at the peach I hold.

But the song is broken.

I leap up from my seat, dropping the fruit, which rolls away, becoming once more that small, severed head. My whole body convulses with horror at the sight. It's all I can do not to bend double and be sick.

A hideous shriek erupts from the end of the table. The demon lurches from her seat, her frame elongating in a grotesque series of breaking and stretching limbs, until she stands twice as tall as she was before. She leans heavily on the table, one hand knocking aside a platter of fruit as it plants into the stone tabletop. The other hand stretches out, the long arm reaching straight for me. I stagger back a step, my eyes widening. Fear chokes me, blocking the scream welling in my throat.

Suddenly, there's a blur of dark gray fur. Dire is there. Half man, half wolf, he latches hold of the demon's arm with his powerful jaws, teeth plunging deep to the bone. The demon shrieks again and shakes its arm, trying to dislodge him. He holds on like a bulldog, growling and snarling.

And I'm still standing there.

It takes me a full three breaths before something sparks in my brain, driving me to leap away from the table, to put some distance between myself and that mayhem of rending flesh and breaking bone. Instinct makes me grab my half-forgotten bow from where it stands propped against my chair. I turn, prepared to flee, but take only three steps before I stop.

I look back. Back up at that tree.

This is my chance.

Inhuman sounds lance my ears, and a whole hellish tumult of slashing claws and gnashing teeth plays at the edge of my sight. I shut them out, focus on my goal. Leaping onto the table, I kick aside a bowl of tiny heads, sending them scattering. My gaze fixes on that topmost bough of the apple tree, gleaming bright in the moonlight. I nock an arrow, take aim.

The roars fade to nothing. There's just me in that moment. Me and that apple, so high above. Me and the long breath I draw into my lungs.

I won't have a second chance at this.

I let my breath out slowly.

Then my arrow flies, speeding in a sure and perfect line as though it will pierce the moon itself. But it does not need to go so far. Its sharp head cracks through the delicate gold branch, which breaks, droops, hangs suspended.

Then the weight of the apple pulls it tumbling free.

I'm already in motion, springing across the table, vaulting over platters and bowls. Something whistles to my left, and I'm vaguely aware of curved, black nails slashing the air just inches from my cheek.

I don't turn. I don't stop.

I leap from the table, hand outstretched. My fingers close around golden fruit.

With a gasp, I land hard, falling to my knees, the apple pressed close to my heart. For a few breaths, I can't move, my very bones jarred by the impact of that landing.

But I can't linger. Not here.

Gathering strength, I spring up and whirl, just in time to miss the lashing hand of the demon, which crashes into the paving stones where I'd knelt an instant before. I stagger back, catch my balance, then run along the length of the table. Some part of me wonders where Dire is, whether he's still alive. There's no time to dwell on such thoughts, however. I've got to get out of here, I've got to find my way back to the gate.

Something hooks around my shin. I gasp, cry out, and fall, only just managing to catch myself before I smash face first into stone. The apple is still in my grasp, cradled against my chest. I kick, feel a single claw resisting then loosening its hold. With a desperate roll, I get onto my back, looking between my feet. The demon lies on the stones, stretched out at full length, her horrible face twisted and leering. Where there was no mouth at all before, now a slit has opened in the bottom half of her face, and a forked, purple tongue flickers between sharp teeth. Her third eye glares wildly at me, and I can hear the beginnings of her poisonous song tickling the edge of my awareness.

I scream, trying to block out that sound, and roll again. This time I manage to push my way between two chairs and crawl on my belly under the table. That clawed hand strikes out at me, but only manages to catch hold of a chair leg. She wrenches the chair back, hurls it behind her to crash and shatter against the stone wall of the atrium.

I burst out on the far side of the table, pushing up on my hands and knees. I get one foot under me, gasp desperately for breath, stand upright. In a moment of idiotic terror, I turn my head, look back over my shoulder.

The demon is hauling herself up onto the table, massive and many-jointed, her hair a wild storm in the moonlight. She roars at me, stretches out her hand . . .

Dire is there again.

He appears as though from nowhere, hurtling into the side of her face. His jaws rip into her cheek, opening a gaping wound. The demon's shrieks of pain and horror are almost paralyzing to my senses as she tears at her own head, trying to dislodge her attacker.

I turn and flee the atrium, out into the empty lawn. My heart thunders in my ears, but not loud enough to drown out the terrible sounds behind me. I run as hard as I can, making for the shrubbery up ahead. It's probably a trap, it's probably ready to swallow me whole. In that moment, I don't care. I'd rather be devoured by a poisoned maze than fall into the Quisandoral's clutches. And maybe, just maybe, I can push through, can still reach the gate—

I hear a yipe of pain.

The sound shoots through me like an arrow to the heart.

I shouldn't stop. I mustn't. I should run, run, run, never looking back.

Instead, I pivot on my heel, my hair flying wildly around my face as I stare back down the incline to the atrium below.

Dire lies on his back in the middle of the broken table. His huge body is splayed, his arms wide, his hideous wolf head thrown back. I can see his chest rising and falling, a sign of life. But he doesn't move.

And the demon—its face bleeding in long silver streams, its skin hanging in tatters from innumerable bite wounds—crawls toward him down the length of the table. It hardly looks like a woman now, so awful and jointed and strange. Its spine seems almost to ripple like a serpent, and its feet and hands tear into the tabletop, sending cracks through the stone. It lifts one arm, its claws flashing in the moonlight, and I know it's going to plunge those claws through Dire's heart.

I have a second in which to decide. Run, or . . .

I drop the apple to the grass at my feet. Whip out an arrow. Take a firing stance.

"Hey!" I shout. "Over here, you big ugly!"

The demon turns its head.

I shoot.

My arrow flies swift and true, cutting through poisonous vapors and songs. It embeds directly in the center of that gemstone eye.

# 10

## DIRE

I stare into the face of looming death.

I don't feel any fear. I don't feel anything. All feeling, all sense has been knocked from my body as I lie in the middle of that table. I can do nothing but struggle to catch a breath and stare into that gleaming, faceted eye.

The demon raises its head. I have moments left. Less than moments.

I wonder if I'll feel liberation at the point of death. Or will the pain be too great?

"Hey!"

A voice, bright and clear as a bell, breaks through the dull thudding in my head.

"Over here, you big ugly!"

Is that . . . Brielle?

The gemstone eye blinks. Turns.

The next instant, it's as though something has blossomed from its center—a quivering stem with a fletched, feathered flower. I stare, lost in wonder at that sight, unable to comprehend what it is I'm seeing.

Then the demon utters a terrible cry and lurches backwards, huge hands tearing at its face. It screams and screams, and some strange dark force bursts from its core. That force spreads fast, like the rippling of water disturbed by a stone. It washes over me, vibrating through my bones. It's magic—ancient magic. More ancient than anything I've ever before encountered.

For a moment, I think it's killed me.

The next moment, I blink again. I'm still alive. What's more, I feel a surge of strength that wasn't there before. Rolling, knocking platters and bowls every which way, I push through chairs and land on all fours on the ground. I shake my head, force my eyes to clear, my mind to focus. When I look up again, I see the results of that dark shockwave.

The garden—it's gone. Completely gone. Barren nothingness surrounds us, not unlike the nothing contained within the walls of Elorata Dorrel's home. This whole world, this whole domain . . . it was nothing but illusions as well.

I squeeze my eyes shut then open them again, trying to force my vision to clarify, to make sense of the murk around me. When I look again, two things stand out crisp and clear to my sight. The first is Brielle, standing some thirty yards away, her bow still up, her arm still poised from the arrow she's just loosed.

The second is beyond her. The gate. Our escape.

Another horrible shriek shocks me from my stupefaction. I whirl and look back at the demon just as it yanks the arrow from its bloodied eye socket. It swings its heavy head around, searching for me, its jaw sagging, and a long, forked tongue flicking through sharp fangs.

I'm already in motion.

Pulling myself up, I lumber on all fours, staggering at first, then faster and faster. I make straight for Brielle. She sees me coming, and her eyes widen. She lowers her bow, starts to turn, to flee.

I'm already upon her. Scooping her up in my arms and racing across that emptiness for the gate. I run on only my hind legs now, but even so I'm faster than she would be on her own. Holding her against my hairy breast, I feel the fingers of her free hand tangling in my fur. Her other hand still grips her bow, and thankfully she has the sense to keep it up and out of my way.

An inarticulate cry bursts from her lips. In the same instant, a pungent stink of pure fear rolls out from her pores. I don't need to look to see why. The pound of the demon's feet reverberates behind me. It's gaining on us.

If I'm wise, I'll toss the girl to one side, leave her to face the demon on her own, leave her to distract it while I cover the last of this distance to the gate on my own and dive for safety.

But I hold the girl a little tighter, tuck my head, and *run*. The gate looms before us, taller than I realized. I feel the change in pressure in the air behind me, and I know with the instinctual knowledge of all prey that my predator has just sprung, that it even now flies through the air, straight for me. I feel the scrape of claws against my back, slicing across the flesh of my shoulders . . .

Then I'm through the gate arch, through the thin place in reality, and tumbling head-over-heels.

I cannot think, cannot breathe. I can do nothing but tighten my arms around the girl. Flashes of green and light and dark flare across my senses.

At last, the fall ends. I lie at the bottom of a steep incline, my head throbbing, my vision spinning. Beneath the stench of fear, I detect the many layered scents of the ancient forest all around me. My chest rises and falls as I struggle to regain my breath. But my lips twist in a smile.

We made it.

We're out of the demon's garden. Back in Whispering Wood.

I close my eyes again, and for a little while, simply concentrate on breathing. Slowly, my numbed awareness clarifies, and I realize my arms are still wrapped around a small, bony body. A body which lies on top of my chest, fingers curled in the long fur of my neck, face buried in my shoulder. There's a subtle change to the smell of her now when I breathe in. The fear is still there, of course, thick and putrid. But underneath, there's another, subtler aroma. Something like . . . *comfort. Trust.*

It should be impossible. Utterly impossible. But the smell is there. My werewolf senses don't lie.

She feels safe in my arms.

My chest tightens. My breathing, already ragged, hitches uncomfortably. In that moment—however brief, however foolish, however wrong—I don't want to move. I just want to lie there, hold her, and feel that trust. Feel as though perhaps . . . I even deserve it.

But it's not real. I dare not indulge these feelings.

Closing my eyes, I force my arms to relax their hold on the girl, to drop away to my sides. "It's all right," I growl, my voice a dreadful rumbling in my own ears. "We're safe now. We're out."

Am I imagining her fingers tightening their grip in my fur? I must be. For the next moment, she utters a little growl and lifts her head, giving it such a ferocious shake her brilliant hair pulls free of its knot and tumbles about her stern little face in tangled snarls. My breath catches in my throat.

Before I've had a chance to recover, she rolls off me, landing hard on the ground with a little, *"Oof!"* She grimaces and adjusts how she lies so that she's not on top of her quiver. There she remains for several breaths, staring up at greenery overhead so thick one can barely catch a glimpse of sky. A single stray sunbeam makes its way down, lighting the lower part of her face. Drawing my gaze straight to her parted, panting lips.

What is wrong with me?

With a snarl, I heave my awful, bestial body upright, shake out my coat, and sit back heavily on my haunches. The morning is much progressed by now, and I'm well on my way to full-bodied wolfhood. Already, I'm finding it harder and harder to concentrate on a human arrangement of thoughts. My mind wants to slip into animal ways of reasoning. Smells. Tastes. Urges . . .

I growl again, turning away from the girl, and look back the way we've come. "No sign of pursuit," I say. My voice is scarcely understandable. I'm not even sure I'm actually *saying* what I think I'm saying.

But Brielle seems to understand. I cast her a sideways glance and see her close her eyes and shake her head. "It wouldn't follow us," she says. "Not out here. A creature like that *needs* its domain to exist. Maybe there was a time it could venture out. Not anymore."

A sudden image flashes through my head—an image of Elorata Dorrel standing just within the boundaries of her house, close to the gate but never too close. Is she like this demon then? Something too old and too frail and too evil to survive beyond the strict boundary lines she's drawn for her existence?

Brielle pushes a tangle of hair out of her eyes and back across her forehead. A little unsteady, she gets to her feet. "I suppose we'd better be off," she says.

"Yes," I agree. Then, "Too bad we didn't get that apple."

She casts me a look, one eyebrow upraised. Reaching into the front of her tunic, she withdraws a small gold object, so perfect and glittering in that single beam of sunlight, it looks more like a dream than reality. But no. Of everything in that demon's garden, *this* at least was real all along. The *tarathieli*—the apple of the goddess's tree.

My heart plummets at the sight. At the *smell*. For as I draw the delicate perfume emanating from that ripe, golden fruit into my nostrils, I recognize it. I've encountered that scent before, mixed with other things, but identifiable.

I know now what Granny intends to do with her prize.

# 11

## BRIELLE

I watch the wolfman stalking through the trees ahead of me.

He's mostly wolf now. His forelimbs are of nearly equal proportion to his hindquarters, with only hints of the sloping humped spine that is usually prominent when he ambles along on all fours. He moves with the grace of a natural-born predator, almost silent as he passes through the underbrush.

If I were to encounter him suddenly, I would never guess that a man's form lurked not so deep beneath the surface, and yet . . . and yet . . .

I shake my head, closing my eyes and grinding my teeth. Why can't I fully banish that memory from my mind? That memory of being held in powerful arms, cradled close to a strong, warm chest. It was terrible, so terrible. I'd felt as helpless as a mewling kitten.

But at the same time . . . Oh gods! It's been so long since anyone *held* me. Since I experienced that sensation of safety and shielding. I've always been the strong one, ever since I was a child. Strong and self-reliant, the protector and provider. When I was quite little, Valera did the best she could to shield me, but she was scarcely more than a child herself. She offered everything she had, but she had so little, and I learned not to ask for more.

But in those few moments after passing through the gate—moments so bright and alive with sheer, heart-pounding terror—is it wrong that I also felt such a wave of comfort? As we lay on the forest floor, and I pressed my head against his chest and listened to the thump of his heartbeat . . . is it wrong that I wanted to continue lying there? Just a little longer. Reveling in the sensation of arms bigger and stronger than my own wrapped around me.

For a few breaths at least, I didn't *have* to be the strong one.

Foolish! These are dangerous thoughts, dangerous feelings. I know better than to let myself depend on anyone. Ever. Dependence is weakness, and weakness is a luxury I can't afford.

Besides . . . I look again at that huge, shaggy, terrible animal prowling up ahead of me. What kind of an idiot would take comfort in the arms of such a monster?

With an effort of will, I push these thoughts down and slam the lid tight. I really ought to have found a holly bush and opened one of the Hinter Paths back to Granny's house. But Granny did give us until sundown, and it's only a little past noon now. We have time for a more leisurely route, following whatever trail Dire manages to sniff out for us. And while he may not be the best of company, he is, at least, silent.

So I stroll along at an easy pace and keep my mind firmly turned away from things I shouldn't be thinking. Instead, I let myself remember those days long ago when I was a madcap child making dashes into the Wood, daring myself to go just a little further each day. Back then, the secrets and shadows beneath the trees had seemed full of tantalizing possibilities which I could never name but which, if I closed my eyes, I could almost *taste*.

Those were good days. At the end of them, I always got to return to Valera and her scolding. I knew both where I belonged and where I wanted to escape to.

Not like now. Now I just belong to Granny. And as for escape? There is no escape. Not for me, anyway.

After a while, I notice Dire is slowly transitioning back into semi-human form. His easy, trotting wolf-pace transitions into something more lumbering and awkward. Eventually, he begins to walk upright again, dragging his long arms behind him.

"I think it's time we took a rest," I call out, breaking the silence that has hung between us for several hours now.

The fur down his spine ripples. He turns, fixing those intense, yellow eyes of his on me. My heart gives an extra thump of fear, but I take care it doesn't show in my expression. "Here's as good a place as any," I say, indicating a young oak tree near at hand. A living oak, not like the poor dead thing in which the owlkin roosted. I feel a wave of friendliness roll out from it as I step into the shelter of its branches and take a seat among its roots.

Dire, however, stands aloof. His face, still mostly wolfish, has traces of humanity around the jaw and brow. His eyes are narrow, and his tail twitches faintly. "We should keep going," he growls.

I adjust my seat to get more comfortable and shoot him a swift look. "Oh, come on. I don't know about you, but I'm in no rush to get back to Granny's!" I pull my waterskin from my belt and take several large gulps. When I'm through, I wipe my mouth with the back of my hand. "Want some?"

To my relief, the werewolf shakes his head. I'm not sure how a mouth like his would drink from a waterskin anyway. I'd probably have to pour it out in a stream and let him lap it as it fell. Which would be awkward. And a waste of good water.

Instead, I reach into another pouch on my belt and pull out some hard deer jerky, tossing a piece the werewolf's way. He snatches it a little too nimbly in his jaws, then seems to realize what he's done. For a moment, embarrassment flashes across his face. He turns away quickly, but I can hear him gnawing away at the jerky.

I take a bite of my own piece and chew thoughtfully, leaning my head back against the oak tree. When all is said and done, this hasn't been such a bad day. Compared to yesterday's mission, facing down the Quisandoral was practically jolly. Actually . . . I rather enjoyed it. The hunt. The adventure. The rush of blood. The real, raw feel of *life* one feels after such a close brush with death.

Reaching into the front of my tunic, I pull out the apple again and turn it around slowly. It is beautiful, strange, and ethereal. I can sense the old magic rippling from it. What kind of magic exactly, I couldn't say; I'm not particularly knowledgeable about such things. But it's definitely old. And potent.

What kind of spell does Granny need it for?

Frowning, I glance up and meet Dire's yellow wolf-eyes fixed on me. "What?" I demand.

He grunts and growls like he's clearing his throat. Then he opens his great red mouth and a rough, animal voice emerges through sharp teeth. "Are you going to turn it over? To her?"

"What, to Granny?" I heft the apple, toss it lightly three times, then return it to the safety of my tunic. "That's the job, isn't it?"

"You shouldn't." The werewolf turns his heavy head to one side. Is that a note of . . . *pleading* I hear? It's so hard to tell. Wolf voices weren't meant for pleading. But the human side of him is creeping back more swiftly every minute now.

"Shouldn't, wouldn't, couldn't," I say with a shrug and a lift of an eyebrow. "You know I haven't got a choice."

"There's always a choice."

"Not where Granny's spells are concerned." I sigh, my jaw hardening. "Remember, you're not the only one sworn to her service."

To my surprise, Dire rises from his haunches and stalks closer to me. The oak tree shivers and wafts its branches in a subtly threatening manner. Dire pauses, his nostrils flaring, his gaze shooting up at the tree.

"It doesn't like you," I say, adjusting my seat on the roots, which ripple uneasily beneath me. "Oaks only like humans."

"I *am* human."

I shake my head. "Maybe once. Not anymore."

Dire licks his lips with a long red tongue that flicks across the end of his black nose. Then, with a snarl, he steps closer. To my surprise, the tree merely shivers again but otherwise makes no further threat. Is it afraid of him? I start to gather myself together, ready to rise. But before I can get my feet under me, he drops in a crouch in front of me, reaches out and takes my hand. I'm so shocked by the gesture, I freeze, my mouth gaping, my eyes wide.

"There's always a choice," he says again. Suddenly I realize that his eyes are human again; gray and glittering with . . . are those tears? Surely not!

I try to pull my hand away, but his grip firms. "It may not be much of a choice," he continues. "It may not be more than an instant's worth of resistance. But . . . but I've seen you make that choice; I've seen you resist."

My dry throat thickens. I blink, and in that instant of darkness behind my eyelids, I flash back to the moment in the forest when I had the red werebeast in my sights. The red werebeast I'd been compelled to hunt, to kill.

But I hesitated.

I'd *resisted*.

Not long.

Just long enough.

My lashes rise. "Seven gods!" I bite out viciously. "It's not as though it does any *good*. A moment, a breath . . . even an hour or a day! In the end, Granny *will* have her way. There's no stopping her."

"There is. There is!" Dire squeezes my hand tighter. There's terrible strength in his half-animal fingers. "Maybe not for all of us. But you're different. You are of her blood."

"What?" With a gasp I wrench my hand free. His long claws scrape along my skin, and I yelp at the sudden pain. He looks surprised, ashamed, and backs away, hunching into himself. "What are you talking about?" I demand, shaking my hand and pressing it against my chest. "You think because I'm her granddaughter I can . . . what? Break her binding over me? Ha! Don't get your hopes up."

"You could do it." His voice sinks into that awful pleading. "If you really wanted to—"

"Oh, you think I *want* to be at the old witch's beck and call all hours of every day and night? You think I *want* to be her tool, her . . . her . . . her *slave?*" I stand and step away from him. The oak, responding to my distress, moves its roots threateningly around Dire's feet until he's forced to back away, beyond the circle of their reach. He gazes at me, his expression dark, his human eyes still strangely wolfish in their intensity.

"None of us want this," he says. "But the rest of us truly have no choice. You do. You may not like to admit it, may not like to face it. But deep down, *you do have a choice*. And I think you know it."

I want to spit curses at him. How could he even suggest that I would choose this enslavement? That I wouldn't fight tooth and nail against it if I thought I had even half a chance at freedom?

I reach for the apple inside my tunic again, my fingers brushing the crisp, hard skin. What if . . . what if he's right? What if I could resist Granny's thrall? After all, there is some truth in Dire's words. I *am* born of Granny's blood, so I do carry at least a small measure of her power inside me. And Mother Ulla—the ward witch back home—she said several times that both Valera and I carried power inside us. I've seen Valera's power firsthand, and it is incredible, if not exactly honed.

If she possesses that kind of power, isn't it possible I might too?

Slowly I withdraw the apple and hold it in front of my face. It's so perfect, so pristine, more like a delicate glass ornament than a real apple plucked from a real tree. It would smash so easily. I could crush it in my own hands if I tried.

And what does Granny want it for anyway? Something horrible, judging by Dire's desperate expression.

Closing my eyes, I search down inside myself, trying to find the strength, the courage to destroy the apple. I'm no coward, after all. I never have been. Valera used to say I was brave to the point of reckless. I could use that recklessness now. I could draw my arm back, hurl this apple, watch it break into a thousand juicy pieces against the tree trunk. Then return to Granny and tell her that I *won't* be made into her errand girl or assassin-on-call.

I could . . . I might . . .

*I want* . . .

I want to turn right now and run into Whispering Wood. And run and run and run and never look back, losing myself in those shadows. I want to not be this person. This terrible person I've somehow become.

I want . . . *so much* . . .

But it's all foolishness. And I know better.

Letting out a long breath, I tuck the apple back in the front of my tunic. Granny's bindings are too strong. Dire can believe whatever he likes. He might think I'm weak, spineless. But he's not standing in my shoes. He doesn't know.

I turn and face him. There's enough humanity in his face that I can see the disappointment fading away just before it's masked behind a wolfish grimace.

"Go on," I say. "Lead the way, wolfman. We've got to get back to Granny's before sunset."

Dire blinks once. Then he rises and, using his elongated forelimbs for support, lumbers off into the trees, following his nose as he sniffs our way. I shoulder my bow, adjust the set of my quiver, and fall into step behind him. The apple weighs heavily in the front of my tunic. Like a stone lodged where my heart should be.

# 12

## DIRE

The witch requires me to serve at her table again tonight.

I stand at the wall, clad in the glamoured server's uniform, my beard trimmed, my hair slicked back and tied at the base of my skull. I'm as still and silent as any other decorative feature in the elaborately magicked dining hall.

This time, Elorata has me dressed and ready before the guests arrive, and I'm left on my own for some time. This I do not like. It would be better if my duties began at once, if I could fill my mind with the monotonous bustle of ladling soups and handing around plates of cut meats.

It would be better than standing here, seeing that image in my head over and over again . . . that image of Brielle, her bow upraised, her eyes bright, her arrow newly loosed.

She'd saved my life. When she could have simply fled for cover and left me to my fate.

I close my eyes, trying to drive out those recent memories. But it's worse now. In the darkness of my mind, I see again the look on her face when she held that apple in her hand. When I begged her to destroy it, to not fulfill her mission. It had seemed for a moment as though she really did want to resist. And I had dared hope my suspicions were true—that her lineage really did give her a leverage against her grandmother's magic. I could almost smell the movement of blood in her veins, working, churning, pushing against the equally potent flow of enchantment.

In the end, she'd given in to the spell. Succumbed. Just like I did. Just like we all do.

Elorata is too powerful. And now that she has the *tarathieli*, the cycle will continue.

I am startled from these dark thoughts by a sudden hum of voices just outside the dining room door. Someone exclaims in a pitchy, nasal tone, "*What* a most *intriguing* collection! Did you send out for these specimens, Granny dear?"

"Why no, they were all hunted within the boundaries of my wardship," Elorata's voice trills back, silvery bright and full of cheerful hospitality. "You simply wouldn't *believe* some of the things one finds in this particular ward."

"Gracious gods!" someone else exclaims, a man's voice, a bit raspy on the edges. "How vicious they look! I don't know what the little people of my county would do if they knew things like these lurked so near to their borders. They'd go quite mad with fright."

"Well, my darling, the trick is to never let the country people know just how close they stand to peril," Elorata responds smoothly. "I've never permitted any of the fiends to breach the boundaries of the Wood, of that you may be certain. But they *will* try, won't they!"

She ends with a pretty laugh, opening the door to the dining room. I see her standing there. For once, she does not wear her brilliant colors, but is clad instead in somber black, which serves only to emphasize the vibrancy of her hair and the pure porcelain of her complexion. She doesn't look quite as young as usual but has donned the face of a dignified dame of fifty-odd years rather than the youthful countenance she prefers to wear.

Still outrageously beautiful, of course. So beautiful, it makes me sick.

Compared to her company, she is positively otherworldly. Eight figures shuffle into the room behind her: five women, three men. Most of them seem to have made at least some effort to pull themselves together. One of the women wears a richly embroidered shawl around her bowed shoulders, and it keeps slipping and dragging on the floor behind her. One of the men—a goggle-eyed fellow with a throat like an old turkey—has pinned a bit of discolored lace to his black lapels after a long-outdated fashion.

Only one of the party looks downright disreputable. She's a squat, fat little waddling thing in the traditional peaked witch's hat with a wide, floppy brim. Her gown is made up of so many patches that the original pattern and style has long since disappeared. She stumps along on bare feet, her gnarled staff clunking in front of her.

The other seven carry their staves as well but take care not to make such a clatter as they go. Elorata also carries a staff this evening, though it is not in her habit to do so. It's an elegant black cane topped with a carved crystal in the shape of a wolf head. I look away from it quickly.

Seven of the eight guests catch their breaths at the sight of the dining room. They are, I'm sure, well aware of the glamours being used. They must be, for they are all witches and warlocks, keepers of the eight nearest wardships along the boundaries of Whispering Wood. Workers of magic, maintainers of barriers, they stand between ordinary folk of the counties and all the terrors of Faerieland.

I was brought up revering my own local ward witch. She was a mysterious figure, only ever glimpsed at a distance or whispered of in rumor. But I knew whenever her name was mentioned to make certain signs of respect and veneration. We all feared her. Even as we depended on her. Our champion, our protector.

My mouth forms a grim snarl behind my beard. I hastily pull it into a straight line.

One of the witches—the disreputable creature in the patchwork gown—grunts disapprovingly as she surveys the dining room. She totters right up to the wall by which I'm standing and prods it with the end of her stick. For a moment, a flashing red sigil appears, implanted behind the wallpaper.

"Hmmph. Fancy," the old witch says. Her tone is not complimentary.

"Dear Mother Ulla." Elorata stands by the table and ushers the fat witch toward a chair. "Do please have a seat. I know my little charms and runes are not to your liking. You were always one of the *natural* aesthetic, were you not?"

"Don't mind a bit of glamour here and there," Mother Ulla said, casting a narrow look my way and ignoring Elorata's beckoning. "It's the excess that gets to me. Why waste good magic on wallpaper and chandy-leers?"

Her gaze roves up and down, from the top of my head to my boots and back to my face. I meet her eye for half a second before turning away and facing forward into an empty middle-distance.

"Well, to each witch her own, don't you agree?" says a bird-like little woman in a faded, flower-embroidered smock. She sits daintily in a chair that completely dwarfs her tiny frame. "Oh, Granny Dorrel, it's all *so* lovely. I don't know how you manage it! You truly have a gifting. Blessed by the gods themselves!"

Elorata accepts this praise with a nod, then flicks another swift glance Mother Ulla's way. She pointedly clears her throat.

The fat witch, not to be hurried, twists her lips to one side thoughtfully before finally turning from me and waddling to her appointed seat. She's placed at the center of the table, a place of some honor. By this, I gather that, disreputable-looking or otherwise, Mother Ulla is one of the higher-ranking witches present.

Not so high ranking as Elorata, however. She takes her seat

grandly at the head of the table and claps her hands smartly. I don't need a spoken word from her to feel the compulsion come over me. I lurch into motion, pushing my little soup trolly around the table. As I do the rounds, ladling soup into bowls, seven of the eight witches exclaim over the convincing glamour, the subtle spices, the creamy texture . . . all as delighted as though the glamour were more than a mere fabrication. They know better, don't they? They must! Yet they don't seem to care.

Old Mother Ulla, however, sniffs at a spoonful of soup, making quite a loud to-do over it. Then, her lip curling slightly, she takes a single, loud slurp. Following that, she pointedly puts down her spoon and sits back in her chair, folding her hands across her stomach.

The other witches eye her uncomfortably, their gazes shifting from her to Elorata and back again. Elorata only smiles graciously and turns to the warlock seated on her right, asking him about his journey to her humble abode. He, a pudding-faced fellow of no more than thirty-odd years, probably still new to his wardship, swallows hard and stammers an almost unintelligible answer. While he must know Elorata is wearing beauty glamours, that doesn't seem to alter his total intimidation in her presence. I sniff the air softly as I pass behind him, my wolf senses detecting the stink of pure attraction warring with terror in the poor fellow's veins.

The meal progresses from soup, to bread, to little cups of fruit, and on to the main course. Throughout, Elorata maintains a steady stream of conversation, all without seeming to miss a single bite. The other witches take it in turns to engage with her, each one starling slightly when she addresses him or her by name.

When it's Mother Ulla's turn to be addressed, she alone exhibits no sign of fear.

"Mother Ulla," Elorata says imperiously, turning her sky-blue eyes the old witch's way.

"Yup," Mother Ulla meets that gaze and blinks slowly, like a cat.

"I understand you had a little... *intrigue* in your wardship recently." The old witch shrugs. "Well, if t'aint one thing, it's t'n'other."

"I heard," Elorata continues relentlessly, dabbing her red lips with a linen cloth, "that a few years back, a girl was stolen from your village and made to become a fae bride. That she returned after many years, having not aged a day, wearing next to nothing, but carrying with her a gold necklace full of magic."

"Mmmph," Ulla answers. She blinks again.

"I heard as well"—Elorata's gaze sweeps round to the other witches, who are not quite certain which way to look—"that the same girl left your wardship again soon thereafter, disappearing into Whispering Wood, and taking her magic with her. Tell me, is it true?"

"Might be." Mother Ulla squints Elorata's way. "What of it?"

"Well, my dear!" Elorata tilts her head to one side, allowing one long red curl to fall across her cheek and over her shoulder. "It seems rather *careless* on your part, I must say! To allow a fae to slip in through your boundaries and steal a girl away?" She turns and looks the flower-smock witch in the eye, asking sweetly, "Have *you* ever lost a girl as a fae bride before?"

"Oh, I, um . . ." The flower-smock witch blinks her watery eyes, her pale lashes fluttering. "It's not one of those things one—"

"And *you?*" Elorata turns to the pudding-faced man on her right. "Would you ever allow the Pledge to be thus broken within your own wardship?"

"Well, strictly speaking—" The man interrupts himself with a self-conscious cough. "Strictly speaking, it's not a break of the Pledge if there are certain mitigating circumstances such as—"

"But we are not here to debate the subtleties of the Pledge, are we?" Elorata says, smoothly cutting him off. The warlock quickly swallows whatever he was going to say, placing two fingers firmly against his mouth as though to suppress any further offending words. Elorata turns from him, leans over the table—just a little, just enough to imply a barest hint of aggression—and fixes Mother Ulla with her stare.

"I wonder," she says, "how *safe* the folk of Ellee County feel, knowing that one of their own may be so easily spirited off to Faerieland. And right out from under their ward witch's nose." She *tsks* softly, shaking her head. The diamond combs holding up her elaborate curls glint in the chandelier light. "It's a wonder the wardens haven't gathered to coven years ago to discuss this grave situation."

The witches and warlocks stare, their jaws sagging, breath caught in their throats. But Mother Ulla's lips quirk in a half-smile.

"Nice try, Granny," she says, slightly emphasizing the senior witch's title. "Elegantly done, even. But you ain't foolin' no one. No one what gots any brains, that is."

Elorata draws back, placing a hand against her heart. "What are you trying to say, dear Ulla?"

It's the fat ward witch's turn to lean in. She smiles, showing mostly empty gums and three stout white stumps of teeth. "Now, now, don't go playin' with me. You knows exactly why we've gathered here tonight. No amount of deflectin' is goin' to do you any good."

Elorata looks round at the gathered witches, none of whom quite find it in their power to meet her gaze directly. "Whatever can she mean?" she asks, all sweetness, all innocence.

She makes my skin crawl.

The witch with the colorful shawl coughs and sits up a little straighter than before. "Granny Dorrel," she begins, trying to make her voice prim and imperious but failing by sheer comparison to Elorata's poise. She knows it too, which only adds to her nerves. It's like watching an avalanche of insecurity slowly crush the poor creature into her chair. But she bravely forges on. "It has come to the attention of your local coven, that is, us, that you have not turned out a . . . a trained apprentice. In four decades."

"Really?" Granny tilts her head to one side. "Are my training practices so closely monitored?"

"Well, Granny," the flower-smock witch manages, "you *are* the senior-ranking witch of ten wardships. Everyone looks to you for . . . for . . . for . . ." She casts about desperately for help.

Mother Ulla steps in. "We's all watching you. All the time."

The flower-smock witch whimpers and wilts. This was decidedly not the help she was hoping for.

"Indeed?" Elorata's lips thin in a mirthless smile. "How flattering."

"Not so much." Mother Ulla leans back in her seat, balancing on the back two legs. "We knows for a fact that you've taken in no fewer than *eight* apprentices in the last four decades. Yet there ain't been no witch produced from Virra County in all that time. Ivis County took on Brother Darcassan, who was trained under Mother Zylphie. Jearis County took Mistress Fenna five years back. And Mistress Enharice"—she nods to the flower-smock witch—"were one of my own, and she took Alna County just south of here."

"Yes?" Granny looks at the flower-smock witch and pudding-faced Brother Darcassan and smiles. "And I'm sure they are grateful for the opportunities afforded them."

"Grateful, my eye!" Mother Ulla snorts. "You know as well as I do, we's stretched thin. Enharice here were meant to take on part of Ellee County for a good five years, and I had to rush her off to take the vacancy at Alna instead. Now I gots to find me a new apprentice with stirrings in the blood, which we all know is easier said than done."

"I think what Mother Ulla is trying to say," the lace-pinned warlock butted in, using a painfully soothing tone, "is that all the wardships feel the lack of your expertise and training."

"That ain't what I'm trying to say at all," Mother Ulla snaps. "I'm saying, what in the seven gods' names *happened* to all those apprentices of your'n? Eh, Elorata?"

Elorata stiffens at the obvious neglect of her title. She draws herself a little straighter in her chair, her nostrils flaring as she takes a slow breath. "Have a care, Ulla," she says, her voice gone icy.

"We's all been having a lot of cares. A lot of cares we shouldn't oughts to have been carin' for. So where are they? It's a simple question. You've taken eight apprentices and turned out not a single witch or warlock in all that time. *Where did they go?*"

Elorata's eyes narrow. One of her fingers is moving slightly against the arm of her chair, and I can *just* smell the stink of magic. Is she drawing a rune? Right there, seated at her own table? Does she plan to blast Mother Ulla with a curse in front of all those watching eyes? And if she does, is there a gods-blighted thing any of them could do about it? Combined, their powers must be tremendous. But not one of them could stand alone against the accumulation of magic simmering within Elorata Dorrel.

All that magic . . . all that stolen magic . . .

"*Can you believe it?*" a sweet, gentle voice speaks in my memory. "*I never thought I had a chance! I mean, I know I've got a little something, but I never thought it was enough to attract any real interest my way. But now I'll get to really learn! To use this gift as it was meant to be used!*"

I close my eyes, leaning my head back against the wall. I'm practically unseen here in the dining room, where all the attention of the guests is fixed on either Elorata or Mother Ulla. No one has even noticed yet the fur beginning to creep up from beneath my collar or across the tops of my hands. Maybe they can't notice.

Elorata added extra layers of glamour when she made me ready to serve this evening. Maybe she's made certain no one in that room will see what I'm slowly becoming.

She has not yet given an answer to Mother Ulla's question. The silence has held the table captive just a little too long. At last, however, she lets out a charming, tinkling sort of laugh.

"Oh, well! If you must know, I *have* been more than a little particular in my standards these last few years—"

"Decades," Ulla interjects.

"*Years,*" Elorata laughs again, but there's an edge to it. "Finding an apprentice who can live up to the high ideals of our noble calling is no easy feat. I'm delighted that so many of you have been more fortunate in the selection of magical talent sent your way. Unfortunately, Virra County has never been one for producing great magical effect. Not since I took over the wardship, that is. Perhaps if I were laxer in my duties, a touch more of the *influence* would seep through from the Wood, but there you have it! I've always made the protection of my wardship my first priority."

"Ah!" Mother Ulla leans back in her chair again, her great bulk tilting dangerously on those two back legs. "So that's how you're playin' it, eh? The rest of us, we ain't so good at our jobs. That's why we manage to find such magically inclined help to train up."

"Well, Ulla dear," Elorata says, her voice rich and plummy, "I would never state it so baldly . . ."

The pudding-faced fellow sitting next to her clears his throat for probably the fifth time, finally managing to draw some attention his way. "I think we should all be most satisfied, Granny, if you were to assure us that the *next* apprentice you take on will indeed be . . . be . . . suitable. Should a proper vacancy need filling."

"And how can I promise so much when I control so few of the variables?" Elorata asks, turning his way. "You have my ongoing assurance that I will do everything in my power to *make something* of my next apprentice. Indeed, I expect to take on a new one before the year is out."

My heart plunges sickeningly at those words. But then, I'd known it must happen. Ever since Dreg's term of service came to an end, I'd known it was only a matter of time . . .

"Does that satisfy all of you?" Elorata looks round the table, smiling with that queenly grace that so easily cows her subordinates. Every gaze she meets flashes then darts away. Every head bows. A few grunts and several uncomfortable nods answer her question.

But Mother Ulla rolls her eyes hugely. "You lot of wet lambkins!" she growls and pounds the table with one tiny fist. "Sure'n it don't satisfy none of us. There's rumors of Black Magic goin' about. Don't play stupid with me, Granny! You know it as well as I do, for all you never leave this little glamour-world of yours. Now I don't deny you've done a fair job keeping the Wood at bay and protecting your wardship. But Black Magic don't fly with this coven."

"I don't like your tone, Ulla," Elorata says coldly. "If you have evidence of Black Magic, lay it before me. If not, I would appreciate it if you kept your slander to yourself."

"You know we ain't gots no evidence," Mother Ulla growls. "If we had, we wouldn't be sitting down to dine on your **glamour-feast** like so many children nibbling at the gingerbread walls. We ain't here to present evidence. We's here to let you know—we be watching. This new apprentice of yours, she better be a good 'un. And if not, we'll know why."

Elorata's eyes flash dangerously behind dark lashes. "Very well, Ulla," she says. "You've spoken your piece. Now let me speak mine: if I discover any sign—even the barest *hint* of a sign—that any one of you has been *spying* on me within my own wardship, I shall immediately demand satisfaction by Witch Trial."

That seems to take the breath out of every member of the party. They drop their faces like so many scolded children. Only Mother Ulla keeps her head up, her whiskery chin quivering with rage, her eyes sparking like flints from behind deep folds of wrinkles and fat. But for the first time that evening, I catch the faintest scent of fear from her. For all her courage, for all her plain speaking, the old ward witch doesn't relish the idea of facing Granny Dorrel in single combat.

Elorata looks round at the company, her wrathful expression melting back into a hostess's calm. "Well now, if that's settled, who's ready for coffee and cake?"

# 13

## BRIELLE

Time passes.

Slowly, but it passes.

Days turn into weeks, weeks into months. And somehow, I wake up one morning to discover that I've been in Granny's service a full three months.

I lie there in my rose-colored, glamourized room, staring up at the ceiling, and sigh. When all is said and done, I suppose it hasn't been too bad. A few quests to fetch more rare ingredients from strange parts of the Wood. A handful of hunts—first a stray cockatrice, followed by a grindylow in a nearby river, then a serpentine thing that shot burning balls of goo from its nostrils. Fair game as far as I'm concerned. I was more than happy to put an end to each of them with a well-placed arrow.

No more werebeast hunts. Not yet anyway.

Lately, Granny has put me on patrol, marching the boundaries of her ward day after day, searching for signs of spying. I'm not certain who she thinks is spying on her, but she's grown a little paranoid in the last few months. I don't mind, though. Patrol marching is simple enough, and it keeps me away from Granny for the majority of each day.

With a little grunt and a growl, I sit up in bed, push back the counterpane, and rub my sleep-heavy eyes with the heels of my hands. Today is another patrol, this time across the northernmost borders of Granny's territory. I'll be gone most of the day, might not even make it back to Granny's house before sunset.

I climb from bed, pull on trousers, shirt, outer tunic, boots. First knotting my hair at the nape of my neck, I cover my head with my green hood. Then it's time to don my assortment of pouches, blades, buckles, quiver, and bow. Now I'm ready for anything.

Stamping my boots three times each to adjust the tightness, I move to my bedroom door and step out into the passage. There will be breakfast waiting for me in the dining room, but I don't head that way. Granny will be there by this time, sitting down to a steaming, glamorized coffee from an equally glamorized porcelain cup. She'll ask me about the previous day, smile sweetly, pretend to make conversation as though we are just any grandmother and granddaughter, not mistress and slave. I won't play that game.

Instead, I grab of bite of deer jerky from my travel pouch and gnaw on it as I step through the front door and out into the indistinct garden-scape, making my way to the iron gate. The gate opens at my approach, used to my comings and goings by now. As always, it's a relief to pass from Granny's innermost domain into the unglamorized world beyond the walls. Though I've adjusted somewhat to all the glamours over these last few months, that doesn't mean I like them.

I stride into the forest and slip into the greenery and shadows as easily as a duck gliding into water. This is my natural element, after all. This is where I belong.

I don't bother opening a Hinter Path; I don't need one for where I'm going. Instead, I set an easy, loose gait, swinging my arms, breathing deep, and letting my mind fall into that perfect equilibrium of thoughtless alertness. It doesn't pay to let one's guard down in Whispering Wood, either by sinking into a stupor or by allowing one's thoughts to wander. Best to stay present, focused, in the moment. Like a creature of the Wood myself.

It's not long before I become aware of the shadow trailing in my wake. My mouth hardens into a grimace.

*Dire.*

He's always there these days, dogging my footsteps. I'm not sure if Granny sends him to watch me because she mistrusts me or because she's concerned for my safety. Neither of those scenarios appeals, truth be told. More than once I've considered telling her to call off her watchdog, to let me do my job without his unseen eyes following my every move. It's irritating. Unnerving. Not that Granny cares.

Oh well. At least I rarely find it necessary to interact with the beast-man. In fact, since our tense conversation under the oak tree all those months ago, we've exchanged maybe ten words altogether. He does his job, lurking in my shadow. I do mine. Thus far, our paths have not crossed again.

I shake thoughts of him away so hard, my hood slips from my head and falls back over my shoulders. I don't bother to pull it back into place but quicken my pace through the forest. It takes a good two hours of steady tramping to reach the northernmost boundary of Granny's territory. It doesn't *look* like a boundary, if I'm honest. There's forest on this side and forest on that side, and only the very faintest shimmer in the air to indicate any sort of a boundary line. Every now and then, Granny sends a little pot of sticky, tar-like substance along with me, and has me smear dabs on the trees along the boundary edges. I'm not sure why, but I'm guessing it somehow regenerates the rune spells she's planted here.

Today, however, I'm merely to walk the boundary and check for any signs of disturbance. Simple enough. I continue my easy pace, keeping the boundary edge on my left and skirting round thicker clumps of undergrowth and fallen tree limbs as necessary. Here and there I pause to pull out my knife and clear the path for future use. For the most part I leave the forest untouched.

All the while, Dire haunts me. Just out of sight. Just out of hearing. Just beyond range of true perception. But I *know* he's there. The prickling up the back of my neck does not lie.

After several hours of marching, finding nothing interesting along the way, I decide to take a break. There are no oak trees near at hand, but I find a mossy knoll that looks comfortable enough and sit. It's more dried venison for lunch, washed down by mouthfuls from my waterskin. I don't really mind. I've lived on worse. And at least I know it's not glamorized.

While I eat, I take special care not to twist in place and try to peer into the greenery behind me. Not to search for a glimpse of gray fur or flashing yellow eyes. As always, I maintain a demeanor of firm disinterest. I don't know if it fools the werewolf or not. Gods know, he can probably *smell* my awareness of him from a good half-mile off! But it makes me feel better.

No matter what, I won't let myself think about that last moment under the oak tree. That moment when his eyes had gazed into mine with such human desperation . . .

A growl rumbles in my throat, as savage as any werebeast. I shove a hunk of jerky into my mouth and tear at it, trying to force my teeth through the tough, smoky meat. I've no sooner torn free a long strip when I become suddenly aware that I'm not alone. Someone else is here. Someone besides me and the unseen werebeast.

I pause, lift my head, the strip of meat still dangling from my lips. A figure stands just on the other side of Granny Dorrel's border. A figure who seems to manifest out of thin air. She's little more than a shadowy outline, but I can still discern the faded, patchwork gown, the broadbrimmed hat, and the gnarled staff on which she leans heavily.

I break off my bite and swallow it unchewed. Choking a little, I stand up, brace my feet, and lift my chin.

"Hullo, Mother Ulla."

When I speak her name, she comes more completely into view, all her faded, blurry edges hardening until I can see her plain as day: the old ward witch of Ellee County—the county where Valera and I grew up.

"Well now, fancy meeting you here," she says, giving me a once-over. "I've heard tell of something like this. There's rumors all over of Granny Dorrel's new huntress. The description sounded just a bit too familiar for my liking."

"What?" I ask warily. "Scrawny and flame-haired with a face full of freckles?"

"Nah." Mother Ulla sucks on a tooth, her expression sour. "Hard-headed. Reckless. The kind of fool creature who'd jump into the Quisandoral's domain without a second thought and steal a golden apple." She rolls her lips around, then spits. "Sounded 'bout right."

I adjust my stance slightly. "What do you want? I know, sure as sin, you haven't come to help."

"Do you need help?"

"Not anymore." Bitterness roils in my gut. How many times had I gone pleading to Mother Ulla to help me in those early weeks right after Valera was stolen? Valera went to her as well, trying to find a way back to her lost fae husband. Mother Ulla refused her same as she'd refused me. As a result, the two of us went to Granny instead. And the rest is history. Bad, bad history.

"Never did need your help," I persist stubbornly. "Not really. I had everything I needed to get what I wanted."

"And this?" Mother Ulla lifts a hand from her staff and waves vaguely at me then around at the forest looming over us. "This is what you wanted? To be Granny's little runner-around girl?"

"I wanted to help Valera. And I did."

She grunts and sucks her tooth again, thoughtfully. "Where is that lovestruck sister of yours then?" she asks at last. "She hereabouts as well?"

I don't answer. Slowly, my hand moves to the knife at my belt. A stupid gesture, and well I know it. What am I going to do, threaten the old witch? But my fingers play along the hilt, nonetheless.

Mother Ulla snorts and twists her staff around in her nimble little fingers. "It don't take special sight to see that you've gots yourself in a bad way, girl. Maybe we can help one another."

"I don't need your help," I answer sharply.

"That's as may be. Hear me out, even so." Mother Ulla narrows her old eyes so that I can scarcely see them glittering between wrinkles. "It's in my mind that your Granny is up to something not quite right deep down in that wardship of hers. Something by way of Black Magic. Runes is one thing. Even some potions; I ain't against a good potion now and again. That's a natural outflow of magic and can generally be controlled without taking control in turn. And I ain't never seen a one like your Granny for a glamour,

I'll grant you that.

"But . . . it's my belief she's gone and dabbled in the Deep Secrets. Things what ain't safe for mortal minds. Things what require bargains and pain and the taking of things what don't belong. Things what warp the shapes of souls. And, over time, the shape of wardships as well.

"There's warping in the air here." She reaches out and just barely touches her staff to that empty space in the air, that invisible boundary line between her wardship and Granny's. "I can't quite see it. I can't quite sense it. But I *know* it. I know it deep down in my bones. And the longer you stay in there, girl, the more you're at risk being caught up in the worst of it."

A shudder runs down my spine. The truth is, I don't doubt what she's saying. The wrongness in this wardship . . . I felt it the very first time I set foot here. These last few months have only intensified that feeling. But what can I do? I still have most of seven years of service ahead of me.

I meet Mother Ulla's knowing gaze. Should I tell her? Should I tell her about the agreement Valera made with Granny to spare my life? Tell her what Granny expects of me, what she has already made me do?

There's no point to it. Mother Ulla isn't my friend. She never was. And unlike Granny, she doesn't even pretend to be sympathetic. All too vividly, I remember that little eleven-year-old girl I once was, standing outside the cottage door, pounding and weeping and begging the old witch to come out. To help find Valera.

Nothing but silence answered.

"Have you said your piece?" I demand, setting my chin in a hard line.

Mother Ulla's eyes flash through the wrinkles. "Yeah. Yeah, I guess I have."

"Then I bid you good day, Mother Ulla." I pull up my hood to shadow my face, turn to go, but pause. Looking round, I fix the witch with a studying stare. Then I step up to the invisible boundary and the young poplar tree growing right on the line. I look it up and down, uncertain what it is I'm sensing. Maybe it's nothing, or maybe . . .

I whip out my knife and plunge it into the trunk. Immediately, there's a flare of green light, and just for an instant I see the shape of a rune. A rune that is *just* on Granny's side of the boundary but is definitely *not* Granny's magic.

Ruthlessly, I dig my blade into the trunk, peeling back bits of bark and layers of wood, ignoring the shudder in the branches overhead. I tear a long strip of bark and toss it to Mother Ulla's side of the property line, then meet the old witch's eye.

She stares back at me. Slowly, deliberately, she grinds the end of her staff into the bark. There's another flash of green magic as the rune disappears.

Without a word, I turn and march on my way, following the line of the wardship. I feel Mother Ulla's eyes on me as I go . . . and from the deeper shadows on this side of the boundary, another pair of eyes, even more intense, even more deadly.

I glimpse two other werebeasts when I return to Granny's house a few hours after sundown.

I don't often see those two, though I know they're always nearby. One is a shaggy gray-and-black creature, the other red like Dreg but smaller and lither. I've never seen them in their human state, though I think one is female, the other male. For the most part they keep to themselves and avoid me like I'm plague-ridden.

They seem to be patrolling close to Granny's house tonight. I don't know why. Perhaps she sensed some extra threat in the air and called in her security. Now that Dire seems to spend most of his time tailing me, these other two are probably kept much busier fulfilling Granny's various tasks. And they don't have Dreg to help them anymore.

*Dreg . . .*

Even as I reach Granny's gate, I pause, a sudden shiver of sickness rippling through me. One hand gripping an iron bar, I close my eyes, bow my head, waiting for the sensation to pass. But that's a mistake—for now, in the darkness behind my eyelids, I see again that horrible moment when Conrad pulled back the red werebeast's head and ran his knife along her exposed throat. I see the blood gush; it seems to overwhelm everything, drowning me from the inside out.

This is the image that haunts my dreams. Night after night

after night. And how much longer before I'm the one required to do that throat-slitting?

With a sharp creak, the gate begins to move, startling me. I take a step backwards, blinking into the darkness on the other side. The sun is down, and my eyes have only partially adjusted to the pale moonlight of the forest. The murk of Granny's garden is almost impenetrable.

Drawing a long breath, I stride through the gate and make my way across the indistinct garden. Tonight I feel the undeveloped glamours like a thickness in the atmosphere, ready to choke me. I put my head down and hurry. Hopefully, I can get inside, make it to my room, eat whatever glamorized food I find there, and collapse on my bed fully clothed, all without encountering my grandmother.

The front door opens at my approach. Not a good sign. Usually if the house itself responds to me like this, it means Granny is aware of me as well. And if Granny is aware of me, it's because she wants something.

"Oh gods, what now?" I mutter as I step inside.

To my surprise, I enter immediately into the hall of werebeast heads, without any of the regular twisting and turning passages. I stop in my tracks, my heart thudding, half-ready to retreat into the garden. But a door at the end of the hall opens, letting a square of warm light fall upon the floor. It's as good as a summons.

Swallowing hard, I tuck my chin and move quickly to the door, avoiding the glassy stares of the werebeasts as I go. Only once do

I glance up . . . as I pass beneath the poor little weredeer with her frightened, gentle eyes. But I only shoot her a swift glance, then focus on what lies ahead.

The open door leads into a pretty sitting room. I've been here before, of course. Valera and I both sat in this room with our grandmother months ago, when we came to her for help. There's a big fire on the hearth and a lovely, tall-backed chair pulled up close to it. Granny sits there, splendid as always, in a golden gown of crushed velvet. She's got a little bit of embroidery in her hands and is delicately stitching bloodred petals against fine white muslin.

"Good evening, Brielle," she says in her softest, most welcoming voice. It makes my skin crawl. "Leave your weapons outside."

I obey, propping my bow and quiver against the wall of the passage. I remember to slip off my knife belt as well and leave it with the rest. Only then do I step into the room and take a position just outside of the firelight, my hands clasped at the small of my back, my gaze staring into the space above Granny's head.

Granny looks up from her embroidery. "Sit, if you please."

There's just enough suggestion in her words to not quite count as a command. So I remain standing, silent. Granny's eyebrow rises slightly. We both know she could force the issue if she wished. My heart thuds in my throat as I wait for her decision.

But Granny merely sets aside her needlework and picks up a little cup of aromatic herbal tea sitting on the table at her elbow. She takes a sip . . . and for a split second, I see her wince. What is she actually drinking beneath the intense glamour of herbs and sweetness?

Granny puts the cup down in its saucer and turns her gaze back to me. "You've done well in your service thus far, child." Her voice is kindly, like she expects me to flush with delight at the compliment.

My stomach hardens in a knot. I say nothing.

"You've managed to survive three months, which is rather more than I initially anticipated. My borders have never been so secure, my supplies so well stocked. I am pleased with our bargain."

Something bitter builds up on my tongue. I swallow it back with an effort.

"But," Granny continues, then takes another delicate sip from her cup, swallowing slowly, "there is one task you have not accomplished for me. The primary purpose of your service to me as huntress." She lifts her gaze, meeting my eyes. "So far, you've managed to bring down a cockatrice, a grindylow, and a yelric wyrm that have strayed into my wardship. And yet, the disaster of that first hunt stains your reputation. But rest assured! You will now have the opportunity to prove your true worth to me."

The room around me seems suddenly to pitch. It's all I can do to stand upright, to not sway or betray myself in any way. I know what's coming. I've known it was coming all along. But now it's here. And there's no escape.

Which of the three werebeasts will it be? The big gray-and-black fellow? The delicate red female? Or . . . or . . .

Granny sets her cup on the table, props her elbows on the arms of her chair, and loosely interlaces her fingers in front of her chest.

"Dire's term of service is coming to an end. At dawn tomorrow, he will be free."

Free like Dreg.

Free to run.

Free to die.

"Once the bonds that kept him loyal to me are severed," Granny continues, "he may go where he wills and do as he chooses. Unfortunately, that rarely bodes well for me." She smiles again, her lips pretty, her expression harsh. "I expect he will try to kill me. I need you to settle the matter. Before it gets out of hand."

She tilts her head slightly to one side, the firelight catching in her curls just so and heightening the warmth of her complexion. She looks so lovely, innocent even. One could almost miss the viper in her eye. The compulsion of her power settles around me, like chains binding me body and soul. There's nothing I can do. And only one thing I can say.

"Yes, Granny."

I turn and start for the door.

"A moment."

I freeze in place, my hand on the doorknob, unable to draw a complete breath.

"Given the results of your last werebeast hunt, I've decided to take no chances." Her words cut into the back of my skull like so many razor blades. "Conrad Torosson will be joining you. Just to make certain all is done right."

I'm trembling like a frightened child. But I can't let her see. I can't let her know. I summon every ounce of strength I have left in me, and say, "Of course, Granny."

"You may go now. Rest well tonight, my darling. Tomorrow will be . . . important."

With that, her hold on me loosens. I escape through the door and shut it fast behind me. Pausing only long enough to snatch up my weapons, I stumble down the hall of trophy heads, feeling their gazes on me as I go. I reach the end and turn into an indistinct corridor before I fall to my knees, holding my stomach and trying desperately not to be sick. For some while, I can do nothing but kneel there, eyes closed, rocking slowly back and forth. Eventually, however, the churning in my stomach calms. A dullness settles over my spirit.

After all, this is what I am now.

Granny's huntress.

Granny's executioner.

## 14

### DIRE

Dawn has come.

The dawn of my first day of freedom in twenty years.

Dawn of the day I will probably die.

I stand in my human form, naked before the gates of the witch's house. It all feels surreal somehow. As though these moments must be happening to someone else, not me. After twenty long, excruciating years of torment, of slavery, how can I possibly be here? How can this possibly be now?

Perhaps it's all just a dream.

I look down at my naked self. Only a little bit of cloth hangs loosely from my hips, a pathetic excuse for modesty. I tremble in the cold air, gooseflesh rising along my bare flesh. It won't be long before the fur begins to regrow, however. My freedom from

Granny's thrall does not mean freedom from my beast-self, after all. That lesson I learned long ago, at great cost.

I close my eyes. Trying not to feel. Trying not to hope. The truth is, it's been so damn long since I was my own master! Even if this so-called freedom can only last a day or two, I can't help myself. I *want* it. I want those precious hours, those precious moments of knowing I belong to myself and not to Elorata Dorrel.

I wait, peering through the iron bars at the nothing of her world on the other side. The sun rises slowly, spreading golden light through the trees, but when it falls through those bars, the light cannot penetrate more than a foot or two. But I can feel Elorata approaching. In the same way I might feel the looming threat of a storm.

Suddenly, she appears before me. And my heart lurches at the sight of her.

She is breathtaking—like an angel come down from the heavens, clad all in a gown of white belted with silver, her hair loose about her shoulders, falling nearly to her waist in wave upon wave of rippling crimson. Her face looks gentle, almost saintly in its softness, in the curve of her sweet mouth and the roundness of her chin and cheek. Beholding her, a painter would long to create works of holy art, a poet to write a sacred sonnet, a musician to compose an oratorio to the holiness of beauty.

This is Elorata as I first met her. All those years ago, when I first braved the shadows of Whispering Wood, searching for . . . for . . .

A bolt of pain lances through my head. I can't remember. I

never can. And when I close my eyes, when I try to see that face I once knew so well, all I can see is the poor, twisted creature whose head is now mounted on the witch's wall.

I open my eyes, meet Elorata's gaze. She's still just as beautiful as she was a moment before. But the spell is broken, never to be restored. I know her for the devil she is.

She smiles prettily. "Dawn is upon us, my beautiful Dire." Her gaze travels up and down my exposed body. She shakes her head and *tsks* softly, regretfully. "By the seven gods, how it pains me even now that it should have come to this! Will you not repent of your stubbornness? Will you not return to where your heart belongs?"

My lip curls beneath my beard. "My body may have belonged to you," I growl. "My service and even my soul. But never my heart."

"Ah, but it could have! It should have." She takes a step nearer, bringing her face up to the iron bars. Her sky-blue eyes gaze into mine, limpid and alluring. I feel the glamour going out from them, as powerful as any fae's charm. But I hardened to her tricks long ago.

The sun breaks suddenly through the trees, shining full upon me, warming my nakedness. In that same moment, I feel it—the last of my bindings disintegrating. The sensation lashes through me, like lines of fire under my skin, and I cry out, fall to my knees, the pain overwhelming everything else.

Then it passes. My darkened vision clears. I'm staring down at the ground between my two hands, listening to the rough breath heaving in and out of my lungs. I shudder, close my eyes, force back the sickness rising in my throat.

My twenty years of service is complete.

I'm free.

"I could have loved you, you know."

I wince at that lovely, sultry voice caressing my ear. With a growl, I lift my head, stare up into the witch's eyes. For a shocking instant, I see something true shining behind her glamours. A real and painful *sorrow*. She shakes her head and extends a hand between the iron bars toward me.

"I could have loved you. Truly. Deeply. I could have given you my whole heart."

Her fingertips hover in the space just before my eyes. It would be nothing at all to lean into her touch. And I know just how soft that touch would be, how gentle and yet how full of promise of stronger, sweeter sensations.

I pull back. Panting, I get to my feet, sway heavily where I stand. I'm weak as a newborn pup. But I belong to myself again. Whatever life remains to me, however twisted with curses and fear, I will never again take that belonging for granted.

Elorata withdraws her hand, gripping the iron bars so tight her knuckles stand out. She bares her teeth, and her glamour cracks, revealing a glimpse of the truth—a glimpse of the haggard, wizened shell of a woman who has seen far too many years of vicious magic. The image vanishes in a blink, however, and the glamour redoubles, her beauty almost strong enough to knock me off my feet.

"Very well, sweet one," she croons through her teeth. "You've made your choice. May you not regret it in your final moments. Now go! You have until the sun reaches its zenith. Then your head is mine."

I don't want to break her gaze. I don't want her to know that she can still frighten me. Not now. But time is passing. If I'm to have any chance at all . . .

I turn and flee into Whispering Wood.

## 15

## BRIELLE

Time for me to go.

Just as the sun reaches the highest point in the sky above, I step through the iron gate, leaving Granny's house behind me. Granny isn't here, thank the gods. I'm not sure I could bear to look her in the eye just now, not sure I could stand to hear her speak in that gracious, controlled voice of hers. My limbs are shivering, my veins pulsing with the compulsion I am bound to obey.

Whatever Dire may once have thought—whatever power he believed flowed in my blood—I know the truth. There's no backing out of this hunt.

I close my eyes, trying to remember how to pray. It's been so long since I bothered, so long since I sought aid from the gods.

From anyone. Why should I expect the gods to help me now?

A crackling of underbrush. I open my eyes just as Conrad emerges from the Wood into the clear space before Granny's gate. Gods on high, he's bigger than I remembered! Almost as tall as Dire in his werewolf form, and nearly as broad too. Armed to the teeth, clad in leather armor, an intimidating presence whom even the fae would hesitate to cross.

I meet his gaze and nod grimly. "So. You're working for Granny again, are you?"

He comes to a stop in front of me and blinks slowly. "Aye."

My lip curls. "How do you like being my grandmother's watchdog? Is it as fun as it looks?"

That one good eye of his narrows slightly. "Pay's good."

Is that a trace of defensiveness I hear in his voice?

I step around him and make for the forest. No point trying to engage in conversation. Besides, the day is lengthening, and my quarry's head start is only growing the longer I delay. Best to get this hunt over with.

It isn't hard to find Dire's trail. I watched from the shelter of the garden when he broke from Granny and fled into the Wood, taking note of where he vanished among the trees. In the human form he wears at dawn, he's not as stealthy as he is by this late in the day when his monster shape is dominant. I easily find broken twigs, stirred up leaves, and even one distinct footprint in the dirt. That footprint I immediately distrust, fairly certain he planted it purposefully to point me in the wrong direction. I'm not so easily deceived.

His real trail seems to lead in an altogether different direction. Part of me hopes I'm wrong, part of me hopes that I will fall for his tricks, giving him that much more time to put distance between us, maybe even to escape altogether. But no. I know what I'm doing. And with Granny's compulsion driving me, I have no choice but to do it well.

I set off swiftly, pursuing the trail, Conrad falling into place several yards behind me. He offers neither counsel nor critique. He merely follows. It's a bit unsettling, but I've grown somewhat used to having every footstep dogged over these last three months. A small part of me might even be glad he's here. His presence keeps me from sinking too deeply into thoughts I dare not let myself think, keeps me from feeling the sickness churning in my gut. I must stay present, concentrating on the needs of the moment.

I am a huntress. No more. No less. And Dire is my prey.

It isn't long before the werewolf's trail leads me through a familiar part of the Wood. At first, I'm not sure why it's familiar, only that something about this place makes the hair on my neck prickle. Every little sound—a breath of wind through the branches, a rustling of leaves as a squirrel darts past—makes me jumpy.

Then I step into a clearing. And my heart drops to my stomach.

I do know this place. I remember it all too well. The broad canopy of dead branches overhead. The bulging roots beneath the soil, no longer full of life and vitality. The huge hollow trunk and the gaping hollow in which even now an owlkin is probably sleeping.

I stand frozen in place, my jaw hanging open. The whole

adventure seems to play out before my vision. Dire climbing that trunk. The owlkin emerging, its long-fingered hands grasping the edge of the hollow. The flash of talons, the heart-pounding terror. All of it comes back to me in a flash.

We survived that encounter. Together.

I swallow hard, my throat suddenly dry. I'm being foolish. I'm reading into this, but . . . I can't help feeling as though Dire led me here for a reason. As though he's trying to tell me something.

Conrad steps to my side, huge and solemn, his hand on the hilt of his big hunting knife. "There's something in that hollow."

I nod. "An owlkin."

He turns his head sharply, fixing me with the stare of his one good eye. "In truth?"

"Yup." I adjust the set of my quiver and turn away, striding back into the trees. "But that's not our quarry today."

Conrad growls. As a professional Monster Hunter, it must gall him to let a creature like that live. But no one is paying him to make an end to it. Ultimately, he follows me.

I pick up Dire's trail again, once more noting how oddly clear it is. He's not making any effort to disguise his progress. I worked much harder when I pursued the red werebeast months ago. But Dire is no fool. And the further I follow the winding route he leads, the more I'm sure he's doing this on purpose.

The trail takes a turn, and I push through a stand of young saplings, burst through to the far side. And stop again.

Oh.

Oh, gods on high.

Standing before me, tall and strong, is the very same oak under which I sat for a rest following our encounter with the Quisandoral. Where he crouched in front of me, took my hand in his, and begged me to . . . to . . .

I close my eyes, fighting a wave of nausea. He's still hoping I can fight this. Fight Granny. Hoping I have a choice. Why can he not accept the truth? Why can he not accept the twisted fates that have led us to this dreadful day, this dreadful hunt? Granny may be issuing the commands, but the death she calls for must have been foreordained by the gods themselves.

We don't have any say. Neither of us do.

Conrad stands close behind me. He's silent, but the power of his presence is too potent to ignore. He's watching me, curious, but holding his tongue.

Setting my jaw, I spin on my heel and march on. At first I don't even think about following Dire. I think only about getting away from that tree, away from that memory. Away from that image of compelling gray eyes, begging me to understand, begging me to act, to strive, to resist . . .

No! I can't do this. I can't think like this. He's toying with me, like a cat with a mouse, and I'm letting him get away with it. But I am not the mouse here. I am not the prey.

I retrace my steps and pick up the werewolf's trail, leading away from the oak and on into the deeps of Whispering Wood. His body has changed dramatically by this stage. The few footprints I find are halfway between man and wolf. I'd better hurry if I want to catch him before sunset. Before he looks like a man again.

I'm not sure I can do what needs to be done if I have to look into his human eyes . . .

Somehow, I know exactly where the trail will lead me next. It doesn't twist and wind anymore but cuts a straight route through the forest until it reaches a little rise on which stands a grove of young fir trees. Their branches bend and break as I push my way through, filling my nostrils with their spicy perfume. I emerge on the far side and look down into a valley.

A valley in the center of which lies a small, crystal-clear pool.

It's all just as I remember it. Just as it was when I came to this place three months ago, my bow strung, my arrow at the ready. Only then, the creature crouched over that pool, staring with such despair at its reflection, was red, not gray.

This time, it's Dire.

He doesn't move. Not even when I swiftly string my bow and whip an arrow from my quiver. I know he's aware of me—one long ear twitches back my way, detecting even the slightest noise I make. But he doesn't move. He doesn't turn on me with savage eyes, doesn't lunge and tear at me with tooth and claw. He merely sits, gazing into that mirror-like water. Gazing at the reflected beast, which is now just as much who he is as the man ever was.

I raise my bow, take aim.

My lips quiver. Despite my best efforts, they soundlessly shape his name: *Dire* . . .

As though he's heard me, he turns. Slowly. Almost though he's trying not to startle me. His face is still mostly wolfish, and fur covers his broad, powerful shoulders and his elongated forelimbs. But his eyes . . . gods help me, his eyes are human. So very human.

I draw a long breath. My arm is shaking. I know my shot will go wide if I take it now.

"Nice little sight-seeing tour you've led me on, wolfman," I call out, hoping the bitterness of my tone disguises any tremor. "Bit roundabout, don't you think? You'd have gotten farther without so many detours."

He looks at me. Right down the line of my arrow. And says nothing.

The shot is perfect. I need only steady my arm, steady my breathing, and I can put this arrow straight through his eye. It'll all be over in an instant. And what does it matter if one of those eyes is damaged? Granny will have glass ones set in place when she mounts her new trophy.

*Do it, Brielle.*

The compulsion burns inside me, a driving force as inevitable as the tide.

*Do it. It's what you came for. It's what you're good for.*

*This is who you are.*

"Aren't you going to beg?" I hardly recognize my own voice, so high and strained in my tear-thickened throat. "Aren't you going to try to convince me to resist? I know you think I can. I know you think I have a choice here."

He looks at me. Just looks at me.

Oh gods, why doesn't he speak?

I draw another ragged breath, my arrow tip shaking hard. Then, with a sudden exhale, I put back my shoulders, pull up my arms, haul on the bowstring.

Pivoting sharply, I fire my arrow.

It pierces the ground mere inches from Conrad's foot.

The Monster Hunter, standing off to my right, utters a surprised cry. His own arrow shoots wide, grazing the werewolf's shoulder rather than piercing his throat. As though given a sudden jolt of life, Dire leaps straight up in the air. He whips about and bolts across the clearing, vanishing into the trees on the far side.

"Seven gods damn!" Conrad casts me a ferocious look, his teeth bared to the gums. Then he too is in motion, sliding down the incline into the clearing, regaining his balance, and sprinting after the werewolf.

I'm running too. I'm not even certain I made a decision—I'm simply in motion, my feet pounding the ground as hard as they can. Somewhere in the back of my head, I feel Granny's spell trying to pull me back into its thrall. But something stronger surges through me now, a vicious determination I cannot ignore. My blood feels as though it's on fire.

I duck and weave through low-hanging branches, spring over fallen trunks, sprint around trees, always just keeping Conrad's bulky form in view. The werewolf is ahead of him, loping long and low. If he were fully wolf, he'd leave us both in the dust, but in his half-man state, he's awkward, slower. It won't be long before

Conrad gains on him, and then . . . and then . . .

Tucking my chin, keeping my arms and bow close to my side, I press on harder. A distant roar fills my ears, and at first I don't recognize what I'm hearing. Not until I burst through the trees and emerge at the top of a high cliff do I realize it's a river carving deep into the landscape below.

Dire is trapped.

He stands on the brink, his chest heaving, gazing down at a perilous drop. Could he survive a leap into that white-rushing flow? Can that ungainly body of his even swim?

Conrad stands a few yards to my left, breathing heavily. He must know I'm there, but his gaze is fixed on the wolfman. He nocks an arrow, raises his bow.

In five pounding steps I cover the distance between us. I'm no match for him in breadth and bulk, but I fling my arms around his waist and drive into him with all the force in my body. A shout bursts from his lips as his arrow flies wildly off kilter, over the edge of the cliff. I'm not quite strong enough to knock him down, but he staggers several paces and drops his bow, trying to keep his footing.

One powerful fist clutches my shoulder and wrenches me to one side. "You've gone soft, girl," he snarls into my face. "You can't let these monsters get to you. They *must* die!"

I shriek wordlessly and tear at his arm, digging my nails into his flesh. He winces but doesn't let go. One leg lashes out, kicks my feet out from under me. I crash hard on my back, and he plants a booted foot into my chest. I grab at his calf, gasping for breath, totally helpless.

He looms over me, his long dark hair hanging in his face. "Stay down."

With all the venom I can muster, I spit. Straight in his eye.

He stumbles back. I draw in a great lungful of air and push myself into a seated position, staring up at the huge man. His face is a grimacing mask of rage as he turns to me. He takes a step.

Before he can take another, something massive and gray hurtles into him from one side. Dire. He, at least, is big enough to knock the Monster Hunter off his feet. But Conrad has not survived this long at his job for nothing. He hits the ground hard but manages to roll free of the werewolf's arms. As he comes up on his knees, his hunting knife appears in his hand. Dire lashes out, but that wicked blade strikes back equally fast. I see a splash of red in the air.

Dire retreats, chest heaving. Conrad gets to his feet. "Come on, wolf!" he growls. "Is that all you've got?"

He adjusts the knife into a plunging angle, surges to his feet, and rushes the wolfman. Dire dodges to one side nimbly enough. But the truth is, while he is the bigger and stronger of the two, he's not the fighter that Conrad is. His wolf-self is too far retreated, his man-self too much returned this late in the day.

His lips curled back in something that isn't a smile, the Monster Hunter lunges again. Dire retreats but stumbles on his own awkward hindquarters and goes down hard. Conrad's blade glints bright, aiming straight for the werewolf's eye.

I'm on my feet. I don't even realize I'd gotten up; don't realize

I'd fully caught my breath. I'm simply up and moving, leaping at Conrad's back. I wrap one arm around his neck, and my other hand grabs at his arm. Startled, Conrad twists his torso, dislodging my grasp. I take a step back, stumble.

Pain flares through every sense.

I gasp.

My whole body stands in shocked stillness, my breath caught in my throat. Slowly, I lower my gaze. And see the hilt of that hunting knife and three inches of bright steel protruding from my shoulder.

Conrad is there in front of me, his face strangely gray behind his beard. His eye widens, and his mouth gapes, as though he's trying to speak.

Then a roar splits the air between us. There's a confusion of limbs, fur, leather, and flashing, wild eyes. I hear Conrad utter a cursing cry a mere instant before the werewolf's powerful arms send him hurtling over the edge of the cliff.

But all that seems miles away from me.

I sink to my knees. The small, dull part of my brain still functioning listens for a splash. But that's silly. There won't be any splash, not in those churning rapids. Will Conrad's body be battered to a pulp among the rocks? Or will the rushing water pull him under and fill his lungs before flinging him up on a distant shore far downriver?

Strange . . . I feel a bit sad. He didn't deserve to . . . to . . .

I collapse. Sprawled out on my back, I stare up at the sky above. Slowly I turn my head, blinking against the darkness closing in. A massive, indistinct shape approaches, all foaming teeth and red gums and heaving breaths. A hand stretches out, fingers splayed, claws gleaming in the sunlight.

Then the darkness overwhelms me. I sink gratefully down into it.

# 16

## DIRE

My hands shake as I reach for the girl. Hands that are beginning to take human shape again but are still very much animal with fur and bloodstained claws.

I pull back, not certain I should touch her, not like this. I can't seem to control the shaking. My entire body quivers like a leaf.

It's just the adrenaline of battle. That's all.

"Girl?" My voice is rough and thick in my throat. I shake my shaggy head, spitting foam into the dirt. Then I try again. "Brielle?"

No answer. Her eyes are half open, but she's unconscious. Her face has gone a dangerous shade of white, causing every freckle to stand out in sharp contrast.

Swallowing hard, I bend over to inspect the wound in her shoulder and the awful knife protruding. It looks bad. I'm afraid to draw out the blade, afraid it'll only make her bleed faster. I cast a quick glance around, searching for something I might use to pack the wound, to bind it. There's nothing. And I don't think my animal hands could manage such a task in any case.

For a moment, my mind goes completely blank, hopeless.

Then an idea sparks in the back of my head—or not an idea so much as an instinct. But now that it's there, I can't ignore it.

As gently as I can, I slip my arms under the girl and lift her, cradling her close to my chest. She moans with pain as I jostle her shoulder, but her eyes are shut. Just as well. If she's unconscious, she shouldn't be feeling the full extent of her pain.

I get to my feet, a little awkward on my hind legs. For a moment I hesitate, looking down into that face nestled against my shoulder. She set out to kill me. I could smell the deadly intent on her when we faced each other in the valley. More than that, I could smell the potent stench of Elorata Dorrel's relentless spells wrapping around her. Those spells are still in place, weakened perhaps, but present.

But she *did* resist. What's more, she saved my life. At risk of her own.

A growl vibrating in my throat, I turn and plunge back into the forest.

Twenty years later, I still remember the way.

I walked this path only once in my former life, when I first plunged into Whispering Wood, searching for the ward witch. But the memory etched itself in my brain as though carved into stone.

Now, my wolf senses guide me, my heart sense compels me, and sooner than I would have believed possible, I find myself on a simple dirt trail leading through the trees. I follow that trail, swift and sure, until I come to a place where I know the forest should end. There should be sweeping fields before me. Open country, open sky, leading to a small, neat lawn and garden and a proud, stone manor house.

But it's gone. Overgrown. Trees and underbrush pack so densely, I can't even see the house anymore.

My lip curls back in a snarl. Many times these last twenty years I've wondered what happened to Phaendar Hall after my departure. Folks always said my grandfather built too close to Whispering Wood, that one day the Wood would overwhelm it. But Granddad trusted the ward witch to keep its borders at bay, and the fields in these parts were rich and fertile. It seemed to him a safe bet.

He could never have predicted Elorata Dorrel's vindictive nature.

I push aside low, clinging branches, trying to shield the girl in my arms as best I can. At last I glimpse a wall ahead of me, covered in thick vines but still standing. That's something, at least. The Wood may have swallowed up the hall, but it hasn't totally digested it yet.

Adjusting my grip on the girl so that I can hold her with only one arm, I reach for the front door. My hand is more hand than paw now, and I'm able to manipulate the latch. I half expect it to be locked, but it opens lightly at my touch, the hinges offering only the barest creak of protest.

For the first time in two decades, I peer into the home of my childhood.

The foyer of Phaendar Hall was always dark, heavy with richly carved wood and a massive stairway. Now, however, sunlight pours through a hole in the roof, dappling the floor. A tall, stately cedar grows up from the inlaid tiles and breaks through the ceiling overhead. The Wood really is taking over everything.

But beyond the tree, I spy the stairway still intact.

Growling softly, I push my way through, ducking branches as I go. Brielle moans when I move too swiftly and jostle her. "Shhh, shhh," I murmur. "We're almost there now. I promise."

I look down into her face speckled with light falling through the rooftop and branches. She's paler than ever. Perhaps it was a mistake taking her out of the thick magic of Whispering Wood. Here the magic is diluted by mortal air. It might be too much for her.

But I've got to tend these wounds of hers somehow. And to do so, I must have supplies.

The steps creak under my footsteps but seem stable enough as I climb to the second floor and take a turn down the left-hand passage. I try not to breathe too deeply as I go, afraid the all-too-familiar scents of home will overwhelm me just when I most need to keep my senses clear. But I feel a strange sense of phantom faces and phantom voices on all sides . . . lingering traces of the world and the people I left behind all those years ago.

I push open a door and step into a bedroom, stopping short on the threshold and closing my eyes as yet another wave of familiarity washes over me. This was my mother's room. Even with my eyes closed, I can still see her sitting at her vanity, powdering her already extremely pale skin. I can hear her brittle laughter; I can feel her cool hands touching my face and those rare but welcome kisses dropped on the top of my head.

I never said goodbye to her before I left. She wouldn't have understood, would have tried to talk me out of going. She had such plans, such hopes for me . . .

Is she still alive, out there in the real world somewhere? Or did the creeping Wood take her and my father by surprise before they could make their escape?

I will probably never know.

Now is not the time to indulge in painful speculations. I shake my head to clear it and swiftly carry Brielle to the bed. The top of a young tree is just starting to push its way up through the floor, and there are vines and green moss everywhere. But the room itself is relatively untouched, and the bed is almost free of dust when I lay the girl gently down on top of the faded counterpane. Thick shadows darken the room, and I struggle to see her face. I carefully push back her green hood, revealing her stern, faintly puckered brow. Is she in pain? I hope not. My fingers, rough and still claw-tipped, trail lightly along the line of her cheek and sweep sweat-drenched locks of hair back from her forehead. She's hot. Possibly feverish.

I must work quickly.

"I won't be a minute," I whisper, my voice strained and hollow in the silence of that chamber. I duck my head and dart out hastily, searching out a few supplies. The pump in the stable yard works without priming, much to my surprise, and I fill a basin with water. I locate old but clean cloths tucked away in a linen closet half hidden behind a young hickory tree. In the drawing room I find my mother's old sewing basket and help myself to needles, thread, and shears.

When I return to Brielle's side, the sun is beginning to set in earnest. It casts dying light through the window onto the bed, turning the girl's sweat-darkened hair into ribbons of fire. I gaze down at her, at that terrible, blood-soaked wound in her shoulder from which the knife still protrudes. My heart beats dully in my chest.

I am almost fully a man now. My wolf-self has retreated, my humanity returned. I drop my gaze, taking in my own naked torso, and shudder. Over the last many years, I've grown used to this daily transition from beast to man and back again. But somehow, being here in my own home makes the truth of my monstrous self even more horrible.

With a snarl I shake my head, shake my whole body, and set to work. Brielle doesn't have time for any personal crisis on my part. I may not have much to offer, but this brave girl saved my life today. She deserves whatever I can give her.

I pull a small table close to the bed and arrange my supplies. I know what I'm doing. It's been a long time since I was a student at university, studying medicine—much too long—but some skills don't fade as quickly as others.

I pick up the shears and turn to the girl. Here I pause, just for a moment. Blood pounds in my temples. But now is not the time to be squeamish. She is a patient. That's all. Like any other. And I need to act. I only have an hour of humanity—not a lot of time for all that must be done.

"I'm afraid there's no way around it," I say, gazing into her pain-lined face. "I've got to clean this properly and get some stitches in. No time for modesty."

I set to work with the shears, cutting away her clothes.

# 17

## BRIELLE

Slowly, I come to.

My first impression of the world around me is *comfort*. I wouldn't have expected that. Though I don't quite remember why, I expected to feel pain. I'm fairly sure that's the last thing I felt before darkness claimed me—pain and more pain.

But just now, as I lie here with my eyes closed, I feel oddly relaxed. There's still pain, of course, but it's not unbearable. And my limbs seem to be resting easily, and the world smells pleasantly of dust, forest, a hint of lavender, and . . . sugar?

My stomach rumbles loud enough to push me back into full wakefulness. I crack my eyes open, staring up at an unfamiliar ceiling of white plaster intricately molded into a pattern of garlands. A glamour? But I don't *feel* any glamours around me.

I turn my head, wincing slightly at the ache that shoots through my shoulder. Biting my lip and blinking back a sudden prickling of tears, I take in more of the room around me. A proper lady's room, with fine furnishings and heavy curtains hung from tall windows. It's lovely but faded and partially overwhelmed by a lot of green growth. There's a tree growing up through the floorboards and vines crawling up the walls. No wonder the room smells of forest.

It's very strange . . .

The scent of sugar once more tantalizes my nostrils. I angle my head a little more and discover a bowl of what looks like oatmeal sprinkled with brown sugar on a table beside the bed. It's steaming, fresh. And it doesn't smell like glamour either.

Did someone just bring it to me? Who?

I start to shift, intent on sitting up, but a gasp bursts from my lips and pain radiates through my shoulder. I reach up to gingerly touch the sore place, and my fingers meet soft linen fabric. I tuck my chin, looking down, and find a neat bandage, slightly bloodied but well wrapped.

I also realize that I'm wearing little else. My tunic is gone. My soft linen undershirt was cut and pulled away from the shoulder to allow room for the bandage. Exposing much of my bosom.

I grimace. Then, bracing myself against the pain, I sit up, trying not to put any weight on my left arm. The world spins around me, and I fear I might faint. But that would be a sorry waste of hot, fresh oatmeal. So I hold on, take deep breaths, and wait for the room to stop whirling.

When at last everything seems to have settled, I check the bandage again, lifting it just enough to glimpse the wound underneath. A row of neat stitches meets my gaze, surrounded by a lot of ugly bruising. No sign of infection, at least. Somebody did a good job taking care of this. An expert job, even.

But . . . who?

Once more I glance around the overgrown chamber, trying to discern some trace of my unseen helper. It's a woman's room. Could this be the house of another ward witch? But surely I would sense some magic then.

That oatmeal is going to go cold and lumpy soon.

I gingerly shift my legs over the edge of the bed, lean over the little table, and pull the bowl closer. I'm absolutely ravenous and would have polished that bowl clean in a matter of moments even without the delectable brown sugar to help it go down. It would be better with a little cream, perhaps, but I won't be complaining to the chef!

As the warmth and sweetness runs down my throat and fills my hollow gut, my fuzzy mind starts to clarify. Images begin to play through my memory, a scene taking place on the edge of a riverside cliff.

Conrad.

And Dire.

*Dire . . .*

I close my eyes, setting my spoon down with a clatter. The last clear memory in my head is of the werewolf stalking toward me. Is it possible *he* is my unexpected helper? Is it possible *he* brought me to this place, bound my wound, and . . . and cooked me breakfast?

Somehow, I can't make that idea fit into the proper grooves of my brain.

I finish eating, forcing down the last few bites. Less foggy headed than before, I sit back in the bed, lean against the headboard, and close my eyes. There's something I must do, something I must try before I can even begin to figure out the mystery of this house and my unexpected helper.

*Granny.*

Those memories of the battle, of my fight with Conrad, of my wound, are all a bit jumbled, but one thing is crystal clear: the moment when I turned my arrow away from Dire and let it fly at the Monster Hunter instead.

I did it.

I resisted Granny's compulsion. I fought her hold on me.

And I won.

What does it mean for my seven years of sworn service? Surely I can't have broken that bargain so easily! Not that it was *easy*, exactly, but . . . but somehow I would have expected it to be much harder. Is there still a bargain in place now that I've managed to counter one of Granny's commands?

I search inside myself, hunting in my head, in my heart, in my soul for traces of enchantment. But I'm no trained magic user. I don't know how to sense such things. I'm probably just as cursed as I ever was.

For the moment, however, despite my wounded shoulder, I feel light. Airy.

*Free.*

I sleep again and wake, still sore, but better than I was before. Though I look hopefully, there's no surprise meal waiting for me on the bedside table. Maybe my unseen helper has gone away and left me here? The room is full of shadows, but I can see daylight through the vine-choked windows.

Well, I'll need to get up and try to figure out where I am eventually. Might as well be now.

Wincing and cursing under my breath, I ease out of the bed. I'm still wearing my trousers at least. My cut-open shirt falls around my waist, however, and I struggle to pull it back into place and adjust the ties across my bosom. Not enough of it is left for any real modesty, however. Grunting with frustration, I scan the room, searching for inspiration. An elegant dressing gown, only a little moth-eaten at the cuffs, lies draped over a nearby chair. Did someone leave it there for me? It's a bright blue fabric embroidered in silver threads, much nicer than anything I would normally wear. I feel a little silly to put it on, if I'm honest. I'm not meant for such finery. Still, better than wandering about the place in a shirt that's falling to pieces.

Getting the sleeve on my left arm and shoulder is a challenge, and I fight waves of nausea and pain. But I manage in the end and wrap the dressing gown tightly across my chest, securing the tasseled belt. Then, barefoot and tentative, I pad to the door.

The hall outside my chamber is silent. No sign of Dire or . . . or anyone else. Half tempted to call out his name, I swallow the impulse and instead step out into the passage and make my way to a staircase. The house is quite nice. Overgrown, yes, but undeniably grand, grander even than the beautiful townhouse I grew up in. Better furnished as well. Which is odd. Why would anyone abandon this property without taking at least some of these fine furnishings and fixtures with them?

Clutching the banister for support, I manage to get downstairs in one piece. I'm sweating and trembling. Gods, I must have lost a lot more blood than I realized to Conrad's knife! Holding onto the newel, I pause and catch my breath, taking in the huge foyer and the enormous tree growing right up the center and through the roof. Is this place even structurally sound?

Once I've summoned my strength, I make my way to the large front door. The latch gives under the barest pressure, and the door swings open. Outside, forest meets my gaze—dense, dark forest. Not just any forest, either. This is Whispering Wood. I'd know it anywhere. The smell. The *feel*.

No one in their right mind would build a house like this right in the middle of the Wood.

"There's a curse here," I whisper, gripping the doorknob for support. "There's a curse . . . somewhere . . ."

A shiver trails down my spine. I back inside and shut the door again. I'm not ready to go striding out into those trees without shoes, without weapons, without a plan. But what *am* I going to do exactly? I've resisted Granny's command; how far will that resistance take me? Can I flee far enough to escape her reach? Or will the compulsion finally catch up to me, enslave me once again?

I circle the tree and make my way to the back of the house where a long hall extends both to my right and left. Straight across, however, is a door, which stands partially open. I step through and enter what must have once been a luxurious salon. It's now sadly overgrown, more so than the bedroom upstairs, but I can still discern furnishings and carpeting through the greenery and scattered leaves on the floor. The windows are flung wide, and vines climb in over the sills in bounteous profusion, clambering up the walls. The overall impression should be one of ruin. But it's not. It's almost peaceful.

I turn to continue my exploration of the house, but something catches my eye: a little black hutch painted in an ornate pattern of birds and blossoms. On top of the hutch is a series of portrait miniatures. Even from across the room, I find myself oddly arrested by all those piercing, painted gazes.

Brow puckering, I draw closer. It's the centermost image that intrigues me most—a young man, clean shaven, brown haired, wearing a posh jacket and lacy collar. His eyes are clear and bright, his face full and square and handsome, with a faint impression of stubbornness about the jaw.

I pick up the frame, angling it to catch more of the light coming in through the nearest window. If I didn't know better I'd think . . . I'd think this was . . . No, I'm sure of it. It *is* Dire. Even without the beard and the shaggy gray hair, I couldn't mistake those eyes. Though I've certainly never seen that expression in them. That confidence, that good humor, that certainty of purpose.

It's strange—the only times I've seen him in his human form, there's always been at least a trace of the wolf about him. Seeing him like this, fully human and uncursed, feels *wrong* somehow. Like something is missing. He's just another handsome youth with a firm jaw. I'm not sure I even like the look of him this way.

Not that it matters whether I like the look of him or not.

I set the frame down, frowning. I'm about to turn away again but happen to see the next little frame beside his. I pick it up. This one is much smaller than the others, but the portrait inside is excellent, a perfect rendering of a gentle girl with chestnut hair and warm brown eyes, her pink mouth faintly tilted at one corner. She looks . . . familiar . . .

"You're awake."

I spin in place, wrenching my wounded shoulder rather painfully as I do so. Dire stands in the doorway. Not the young man of the portrait. No, this is the Dire I know. The wolf. The beast. The day has moved on past noon, and he is starting to show some traces of manhood again around the eyes and brow. But he is definitely not human.

I stare at him stupidly. My heart pounds, and I feel like a thief, caught red-handed. I'm afraid to put the portrait down for fear of drawing attention to it.

"I . . . you . . ." What should I say? Where even to begin? "Where are we?" I blurt at last.

Dire steps into the salon. He's hunched over, his forelimbs supporting his huge torso. It'll be hours yet before he's walking on two feet again. His strange yellow eyes fix on me, and I struggle to discern any trace of humanity in them.

Then they turn slightly. He sees the miniature in my hand. I resist the urge to hide it behind my back. The werewolf lifts his gaze back to mine.

"This," he says, his voice mostly a growl, "is my home."

His home? Somehow, my mind doesn't want to accept that idea, not while looking directly into that monstrous face. But then, I've always known that he did not begin life as a werewolf. He must have originated from somewhere.

Suddenly I want both to know and *not* to know more. A hundred questions brim on my tongue, but fear chokes them back down again. Fear of what, I can't entirely say.

The silence between us has lasted too long. I need to say something. Anything.

"It's . . . it's nice," I manage lamely.

Dire's mouth is much too wolfish to allow for a smile, but there's a flicker of amusement in his eyes. "My grandfather built it. Old Edwyrd Phaendar, a humble merchant. Well . . . not *so* humble.

He had Phaendar Hall styled as a proper gentleman's abode. He was a man of ambition. As was his son, my father."

The werewolf crosses the room, lumbering and huge in this once-elegant space. I want to shrink away as he draws near, but I stand my ground. He stops beside me and points to one of the little frames lining the topmost shelf of the hutch.

"Here he is. My grandfather." The claw-tipped finger indicates the image of a graying, square-jawed man of certain years, still handsome if given to stoutness. His eyes are like Dire's: wolfish. "And this is my father." He points to the next portrait. This man is thinner and paler than his predecessor, but in his face, the wolfishness is even more prominent.

"And here is my mother." The werewolf takes up a third portrait, this one of a lovely golden-haired young woman. He hands it to me.

I hold up the image, my gaze flicking from her face to the portrait of the young man in the center of the shelf. They are very alike, mother and son. He inherited his beauty from her. But not *too* much beauty, not so much that he seems delicate. The roughness and strength from his father's side is there in him as well.

"She's lovely," I say at last.

"She was a Morcarin," Dire says, as though that name should mean something to me. "Quite an old family with money and connections. My father was lucky to win her hand, and well he knew it. They both had great expectations of me."

With those words, he turns to the portrait of the young man.

Of himself. I watch his face as he gazes on that image of what once was. It's difficult to read any human expression in those animal features, but his eyes... they reveal a great deal. Sadness. Longing. Regret. And anger. Always that same simmering, burning anger.

I don't speak. I know there's more coming. Maybe I ought to ask a question or two, try to open him up. But I can't. I simply stand there, waiting.

"They sent me to a fine university in Wimborne City," the werewolf says at last. The incongruity of those words coming from that awful mouth is almost laughable. Who could imagine such a beast attending university? "My people," he continues, "may not have been proper gentility, but they had money. Plenty of money. Thus I was given the opportunity to rub elbows with the young lords- and ladies-to-be of the country, making those all-important connections. My family hoped I would marry into a title, but..."

I don't have to guess where this is going. I open my fingers and hold up the small portrait of the brown-eyed girl. "What was her name?" I ask softly.

"I don't remember." The pain etched into his voice cuts me to the quick. "No more than I remember my own name. We lost our names when we lost our souls to Elorata Dorrel."

Blood thunders in my temples as he speaks those terrible words. Am I surprised? I can't say that I am. There's always been a part of me that suspected... though even now, I'm not exactly sure what it is I suspect. It's just that: suspicion.

I look down at the portrait. Suddenly I know why it feels familiar to me. Those eyes, those gentle brown eyes, are the same as those in the weredeer head mounted in Granny's house.

My gut clenches. I'm suddenly woozy, and for a moment I fear I'll drop in a faint. But no. I won't faint. I won't do anything so stupid as that. I'll face the truth, face this harsh reality. And face my own small part in it as well.

"What did my grandmother do?"

Dire reaches out, and his claw-tipped fingers close around my hand. I feel the warmth of his strange touch for a half breath before he gently eases the portrait from my grasp. He looks down at the image. In that half-lit room, I could, for the moment at least, almost believe he was fully human.

"She was magically gifted," he says. "She always was, from the time we were small. When word came that our local ward witch was seeking a new apprentice, it only made sense that she would be the one. She was so excited! I'll never forget the day she told me. I was home from university at the time, and I . . ." He sighs, bows his head. "I tried to talk her out of it. My parents were already so much against the two of us. If she went on and became a witch, what then? We would never be allowed to marry.

"But she told me not to be selfish. If I got to travel and learn more about the world and its workings, why should I begrudge her this opportunity? A chance to expand herself, to learn, to grow. She wanted to be a ward witch herself one day, to take over the care of our small county. She was, in her humble way, ambitious.

"And I . . . fool that I was, I got angry. So I left. And I vowed I would forget her. I vowed I would do as my parents bade me, find a titled young lady who appreciated my fortune and would take me, merchant's son though I was. I threw myself into my studies and into the gaiety and glitter of society in Wimborne. But I never forgot her . . ."

I know what's coming. Not the details, exactly. But some instinct warns me where this story of his will lead. "What happened to her?" I ask. "What did . . . what did my . . ."

I can't bring myself to say the words: *What did my grandmother do to her?*

A heavy sigh eases through Dire's sharp teeth. He sets the girl's portrait back down beside his own image before turning away and lumbering to the nearest window. There he pulls himself as upright as he can, gazing out at the forest. Is he done speaking to me? Is that all of the story he's willing to share? Perhaps I should go, slip out the door, back up to my borrowed bedchamber. I take a step that direction.

Then, abruptly, he continues: "I came home again for the Feast of Glorandal. I always did, every year, to visit my family and see old friends. And this time, amid all the festivities and entertainments leading up to that night, I pretended I wasn't interested in knowing what had happened to . . . to my friend. I didn't see her anywhere, but I told myself this was simply because I wasn't *looking* for her.

"Soon enough, however, whispers and rumors reached my ears. People said she had disappeared following the start of her apprenticeship. No one had seen or heard from her since."

He shudders, the fur down his spine rising, his shoulders hunching. "I tried to dismiss these rumors. Tried to insist I didn't care, that it had nothing to do with me. But when the Feast of Glorandal came and went without any sign of her . . . and when I found myself facing a return to Wimborne without so much as a glimpse of her face . . . I finally had enough.

"I set out into Whispering Wood. Alone. Without telling a soul where I had gone or why. Everyone in Virra County knows the path to the ward witch's house, even if few dared walk it. I found the way and plunged recklessly ahead.

"But the path kept stretching longer and longer, far longer than it should have. Though I'd set out in early morning, the hours went by, and I seemed to make no progress. By sunset, I was still on the path, but hopelessly lost, deep in the forest.

"The attack came a few hours after sunset. A monster lunged at me from the side—a crazed, half-human, half-animal *thing*. I had brought no supplies, no weapons, nothing with which to defend myself. Taken unawares, I fled the path into the forest itself, but was soon run down, knocked from my feet, trampled, and torn. I doubt I put up much of a fight before I was knocked unconscious.

"I don't know how long it was before I came to again. Days? Hours? Mere moments, maybe. But when I opened my eyes, I found myself in a rich room of green velvet and soft firelight. My aching body was wrapped in bandages. And bowing over me where I lay was . . . the most beautiful woman I'd ever seen."

Granny. I don't need him to describe her. I know who it was he saw. Granny, wrapped in her glamours, young and breathtaking and full of dangerous allure. My gut twists. I'm not going to like where this story leads . . .

Dire, still standing at the window, closes his eyes and bows his head. I watch the fingers of his warped hand curl into a tight fist. "She talked me into staying." His voice is heavy. Shamed. "Day after day. Week after week. I lost all track of time. I didn't care. I believed myself in love and never once thought to question that feeling."

The knot in my gut tightens still more. Exactly how far did this *love* take him? I don't want to know. But I can guess. I'm not a fool.

I turn away from him, staring at those little miniatures on the hutch shelf. Staring into the face of that gray-eyed boy. Yes, he was just the kind of pretty fop my grandmother would fancy. And he gave in without a fight.

I wish I could tell him to stop talking, wish I could just turn and leave. But I've listened this far . . . I should probably hear the rest of his story.

"I lived in a dreamlike state," he continues, "all thoughts of home and school and family and responsibility fled. I was like a pathetic lapdog, always trailing at my beautiful lady's heels, adoring her without question, without reason. She dressed me in fine clothes and fed me fine foods, entertained me with sparkling conversation. Flattered me with stolen kisses and chance embraces. I have no idea how long this went on.

"Then, one day, while I was out strolling in the sun, gathering wildflowers to present to my ladylove . . . I glimpsed her. The deer-woman. The same monstrous half-animal creature that attacked me on my way through the forest. Only this time she was human. Or *mostly* human.

"The moment I saw her face, I remembered everything."

He growls softly, turns from the window, and stalks across the room to grasp the back of a chair, claws digging into the upholstery and wood as though he would like to tear it to pieces. But he merely stands there, holding tight, bracing himself. His eyes flash in the shadows, meeting mine.

"I cannot begin to describe what happened next. The witch's spell was broken, and I realized what had happened, what I had become. I fell at the deer-woman's feet—at the feet of my . . . my sweet one. I held her hands and begged her to forgive me, begged her to tell me what had happened to her. She tried to speak, but the compulsions stopped her tongue.

"Elorata Dorrel found us like so. Her jealous shriek was sharp enough to stop my heart. I turned, and for the first time I saw her for what she was—the old crone, the ancient witch. It was only a flashing glimpse before her glamours closed back in again. But it was enough.

"Furious, I sprang up and charged her. I accused her of cursing my friend, of cursing me. And she . . ." The werewolf breaks off a moment, his grip on the chair tightening still more, his teeth flashing in a terrible snarl. "She didn't deny any of it. *Misery*, she said—for that was the name she'd given the deer-woman—*Misery* was possessed of a tremendous magical gifting. A gifting to which

Elorata had helped herself, taking that power as her own. The spell of assumption is a warping spell, and the result was the creature I now saw. The werebeast. Deprived of her power, committed to the ward witch's service for ten years.

"She was Granny's slave. Her monster."

The sound that emerges from his throat is no longer a growl. It sounds much more like a sob. "I begged for her freedom," he says, struggling to master his voice. "I wept, I pleaded. I abased myself before her. But the first price she demanded . . . it was too much. It was more than I could give. You see, in all the time I'd spent in her house, enjoying her gifts and kindnesses and caresses, I had not yet given her *everything*. I'd held back. Some small piece of me, you see, had known that it was all false, that it was all glamours and tricks. Some small piece of me didn't want to give to her what I had intended for another."

I know what he's saying. He didn't . . . He and my grandmother hadn't . . . I can't even bear to finish thinking the thought.

But the knowledge that *it had not happened* fills me with a sudden, unexpected burst of relief.

I blush, tuck my chin, fiddle with the tassels of my borrowed dressing gown, blood pounding in my ears.

"Elorata is not one to give up a good bargain, however," Dire continues. "When she saw that her first demand would not be met, she had a second ready for the offering: my freedom in exchange for Misery's. I would become her servant, not for ten years, but for twenty. I had no magic to offer her, after all, so twice the term of service was, as she said, only fair. But if I agreed, Misery would go free.

"Fool that I was, I leaped at the bargain. I convinced myself that I'd be able to break the curse somewhere along the way. Or that my love would break it for me. I simply could not fathom the reality of twenty years of service. And I grossly underestimated Elorata's power.

"She cast her spell, and I . . . I became as you see me now. Ravenous. Horrible. Totally lost to my own bloodlusts and rage. The last thing I remember before the red haze came upon me was Elorata's laughter—not the lovely, silvery laughter of the glamoured woman I'd known. This was a hag's cackle, full of wickedness and triumph.

"I rushed off into the forest. I could not control the animal now that it was unleashed, and I gave myself over to every impulse of this new, exciting, terrifying nature. In that first rush of the curse, I did not even remember what I had once been.

"It was days later before my humanity slowly returned. The curse leveled out, finding a sort of equilibrium inside me. I woke naked and battle scarred on the forest floor. And when I pulled my head up, when I looked once more through bleary man's eyes, I saw her. Misery. Dead.

"And Elorata Dorrel standing over her body."

Dire looks my way again. The rage is gone from his face and much of the wolfishness as well. I see the man through the fur and fangs. A man plagued by sorrow, by guilt twenty years old and yet still fresh, still painful.

"I underestimated your grandmother," he says softly. "I did not understand the terms of the bargain she made with me. She lifted her control on Misery, set her free . . . but she did not lift the curse. She never does. We all of us die as the monsters she made us. Free, yet never truly free.

"In the dawn light of that new day, Elorata smiled at me. Such a beautiful smile. Then she snapped her fingers. *'Up, Dire,'* she said, speaking my new name for the first time. *'I have much for you to do. Pick up this carcass and carry it back for me, there's a good boy.'*

"Thus began my twenty years as Granny Dorrel's slave."

# 18

## DIRE

I watch her face closely, studying her reaction to my story. She's such a stern creature, it's difficult to read much in her expression. I can't tell if she believes me. I can't tell if she has any sympathy to offer me. I simply can't tell.

I almost wonder if she hates me. And how could I blame her if she does? I hate myself sometimes. Hate myself for how easily I was duped, for how quickly I fell under Elorata's spells. My foolishness, my arrogance, my ignorance of the ways of magic and bargains must seem idiotic to someone like Brielle.

I tilt my head, trying to catch her gaze. I wish she would look at me, would give me some sign of what she's thinking. Why it matters so much, I can't say. I only know it does.

Finally, the silence is too much to bear. I clear my throat and whisper, "Brielle?"

The sound of her name startles her. Her green eyes flash, catching the fading sunlight as they lock with mine. "Is there . . . is there any way to break your curse?" she asks.

I blink, surprised. Of all the reactions I might have anticipated, this one never crossed my mind. Does she . . . is it possible that she *cares?*

"Yes," I admit, my voice deep and low, not quite a growl. "I'm no expert in these things, but from what I understand, a witch cannot cast a curse without some sort of countermeasure in place. But she can, of course, make that countermeasure as difficult as she likes."

Brielle nods once, a quick tilt of her chin. "And what is the countermeasure here?"

I don't want to tell her. I turn away, looking down at my own two hands. Mostly human hands now. In the time it took for me to tell my tale, my body has reassumed much of its human shape. I realize with a grimace how very naked I am, clad only in the little bit of shredded trousers that hang from my hips. I've grown so accustomed to my own nakedness out in the forest, almost immune to embarrassment. But here, standing in my family home, I feel the shame once more.

Gritting my teeth, I take another few steps away from the girl and put a moss-covered chair between us. "My curse," I say, "is not your concern. For now, you should concentrate on your own recovery. You lost a lot of blood, and it would be best if you stay in bed for the next several days."

"Several days?" She fixes that hard, stern gaze of hers on me. Even without my wolf senses, I can almost *smell* her conflict as she tries to decide whether she's going to protest. In the end, however, she merely nods again.

"There are some small stores of edible goods still in the larder," I say, filling that awkward silence. "I'll prepare something and bring it up to your room."

Her eyes narrow. She doesn't like being waited on; she doesn't like being vulnerable. Especially not in front of me. I hold her gaze, keeping my expression carefully blank and still. If I insist, I'll only provoke her. My best bet is to hold my tongue.

Without a word, she marches to the salon door. In the doorway, she pauses, however. For a moment, I fear she's going to turn back and question me further. My heart thuds uncomfortably in my throat as I wait, wait . . .

Then, with a little shrug of her shoulders, she leaves. Not another word. Not even another glance. Nothing.

A sigh eases from my lungs. I bend heavily over the back of the chair, lean my elbows into the mossy upholstery, and close my eyes. Gods on high, what have I gotten myself into? Bringing Elorata's huntress *here*. Tending her wounds. Caring for her.

"You're a fool," I whisper venomously. "Such a fool! The minute she recovers, she'll be after you again. She may have resisted the witch's power once, but it won't last. Elorata will redouble her hold." I shake my head, my long hair falling about my shoulders. "If you had any sense at all, you would have let her bleed out and be done with it."

I'm not wrong. That's what a wise man would have done. What a survivor would have done. And yet . . .

I cannot quite make myself regret my choice, foolish though it may be.

---

Four days pass slowly.

Dawn of the fifth day finds me climbing the stair of Phaendar Hall, wearing my human form. I've taken to visiting my patient at this hour before the wolf inside begins to dominate again. I don't like being indoors as an animal. Especially not here, in my own home. Instead, I spend my days and nights wandering the Wood, seeking out any sign of other werebeasts or servants Elorata may have sent searching for her wayward huntress. So far, there's been nothing.

But that doesn't mean I can relax my guard.

I donned some of my old garments this morning, as soon as my morphing limbs could fit into the shirtsleeves and trousers. An entire wardrobe of fine clothes is still there in my old bedroom, all twenty years out of date, of course, and not quite fitted to my leaner, rangier frame. But at least I'm not naked. Dressed like this, I've even dared several times to venture into Gilhorn, the nearest town, which stands beyond the boundary of the encroaching Wood. I discovered a stash of coin in my father's office, so I have plenty of money with which to pay for bread, cheese, and sausages, all of which I now carry on a platter up the stairs to my mother's old room.

To Brielle's room.

A rush of heat rises in my cheeks as I approach her door. I feel a bit foolish, waiting on her like this. Like a servant in my own home! But, well, if I'm honest . . . I also rather enjoy it. It's nice to have someone to care for again.

I stand outside her door in the gloomy passage, shift the tray to one hand, and knock. There's an answering grunt from inside, followed by a curse and a bleary, "Who's there?"

A grin pulls at the corners of my mouth. "It's me," I answer quietly.

A few more grunts and curses, each sharper than the last. Then, with a loud clearing of her throat, she calls out in a clearer tone, "Come in."

The latch gives at my touch. I push open the door and step into the room. It's still quite dark inside, but Brielle has lit a candle, and by its light I see her sitting propped against her pillows, rubbing the heels of both hands into her eyes. Her hair is a snarled thicket of tangles, framing her pixie face.

I pause in the doorway. Though I try not to let it, my gaze drifts downward. She's wearing a nightdress. One of my mother's, festooned with ribbons and lace along the loose, round neckline. It's so ornate, so completely unsuited to a wild thing like Brielle. But she makes a charming picture, nonetheless. Snarled hair, sleep-drawn face, and all.

Giving my head a quick shake, I stride across the room and

set the platter down on the bedside table beside the candle. She lowers her hands from her face, looking at the plate, not at me. I see her gaze try to flick my way, but she quickly refocuses on the humble meal I've brought.

"You don't have to do this, you know," she says, her sleepy voice more a growl than mine. "Wait on me, I mean. It's not like I'm some fine lady. I'm used to looking after myself."

"Don't worry. I don't intend to make a habit of it." I sit on the edge of the bed. "I need to check your wound, make certain there's no infection. If there's anything wrong, I need to see to it now before . . ." I don't bother finishing but hold up my hands. They won't be human much longer, won't be dexterous enough to manage bandages or salves or needles.

Brielle attempts once more to meet my gaze. She holds it a little longer before lowering her lashes. For a long moment, she simply sits there, unmoving.

Then, without a word, she slides the neckline of her gown down over her shoulder, revealing the bandage. Slipping her arm out of the sleeve entirely, she presses one hand against her bosom, holding the lace and ribbons in place. Her head turns away from me, her gaze fixed on the wall.

My throat thickens.

After all I've seen and done, the sight of one bare shoulder shouldn't be enough to catch me off guard like this. Gods on high, it was only days ago that I cut the garments off her body and treated the open wound! What's a little flesh to me?

But I can't fully ignore the way my pulse rushes as I stare at that smooth white skin dotted here and there by little brown freckles. I can't deny the sudden longing I feel to put out my hand and run a finger down her throat, across her collarbone, the length of her arm, watching the gooseflesh rise at my touch . . .

I clear my throat, set my face in a stern frown, and focus my attention on the bandage. Brisk, businesslike—that's what I am as I unwind the strips of cloth, lifting her arm gently as I do so and watching her wince. There's still a good deal of pain as she heals, but the bandage is only a little bloodstained, and the scar and stitches are neat and tidy, the flesh a healthy pink. I'm pleased at the sight of my own work. Apparently twenty years was not enough to make me forget a basic suturing and field dressing. I may have made a decent doctor if I'd had a chance to finish my studies.

"Good," I murmur, speaking to the stern profile turned pointedly away from me. "This is healing better than I expected. How does it feel when I do this?" I lift her arm to shoulder level and move it slightly outward.

She winces again. "Not nice," she admits. "But not too bad either."

"Well, we can't expect overnight miracles, can we?" I pull fresh bandages from the pocket of my tunic and wind them in place, trying to be mindful of her soreness. Trying as well not to notice how my fingertips seem to spark and tingle at each brush with her bare skin. Once I'm through, I help her guide her arm back into the sleeve, sliding the lace and ribbons up into place on her shoulder, covering the bandages.

Not once does she look at me.

I rise, step across the room to the pitcher and basin on the washstand, and set to work scrubbing my hands, taking perhaps more care with the little lump of soap than is altogether necessary. While my back is to her, I toss back over my shoulder, "I should imagine you'll be fit enough to travel in another day or two."

"Oh?" Her voice sounds small, almost childlike. I've never heard it sound that way before. "Good," she adds eventually.

I stand at the basin, my hands in the water, pretending still to wash. Really, though, I'm just afraid. Afraid to turn around. Afraid to face her.

These last four days, we haven't discussed what will happen once she's better. While in human form, I concentrated on providing for her basic needs—food, medical care, water. While in animal form, I slipped out into the forest and cared for my own, baser needs—hunting, feeding, sleeping. In those strange between times, when I was neither fully animal nor fully man, I tried not to think about what comes next.

But I can't ignore it anymore. Brielle is still bound to Elorata Dorrel's service. The witch must know by now that her huntress failed, that her own powerful compulsions broke down in the moment of crisis. She's most likely gathering her power, ready to reach out and reclaim her prodigal granddaughter.

And as for me? Well, Conrad may have met a watery end, but there are plenty of other Monster Hunters to be had for the right price. Soon enough, another one will be on my trail.

I've got to decide what I'll do with whatever time remains to me.

If only I could travel to the nearest ward and tell the witch there the truth about my enslavement. Judging by the dinner conversation I'd observed all those months ago, the witches of the surrounding wards have no idea what is truly happening in this wardship. Perhaps if they knew, perhaps if they banded together, they could put a stop to Granny.

But there's no point in thinking this way. I cannot cross the borders of Elorata's wardship. I've seen what happens to other werebeasts who try. The moment they set a toe on the far side of the boundary, death spells are activated—swift and dreadful.

Our cruel mistress will never let any of us escape.

I bow my head, grimacing down into the water basin. It's pretty—blue-and-white porcelain with an image of dancing maidens at the bottom, carefree and laughing. They don't dance alone, however. Strange folk twirl with the maidens, folk with horned heads and clawed hands and hooves for feet. It's a pretty depiction of Glorandal—the one night a year in which the fae folk of Eledria are permitted to enter the human world and dance from dusk till dawn.

My brow puckers. The faintest inkling of an idea tickles the back of my brain.

"We need to make a plan," I say. "For you."

Brielle looks up from the food platter I brought her, a large bite of cheese stuffed into one cheek. Chewing hastily, she swallows and blinks at me. "What kind of a plan?"

"If you're going to remain free of Elorata's control, you'll need to escape this wardship."

She takes another bite, chews a little more slowly. Then she sets the cheese down and pushes the plate back on the table. Her fingers fiddle with the edge of the blanket draped over her legs. "Do you . . . do you think it's possible? To escape, I mean."

I step back across the room and sit once more on the edge of her bed, earnestly meeting her gaze. "You are still under the bargain you made with Elorata, which means you cannot cross the boundaries of her wardship. I can't say for sure, but I would be willing to bet that to do so will mean instant death."

"Oh, great." Brielle rolls her eyes and shakes her head. "Sounds like escape is pretty much out of the question then."

"Not," I say, leaning a little closer to emphasize my words, "if you go *deeper* into Whispering Wood."

She frowns. I can see her mind churning, trying to understand what I've just said. She'll get there on her own, of course, but I'm too impatient to wait. "You don't have to actually *leave* Elorata's wardship. Find one of the gates; enter Faerieland. And never come back."

Her eyes grow slowly rounder as she processes what I've just said. Her lips part, her jaw dropping slightly open. I can see a glow of hope dawning in her face.

Then she blinks and shakes her head quickly. "That sounds a good deal like suicide to me. I'm human! I've traveled in and out of the gates here and there, but never for more than a few hours. How long would a human like me even last in Faerieland?"

"You could go to your sister."

"What?"

I reach out with one hand and very nearly take hold of one of hers before I realize what I'm doing. Hastily I snatch my hand back, planting a firm fist on the bedding instead. "Didn't you tell me your sister was stolen away to be a fae lord's bride? She's got to be there somewhere. In Eledria. She would welcome you."

But Brielle shakes her head slowly. "I don't know. I truly don't know. They were . . . she was parted from her husband." She tucks her chin, and I glimpse a flash of shame cross her face. There's some story here that I don't know. Something dark. She rubs the heel of her left hand into her eye again, as though trying to force some unpleasant thought out of her head. "The last I saw Valera, she was on her way into Faerieland to find him. But she's . . . she's not like me. She's not used to the ways of the Wood or the fae. I . . . I don't know if . . ."

I nod gravely. "You don't know if she survived."

Brielle sniffs suddenly and shakes her head. Is that a gleam of tears I see?

This time, when my hand stretches out, I don't stop it. I wrap my fingers around hers and squeeze gently. She starts, and for a moment I think she'll pull away. Instead, she goes very still, like a wild creature caught in a trap.

"Brielle," I say, trying to make her look at me again. "There's always a chance, you know. She may have found him. They may even now be reunited and settled somewhere. Somewhere you will be welcomed."

Her teeth chew her soft lower lip. Finally she speaks again in a low voice. "It doesn't matter. Even if she did, I have no idea where she is. Faerieland is huge—a hundred worlds upon worlds, all layered on top of one another. I can't just go wandering in and hope for the best."

"No. But perhaps we can discover a clue. Something to give you direction."

She looks up sharply. "What do you mean?"

"Glorandal Night," I answer. "It's coming soon, tomorrow night, in fact. The fae will slip out from the Wood to mingle with mortals. If you attend, you could ask around. If a fae lord has taken a human bride, you can be sure word has spread like wildfire throughout the various courts and realms of Faerie. You might be able to pick up some information, some clue to your sister's whereabouts."

A dangerous light of hope sparks in her eye. I could almost kick myself for daring to ignite it in her, for I know too well how painful a new hope can be. But at least it's something. At least it's better than waiting around for Granny Dorrel to find her again.

"If I go," Brielle says slowly, "if I pass through a gate, I'll never be able to return. Not to this world."

I shrug. But when I speak again, my voice is a little huskier than I intend. "Would that be such a hardship?"

She opens her mouth, closes it again, and looks down at her hand, still clasped in mine.

Then she says softly, "I've got nothing to keep me here."

I stand, letting go of her fingers and stepping back from the bed. I don't know why, but . . . but for some reason I'm disappointed. Bitterly so.

"Good," I say, and turn my back to her, striding to one of the open, vine-choked windows. "It's a plan then. We'll attend the Glorandal Dance in Gilhorn tomorrow night. We'll question the fae, learn what we can. And the next day, if the gods are good, we'll set you off on the right path. You should be out of your grandmother's reach before sunset two days hence."

"Yes," she says behind me. "If the gods are good."

Morning is well progressed by now. I look down at my hands. Gray fur creeps in beneath the cuffs of my sleeves. If I don't go soon, my warping body will rip through these garments and leave them in tatters.

"Rest now," I say, turning from the window and making for the door without another look her way. "You want that shoulder as strong as possible for your journey."

"What will you do, Dire?"

I stop short, partway out the door. My head and shoulders bow as though suddenly bearing a tremendous weight.

"Granny will send another Monster Hunter," Brielle continues, her tone edged like a blade. "Are you just going to wait around to be tracked down? Like an animal?"

Slowly, I turn my head, look at her over my shoulder. "But that's what I am. Isn't it?"

I leave the room and shut the door behind me.

# 19

## BRIELLE

I wake the next morning several hours after dawn.

At first I don't quite understand the sinking disappointment I feel when I look out from my bed and see how far the patch of sunlight has progressed along the floor. After all, I slept long and deep, better than I have since first coming here. So why is my stomach knotting like this?

Then I realize: the dawn hour is past.

Dire didn't come to see me, to check my wound.

Which is a good thing! If he didn't come, that means I must be much better and don't need his daily plucking and nagging. Besides, I don't like being fussed over, *cared* for. It's embarrassing. And unnecessary.

I sit up, grimace at the soreness in my shoulder, and gently move my arm in its socket. Certainly not back to normal, but not terribly far off either. I should be ready for whatever adventure awaits tonight.

Pushing back the blankets, I slide out of bed and snatch up the same dressing gown I've been wearing these last several days. I wrap it around the frilly nightgown, trying not to enjoy the softness of the fabric too much. But I can't quite help it. There's something so *nice* about un-glamoured silk, un-glamoured muslin. Granny's fabrications are always convincing, to be sure . . . but knowing they aren't real always dampens my enjoyment of them.

I move to one of the open windows, shivering a little as the cool morning air blows through, stirring the leaves and vines. The Wood seems closer than ever today, but as I gaze through the interwoven branches and tall trunks, I feel almost as though I can see all the way to the edge. Out to where open country lies, with its fields and towns and ordinary folk going about their lives, free of the Wood's treacherous influence. Are they out there now, setting up for Glorandal Night? Stringing lanterns and banners, baking treats and sweets. The musicians tuning their instruments, the young lads and lasses testing their dancing shoes.

It's been a long time since I attended a Glorandal dance. Excitement shivers in my stomach at the prospect. Is it possible I'll discover word of Valera? Is it possible I'll find the information I need to finally escape Granny's clutches? And if so . . .

If so, what will that mean for Dire?

I sink onto the window seat, which is covered in soft moss like a cushion, and lean my head against the wooden frame. Why am I letting my mind wander this way? Why am I letting concern for the werewolf encroach on other, more important thoughts? Yes, he's been kind to me these last few days. Unexpectedly, undeservedly kind. But is that any reason to lose my head?

I close my eyes. For a moment, I feel again that sparking thrill when his fingertips brushed against my bare flesh.

"Stupid!" I growl and shake my head, my brow knotting. "Stupid, stupid girl. You saved his life from the Monster Hunter; he saved your life in return. That's all this is! A give and take. Like a bargain almost. Nothing more."

There can never be anything more between us. Never.

I'm Elorata Dorrel's granddaughter. I'm kin to the woman who brought about the death of his true love. His sweet, gentle true love. A girl entirely unlike me in every particular . . .

I stand up sharply, shaking hair out of my eyes. The abruptness jars my shoulder, and I wince and put a hand to it, rubbing in little circles over the bandage. It's going to be a long day. Painfully long. But gods willing, when it's over, I'll have what I need. Then I'll get out of here as fast as I can, put many worlds between me and my grandmother. As for Dire? Well, he's a big boy. He can handle himself. Same as me.

We are, both of us, meant to be alone.

I spend the day wandering aimlessly about the hall.

Now that I'm starting to feel better, restlessness settles into my bones, like an itch I can't quite scratch. Every hour or so, I force myself to return to the room, to sleep or at least to doze. Dire has many times insisted that sleep is the best medicine.

I wonder a bit about his confidence in caring for my injury. He'd said he was sent to the university in Wimborne, the capital city. Perhaps he was studying medicine back before . . . before everything? Gods! It's so strange to think about Dire in these sorts of terms. A student, with a history, with goals and ambitions. With friends and family and . . . and lovers. I've been so careful to always and only think of him as the monster. The beast.

If only he wasn't avoiding me while in his werewolf form these last few days. He's taken care to only show himself at dawn and dusk, when he is fully human. It's making things difficult. Everything would be so much simpler, so much clearer, if I could just see him again as the monster he is.

I doze again in early afternoon and this time sink into a deeper sleep, waking late in the day. A little gasp bursts from my lips as I sit upright. There's a change in the atmosphere. Subtle but growing stronger by the moment. A change which I have always felt in those last, creeping hours before Glorandal Night: *magic* in the air.

I smile. I can't help myself. There's something undeniably delicious about that pricking in my thumbs, that dance of fine hairs on the back of my neck. Glorandal is the most magical night of the year, a night of wildness and possibilities. Valera never liked it . . . she was afraid of that unnamable *something* in the wind, that scent, that taste, that strain of song. She always wanted to keep me indoors and away from the dancing, but I would beg and plead so hard, and when that didn't work, threaten to climb out my bedroom window and run away if she didn't take me.

Ultimately, I always convinced her. We would run together, hand in hand, to our village's dancing green, there to experience the wonders, to glimpse the strange, shadowy, unnatural figures. And to dance. Not stately dances like the balls I sometimes glimpsed through the windows of the Public Hall. Those dances were dances of manners and propriety and elegance. Glorandal dances were wild. Primal like ancient drums, pulsing magic straight through the veins.

Oh, how I loved those nights!

I close my eyes and sniff the air, delighting in these sensations flooding through me. We should set out soon if we don't want to miss a moment.

I spring up from the bed and take three steps toward the door before I stop and look down at my dressing-gown-wrapped body and the hem of the lace nightgown just visible by my ankles. I can't wear this to the dancing green; I'd be a laughingstock!

Pressing my lips together, I turn to a large, ornately carved chest sitting half hidden by a bramble of wild roses. I push the roses out of the way, receiving more than a few thorny bites for my efforts, and drag the chest out in the open where I can fling back the lid. I tell myself not to expect much—it's been years, after all, and most of Mistress Phaendar's fine gowns must have rotted away long ago. But I might as well have a peek . . .

To my surprise, the gowns are as fresh as though folded and placed in this chest yesterday, sandwiched with delicate paper and layers of dried lavender. A dazzling array of colors meets my surprised gaze. I'm almost overwhelmed by choices.

Then I catch a glimpse of a vivid midnight blue and snatch it out from among the rest, draping it over the bed for inspection. I'm not much of a one for fashion. That's always been Valera's domain, not mine. But even I can't help staring at this gown.

It's beautiful. Dated, yes. Valera had told me that voluminous sleeves, wide necklines, and pinched waists were all the rage these days. This gown has none of those features. Its sleeves are fitted and sport a row of silvery buttons from wrist to elbow. The scooped neckline is much too low for modesty, obviously meant to be worn with a decorative chemise underneath. The waistline is loose but nicely fitted.

I return to the chest and fish out a chemise, a belt, and a front-lacing corset. I've never been a corset wearer, but even my inexpert eye can see that this dress needs something structured underneath in order to fit smoothly. So I set to work pulling myself together—lacing and tucking and tying and buttoning. It's all quite a bother, and halfway through the process I'm about ready to chuck it all and slip back into my comfortable dressing gown.

When at last the job is complete, however, it's not so bad. I anticipated difficulty breathing and severe discomfort from the corset, but instead it gives me a nice sense of protection and support—all that boning around my midsection feels almost like armor. It definitely helps my posture, and since I didn't lace it tight, my breathing is in no way compromised. I could probably dance the whole night away in something like this.

Moving across the room to Mistress Phaendar's tall mirror, I steal a tentative peek. A smile tries to break across my lips, and I fight to hold it back. But the truth is . . . I rather like what I see. The bodice, even with the chemise, is still a little lower cut than I like, but everything feels secure enough. And the way the shoulder line is cut, one can scarcely see the bulge of my bandage underneath the midnight cloth.

I turn to one side and then the other, feeling more than a little foolish. Then I scamper back to the chest, find a pair of slippers that are only a *little* too snug, along with a decorative belt and some hair combs. A few minutes of experimentation with the combs is enough to drive me nearly mad, so I end up tossing them and simply tie my hair in its habitual knot at the nape of my neck. It might not be fancy enough for a gown like this, but it'll have to do.

I stand before the mirror again, surveying the overall effect one last time. Giddy pleasure tickles my stomach despite every effort to quash it. But I can't be silly about this. I'm not going to the dance for fun, after all. I have a purpose, an important mission to fulfill.

And I am certainly *not* going to dance with Dire.

I frown as thoughts of Dire push to the forefront of my mind.

He's been so unselfish, risked so much for my sake, and I can't help but wonder . . . why?

*Because he's a good man.*

*He's a good man. And you're going to leave him behind.*

*To face whatever horrors Granny has in store for him.*

"Great gods above!" I growl and turn away from the mirror, clutching folds of skirt in both hands. It's not like there's anything I can *do*, is there? I've got troubles enough of my own without worrying about the werewolf.

I need to focus.

The room grows darker as the sun begins to sink and the shadows of the forest fall ever more deeply across the ruins of Phaendar Hall. I step out of my room and proceed to the front staircase, peering over the banister to the foyer below. Dire is there. Waiting for me.

He stands before the open front door, framed by late sunlight, and gazes out into the forest. Offering me a prime opportunity to observe him without his knowledge. He's slicked his hair back from his face but not tied it, and it falls in gentle, textured gray waves about his shoulders. From somewhere in this house, he's dug up a suit of green velvet: doublet, hose, trousers, and capelet. All twenty years out of date, but richly made and well fitted.

It's funny—I've seen him nearly naked numerous times, when his wolf form has retreated, leaving him bare and exposed. I know exactly how tight and toned his abdominal muscles are, how broad and strong his shoulders, how powerful his forearms and calves.

But seeing him now—those trousers fitting just so across his hips, and that doublet straining at the shoulder seams—somehow, he feels suddenly more *real*.

I let a slow breath out through my lips. Then, straightening my shoulders and moving boldly to the top of the stair, I clear my throat. Dire turns, looks up at me. His eyes widen. Is he surprised to see me in this gown? Displeased? He must have known I'd have to borrow something. I can't very well attend the dance in a nightdress.

His mouth opens as though he's going to speak, but no words come.

"What?" I demand, my voice ringing in the open space of the foyer beneath the spreading branches of the tree. "Do I look as bad as all that?"

He shuts his mouth, shakes his head. At last he manages, "I . . . I see you found more of my mother's gowns."

"I figured she wouldn't mind." I descend the stair, holding the hem of the skirt up with both hands so I won't trip. As I reach the bottom step, I cast him a quick glance and add shyly, "I hope *you* don't mind?"

"Of course not." He's still staring. His eyes run up and down my figure, but he quickly yanks them back to my face. I get the strong impression he's focusing hard, determined not to ogle me. I'm also not sure that I would particularly mind being ogled . . .

A hot flush climbs up my throat. Gods above, I hope the shadows in the foyer are deep enough to disguise it!

"Well?" I say, putting up my chin. "Shall we then?"

Dire bows solemnly. It's such an unconsciously gracious gesture, it takes me aback. When he straightens, he motions to the door, and I hasten to precede him out onto the front step. There I pause a moment as he joins me and shuts the door behind us.

"How far is it to the village?" I ask.

"About three miles to Gilhorn. But only a mile to the dancing green. It won't take us long to reach it."

I glance at the sky, orange and streaked above the dark silhouette of branches. "Sunset will be half over by the time we get there. What will . . . what will *you* do?" I glance sideways at him, catching a brief half smile.

"Glorandal Night," he says, "is a night of profound magic. Profoundly *good* magic. The marriage of the fae Glorafina and the human Andalius ushered in a time of great peace and prosperity for all worlds. The magic of that union has never fully faded. Which means curses cannot thrive on such a night . . . not even a curse as powerful as Granny Dorrel's." He clears his throat and meets my gaze for half a moment. "I should retain my human form until midnight."

I nod. "Are you sure?"

He offers a little shrug. "If I'm wrong, the folk on the dancing green will simply assume I'm one of the fae. I shouldn't be too conspicuous."

I accept this with a nod. Then, to my great surprise, Dire offers his elbow. He catches my eye again and this time holds it, a smile flashing through his beard. "Would the lady do me the honor of attending Glorandal Night with me?"

Another wretched blush roars in my cheeks. I nod quickly and murmur, "Why thank you, kind sir." I gently lay my fingers on his elbow, feeling utterly foolish and utterly delighted at the same time. Dire guides me down the front steps and sets a brisk pace through Whispering Wood.

And so our Glorandal Night begins.

## BRIELLE

The Wood is alive all around us.

I've been aware of *them* all along, my latent werewolf senses still keen enough to detect the strange scents of strange folk moving through the shadows, flitting from tree to tree. At first, Brielle does not seem to notice, but suddenly her breath catches and her grip on my arm tightens.

"Did you see that?"

I don't think she's afraid. I think this is a hunter's tension, full of wariness, not fear. I wouldn't be surprised if she started to reach for her knife . . . if she's wearing one hidden in the folds of that lovely gown.

I glance the direction her gaze is focused and just glimpse a flutter of movement. "It's all right," I assure her. "It's the fae folk.

The sun is nearly set, and they are arriving for the dance."

"Oh. Right." She sounds embarrassed. Whispering Wood is always brimming with threat; it's difficult to let one's guard down.

We continue through the trees, noting more and more woodland folk as we go. I often wonder why the fae take such an interest in the human world that they flock to its borders on Glorandal Night. Perhaps it has something to do with the passage of time in this world, the way everything blooms and fades so quickly. Perhaps the very brevity of time here compared to the agelessness of Faerieland makes life both more precious and alluring.

I understand this now in a way I never did before . . . now that my life has been so unnaturally prolonged by Elorata Dorrel's curse.

The trees begin to thin around us. The Wood has encroached only as far as the Phaendar estate borders, no farther. The witch's doing, no doubt. She allowed this encroachment to happen, allowed everything my grandfather had built from nothing to be swallowed up. Her malice truly knows no bounds.

I look again at the girl at my side, her face just visible in the last of the golden twilight. How strange to walk with her like this! In this lighting, and wearing that gown, the similarities between her and her grandmother are much more striking.

But that's not fair. In truth, they are quite different. Everything about Elorata is so carefully and precisely beautiful, while Brielle is wholly natural. There's no pretense or effort to her beauty. She's not even exactly *beautiful*. I would scarcely have noticed her twenty years ago, back in my long-lost youth.

But there's such an unruly freshness about her face, in the flash of her eye, in the curve of her lip. It takes my breath away. And seeing her in this gown—so elegant, so refined, so at odds with everything I've come to know about this girl—it's almost as though the tameness and structure of her garments makes the inner wildness of her spirit all the greater by sheer contrast.

She glances sideways. Catches my studying gaze. I frown and quickly yank my eyes forward. What in the seven gods' names am I doing? I've no business indulging thoughts like this. Besides, after tonight, if all goes well, she'll be on her way out of this world. I'll never see her again. It's her best chance. For her sake, I hope it works.

And then I'll face my own grim future . . .

We reach the edge of the forest just as the sun is disappearing behind the horizon. I shiver at the sight and can't help a covert glance down at my own hands and body. But there's no sign of the werewolf returning. Not yet. The magic of Glorandal Night is indeed strong, holding off Elorata's curse.

The dancing green lies before us. My heart gives an unexpected lurch. It's all so familiar! The green and that path leading from it up to the village, with its well-known assortment of rooftops. I used to run that path when I was a boy, eager to meet . . . to meet *her*. My friend. It all comes back to me in a rush, as I stand there beneath the deepening shadows of the forest, gazing down at the village folk making ready for the coming festivities. How many times did I meet her here on Glorandal Night, to dance with the fae until dawn? Each time like a dream, but a dream I never truly expected to end.

"Are you all right?"

I blink and give my head a quick shake, glancing down at the girl beside me. A girl as utterly unlike *her* as any could be, with her stern face watching me so contemplatively. Always a little too knowing for comfort.

Hastily, I mask any emotion from my expression and offer a nod. "Look," I say by way of distracting her gaze, and nod to our right.

She turns and sees what I see—fae folk pouring out of the Wood, venturing down to the dance lawn. They step into the light of lanterns strung all around the periphery, and suddenly those lanterns spark to life, a whole array of shimmering colors. The very air seems to sparkle with magic.

Human musicians, clustered to one side of the green, begin to play their instruments. As they play, the fae folk join them, blending their eerie, haunting strains into the more familiar local tunes. The resulting song is all but irresistible. I feel the lure of it plucking at my soul. Brielle's grip on my arm tightens once more. She's no more immune to that song than I am.

A beautiful fae woman with long golden hair and lavender skin makes her way to the center of the lawn and begins to dance all on her own. Her movements are like water and wind, totally hypnotic. Simply watching her is a joy. I could stand here all night and be satisfied. But then she reaches out and catches the hands of one of the young lads standing on the edge of the green, pulling him into her dance. He goes willingly, a great, stupid grin on his face.

A bareheaded lout of a farm boy, but as he dances with the fae woman, he becomes something nearly as beautiful and graceful and wild as she.

One by one, others join the dance, fae and human alike. Their shadows whirl with the lantern light, and the music rises to the sky above, calling out the stars one by one. I feel Brielle's excitement mounting, can almost *smell* the eagerness in her racing pulse. It beats in time to my own as the magic of the night and the music plays upon our senses.

We need to be careful.

"Remember," I say, speaking in a low voice close to her ear, "you're on a mission. Don't let the fae song get in your blood or you'll forget everything until dawn. Keep your sister firmly in mind and ask everyone you can about her."

Brielle nods without looking at me. "What about you?"

"I'll do the same." I step away from her, pulling my arm from her grasp . . . and feel the cold spot where her warm hand had rested. It's almost painful to be suddenly deprived of even that slight connection. But I won't focus on that.

"I only have until midnight," I remind her. "But I'll meet you here at dawn when I . . . when . . . when I can. We'll compare what we've learned then and, if the gods are with us, set you out on your journey soon after."

Her eyes flash, catching mine and holding them. There's something in her expression, something I can't quite name. For a moment, I think she's going to speak. And whatever she might say, it's important. Something I both fear and want very badly to hear. Then she blinks. The moment is broken.

Without a word, she turns and strides out from the trees, like one of the fae folk herself. Her dark blue gown flows gracefully with the sway of her hips, and the seams emphasize the proud set of her shoulders, the undeniable strength and, simultaneously, the undeniable womanliness of her figure. My throat is thick and tight as I watch her go.

Swallowing hard, I push myself into motion as well, aiming for the opposite end of the green. I weave in among the throng of folk, both fae and human, catching a few eyes among the townspeople. Several of them I've encountered during my recent ventures into town for supplies, but none of them acknowledge me. Though I'm wearing human form, I'm probably as strange and otherworldly to them as any fae.

"Well, hello there, handsome thing."

I turn at that voice and find myself face-to-face with a fae woman—the same fae woman I observed opening the dance. Up close, her lavender skin is luminous, glowing from the inside with the intensity of her own life force. Her golden hair shines like ribbons of pure sunlight, and her eyes are chips of blue sky with no dark centers to mar the perfection of the hue. She's wearing . . . remarkably little, truth be told. A swath of silky stuff draped across her breast and falling negligently over her hips. But there's such an ease to her bearing and manner, she doesn't quite *seem* naked.

"You look like you need a dance," she says, smiling into my eyes.

Her hands are already on my shoulders, and I realize she's leading me into the dancing lawn.

"I'm not here to dance," I say quickly and take hold of her forearms, intending to pry her off. But even as my fingers wrap around her flesh, I feel the incredible strength in her grasp. If I were in my wolf form, I might be a match for her, but as I am, I'm practically helpless.

She sees the startled look in my eye and laughs a birdlike trill. "Not here to dance on Glorandal Night?" Pale white lashes flutter across her blue-sky gaze. "How dare you even *think* such a thing? It should be sacrilege!"

I shake my head, trying to hold onto my purpose. "I'm searching for word of a Moonfire Bride recently come to Faerieland. Have you heard something of this tale?"

The fae woman tilts her head to one side, her large, pointed ears twitching. "I hear many things," she answers archly. "But now is not the time for talk!"

With that, she gives me one last pull, and I find myself in the very center of the dancing lawn. How did this happen? I thought I was ready to resist such lures, yet here I am, having put up scarcely any fight at all. No spell or enchantment compels me, at least none that I can sense. It's simply the night itself, the air of Glorandal. It calls to one, gets into the blood. Makes one feel alive to all manner of terrible and wonderful chances.

I spin and twirl with the fae woman. This dance is nothing like those elegant parties I attended back in my school days. Those were dances made up of stray glances and brushing fingertips, tantalizing in their own way but always guarded by social propriety.

There's nothing proper about this dance. The fae woman takes hold of my hands and places them on her hips, which writhe and sway in time to the melody. She plants her own hands on my chest, and to my surprise, I find that my tunic has come undone, my shirt unlaced, and her palms are planted on my bare chest. I try to recoil, but she merely laughs and draws me closer.

We spin with the lanternlight and the madness, the moonlight and the song. Though the wind bites with cold, I'm flushed and warm, full of fire in my gut. I don't know how long I dance with the lavender-skinned woman, but I am soon passed from partner to partner. Once or twice I brush hands with a village girl, but most of my partners are fae—some women, some men, some beings I couldn't begin to guess. All strange and lovely. The night has me in its clutches now. I am a wild wolf, barely contained within a man's body. I am hungry, ravenous . . .

Suddenly I turn . . . and stare down into Brielle's upturned face.

The whole world stops.

Somewhere, far away, the music continues, along with the fantastical gyrating bodies, the laughter, the madcap merriment and song. But that's not part of here, not part of this little slice of space and time. Here there is only room for the two of us.

Her hair has pulled free of its tight knot and hangs in wild tangles about her shoulders. Her bosom heaves with exertion, and a rosy flush suffuses her skin. Her eyes are bright with fae light.

She's never looked more beautiful.

I catch my breath. A dangerous urge rushes through me, brought to life by the dancing. But I blink, shake my head, force myself to look at her again. To see her, to see Brielle. Not just the beautiful girl, but the person I know, the one I've come to admire, to respect.

The burning of primal instinct fades. I'm not a rapacious beast, I'm not a slave to lustful instincts. There's something more here. Something deeper, something stronger.

"Brielle," I whisper and take a step toward her, closing the distance between us.

She cannot hear my voice over the music. But her gaze fastens on my lips.

I take another step, and she flinches. For a moment I fear she'll turn and dart away, losing herself in the crowd. I want to reach out, to catch hold of her arms, to hold her in place. But that I cannot do. She is a wild thing, beautifully untamed. If I try to hold onto her, try to control her, I'll not succeed.

So I am still, my hands at my sides, my breath tight in my chest. I simply hold her gaze.

She does not flinch again. In fact, she takes a small step toward me.

There's scarcely any distance between us now. Mere inches. Mere breaths.

I stare into those green eyes of hers, desperately trying to read the expression there. But they are so deep, so secretive. One wrong move will set her to flight. But if I make no move at all, something delicate and tentative between us will snap and be lost forever.

I open my mouth. I try to speak her name again.

I can't.

Instead, I lower my head. Slowly, slowly. My hands still at my sides. My gaze glides from her eyes to her lips. How soft and full they are, how red in the shining lights of the magic-infused lanterns. They part softly.

I pause, my mouth hovering above hers. Tasting the sweetness of her breath, feeling the warmth of a connection which is, as yet, merely a promise. She breathes a tremulous sigh. Then her hand rises, and her fingertips brush the side of my face. I look into her eyes once more, so close to mine, I might fall into them and drown.

"*Oof!*"

Someone jostles me roughly from behind. I stumble and stagger into Brielle, my arms wrapping impulsively around her. Her body stiffens, and I quickly let go and back up again, apologies rushing to my tongue. But as I step back from her, I find we are no longer on the dancing green. Somehow, though I couldn't begin to say how, we're standing in the shadows of Whispering Wood. Just the two of us. The dancers are behind us, still whirling to the wildness of Glorandal Night's enchantments, bathed in the glow of magicked lanterns. But here, there is nothing but moonlight.

I gasp and look into Brielle's pale face again. She backs away from me, leaning against a tree, breathing hard. And staring straight at me.

"Brielle," I whisper.

I don't know who moved first, her or me.

It doesn't matter.

Suddenly we are together, my arms around her waist, pulling her closer, her arms around my neck, equally eager. My lips are on hers, hungry, desperate. Full of need I've scarcely dared acknowledge until this very moment. I give her everything in that kiss, everything I shouldn't. I open myself to the agony of vulnerability, to the inevitable pain of our parting.

But I can't help myself. Not here, not now. Of course there will be pain—love *is* pain. The sweetness could not be so sweet without that underscoring bitterness. But to live without love is to never live at all. I know that. Better than most. And I would endure all the shocks and agonies this love has to offer in exchange for this one moment. This one terrible, glorious moment when I'm kissing her, and she is kissing me back.

I turn my head, trying to taste her sweetness from a fresh angle. She grips the back of my neck, her fingers curling in my hair, drawing me back to her.

But as our lips meet again, I feel it—the change.

I pull back, staring down at her.

Her eyes widen, gleaming in the moonlight. A small gasp escapes her parted lips. "Oh!" she breathes. "Oh, Dire . . ."

At the sound of my name—my horrible, witch-given name—I let go of her and step away. I shake my head, which is suddenly heavy on my shoulders, and my hands come up to grasp my skull, claw-tipped fingers digging into my scalp. Somehow, I danced until midnight without realizing it. The protection of Glorandal is fading, and my beast self rapidly returns.

I turn away, hunch over. A roar rumbles in my throat and pain ripples through my skeleton as my bones break and reshape much faster than they usually do. The seams of my garments strain, rip.

"Dire!" Brielle cries again.

It's like a knife to my spine, hearing my beast name spoken from her lips. Lips which had, only moments before, been mine.

"Don't look at me!" I snarl. I don't know why it matters. She's seen me like this so many times. But now it feels wrong.

"Dire, I'm sorry," she protests. I sense her footsteps approaching, her hand reaching out to touch my shoulder. "Please, don't—"

"Leave me alone!" I whirl and snap huge teeth, stopping within inches of her outstretched hand. She leaps back, her eyes wide and fearful in the moonlight. "Go, Brielle," I say, my voice scarcely audible through the animal snarls and growls. "Get away from here, get away from me!"

"No." She plants her feet firmly. There's still fear in her gaze, but defiance flashes there as well. "I won't leave you. I won't—"

An incoherent roar bursts from my throat. I lunge at her, sagging into my heavy forelimbs. She staggers back, trips on the edge of her gown, and goes down hard. I loom over her, gazing through a red haze of wolf rage, watching all her futile defiance vanish as pure terror takes over.

There's still just enough humanity left in me for that gaze to pierce my heart.

    With another roar, I turn and spring away into the trees. My partially human hands tear at my garments as I go, ripping away doublet, shirt, belt, trousers, until I'm nothing but a wild, naked beast racing through the forest.

## 21

## BRIELLE

I lie sprawled on the ground, propped up on my elbows, my legs outstretched, my skirts rumpled to my knees, staring into the shadows in which Dire disappeared. My lips burn. I touch them with trembling fingers. How swollen and warm they feel, even as my heart races and my ears echo with the rumbling growl of his hideous voice.

What just happened between us?

"Gods damn!" I hiss, closing my eyes and shaking my head. Yanking ridiculous folds of skirt out from under me, I pull myself to my feet. "Stupid, stupid!" I mutter as I brush bits of leaves and pine straw from my backside. What got into me? The magic of Glorandal, most likely. All that wildness and music stirred up something in my blood. I haven't danced at a Glorandal Night since

I was a child, so I've never experienced it quite like I did tonight. It brought to the surface everything I've fought so hard to suppress.

*Dire* . . .

I curse again and rub my hands down my face. Even now, even after watching his face transform right before my eyes into that awful wolf . . . I still want him. Want him with an ache I don't understand. I want his kiss, his touch, the heat of his breath on my bare skin.

But I want more as well. I want him in the same way I want . . . *home.*

Which is stupid, of course. What has home ever been to me? The place where my mother died giving birth to me? The place where my drunken father made our lives miserable year after year? The place where my sister's arms once offered comfort and love, only to be taken when I needed her most? No, *home* is definitely not for me.

But I've longed for it, nonetheless. Longed for that safety, that belonging. And beneath the burning heat on my lips and the roaring fire in my veins . . . I long for Dire in that same way.

Am I really going to leave him? Am I going to run away into Faerieland, abandon him to certain death? After what we just experienced together?

Then again, what *did* we just experience? I know what *I* feel about it, but how do I know what he's thinking? He might have taken me in his arms simply because I was *there*. Warm and willing. No, more than willing. Eager. Desperate. What if he'd sensed that desperation and decided simply to indulge himself? Could I blame him?

Would I wish to take the moment back?

Biting my lower lip, I turn away from the forest and gaze back down to the dancing green where the magic of Glorandal Night continues unabated. How long did I dance? I scarcely walked in among the crowds, scarcely began to ask any questions about the Moonfire Bride, before someone caught and dragged me into the fray. Any resistance had been futile, and soon I didn't want to resist at all. I was simply moving with the music like a leaf caught in the stream's current. I've never been a *good* dancer, merely an enthusiastic one. But on Glorandal Night, that didn't matter. I laughed and clapped and stamped my feet and exchanged partners with abandon, letting the melody carry me deeper and deeper.

Until I suddenly stood across from Dire.

I close my eyes, sighing out another bitter curse. Gods above, it felt as though the magic of the night destined us to find each other. As though, for us at least, the song reached its culmination in that one heart-pounding moment when our eyes met.

I rub two fingers against each temple, trying to rub out the thrum and throb still echoing inside my skull. I must get myself together, get back down onto that green, and ask the questions I need to ask. I'm still on a mission, after all.

I open my eyes . . . and yelp with surprise, jumping back a step.

Someone stands directly in front of me. Someone I didn't hear coming. A fae woman with golden hair and lovely lavender skin, her eyes shining in the darkness with their own blue light.

"I understand," she says, speaking in a lilting language that plays across my senses and somehow becomes comprehensible by the time it reaches my ears, "that you and the big fellow are asking after a Moonfire Bride."

I blink. Then with a little choke, I blurt out, "Yes! I am! A Moonfire Bride taken by a fae lord. Have you heard word of her?"

"I may have." The fae woman tilts her head to one side, her lips puckering prettily. "And I could be convinced to tell you what I've heard . . . for a price."

Immediately, my guard goes up. I've made more than a few fae bargains in my time, and I know how tricky they can be. "What kind of a price?"

The fae woman smiles, showing far too many teeth. "Oh, I won't ask for much . . . merely a strand of hair from your pretty head in exchange for all I know of the Moonfire Bride."

I stifle a snort. Does she think I'm an idiot? "No hair," I answer firmly.

She looks hurt. "A tooth then? How about a finger, a very small finger? No? A fingernail would do . . . or an eye, perhaps."

I keep shaking my head. For all I know, this fae woman knows absolutely nothing about the Moonfire Bride. I'm not about to give any part of my physical self into this grasping creature's hands.

At last the fae huffs and crosses her muscular arms. "Fine then. You're such a skinflint, are you actually willing to give *anything*?"

"I'll give a good word," I answer. "A good word in exchange for whatever knowledge you have of the Moonfire Bride."

An eager light sparks in the fae woman's eye. Maybe I offered too much after all.

"A good word I have little use for," she says silkily. "But a good *wish* now . . . one of your sweet, delectable human wishes . . . that might be something!"

My brow furrows. "Why? It's not as though our wishes come true."

"Ah, but a wish made on Glorandal Night always *means* something." She rubs her fingers together, like she's holding herself back from snatching a tempting treat.

"All right," I say slowly and lick my dry lips. "What would you have me wish for you?"

"Oh no, nothing *for* me." She puts up both hands and shakes her head. "This needs to be *your* wish. The first wish you feel in your heart. Give that to me, and I'll tell you what you want to know."

There's something not right here. A trap I should be able to see but can't.

Then again, what's a wish? I've made wishes every single day of my life, and only one of them ever came true. I wished to find my sister again, and I found her . . . but the fulfillment of that wish brought so much pain, I've often wished I never received it.

No, I learned long ago not to base my life on wishes. So if I give one up now, what difference will it make?

"Fine. I'll give you a wish, you give me word of the Moonfire Bride." I hold out my hand.

Now it's the fae woman's turn to hesitate. Then, flashing another toothy smile, she places her long fingers in mine and grasps hard. I'm surprised by the strength of that grasp but refuse to flinch or try to pull back.

"The wish first," she says. "Give it to me."

"How? How do you want me to give it?"

"That, little human, is entirely up to you."

I set my jaw. Then, with a shrug, I close my eyes. What do I wish for? Freedom from Granny? Freedom from everything! Those wishes are such big, all-encompassing things, but are they really the *first* wish in my heart tonight?

No . . . if I'm being honest, there's something else stirring inside me. Something else for which I long, though I know I shouldn't.

I squeeze my eyes a little tighter, open my mouth, and slowly release a long, long breath. With it, I feel the wish go out from me. A small, foolish wish for strong arms to encircle my body, for insistent lips to find mine in the darkness. For the touch of long fingers in my hair, on my neck.

I let the wish go. And as it leaves, I feel the tiniest bit freer. After all, it was a forlorn wish at best. There's no way there could be anything more between me and Dire than that one perfect, beautiful kiss.

The fae woman lets out a sigh. I open my eyes to see her standing with her hand upraised, as though she's just caught something. Her face is wreathed in a huge, satisfied smile. It's unsettling.

"All right," I growl, crossing my arms. "You've got what you wanted. My turn."

The fae opens her pale eyes slowly, fixing me with an expression of perfect self-satisfied smugness. "Here's what I know, human girl," she says through her teeth. "Lord Dymaris of Orican is said to have taken a Moonfire Bride as his own. He has returned with her in triumph to his domain in Lunulyr, and all his people pay homage to her as though she were a great lady."

For a moment, everything melts away. My heart leaps from my chest and soars. This is so much more than I dared hope for! The last time I saw Valera, she was setting off alone into Whispering Wood on a desperate quest to find her husband. Neither she nor I had cherished much hope of her success. But I knew Valera could never be happy again if she did not at least try to reach her lost love.

Did she make it? Could this Lord Dymaris be the same fae lord I've hated so hard all these years for stealing my sister? Did Valera manage to save him from some dark fate, and did they truly return to his home in Lunulyr?

At that thought, I can't fully repress a shudder. Lunulyr—the Court of Moons. It's reputedly a strange, dark, but beautiful realm. I've never traveled that deep into the fae worlds, never even considered it. But if that's where Valera is, then maybe . . . maybe . . .

"I can see you're satisfied," the fae woman says, drawing my attention back to her.

"I am. Indeed. It is a bargain well made."

This seems to irk the fae, who tosses her head and sniffs. "Well, let no one ever say I cheat on my bargains. I do when I can, of course, but let no one ever *say* it!" With that, she holds up her hand again, as though clutching something in her fist. "I'll take good care of your wish, little human. Have no fear."

"May the peace and harmony of Glorandal Night be yours," I answer with a nod.

To this, the fae woman snorts dismissively before turning and gliding off into the night. Soon she disappears into the dancing green among the other revelers. I breathe out a sigh of relief, glad to see the last of her, then turn to face Whispering Wood once more.

Well, I got what I needed from this mad night. Now I have only to find a gate that will lead me to Lunulyr. I should set out at once.

"Can't very well go traipsing across worlds like this," I mutter, looking down at my gown with its scooping neckline and bounteous skirts. I need proper clothes—boots, trousers, tunic. And my weapons. There's no way I'm plunging into Eledria unarmed.

I take a few steps, then pause. Am I simply making excuses to return to Dire's house? Am I still hoping to see him one last time? We agreed to meet at sunrise, but really, what's the point? I have the information I need. Is there any reason to face him, to offer stiff and formal goodbyes?

No more wishes.

No more foolishness.

But . . . I *do* need my weapons . . .

"I'll just go back to the house long enough to get what I need,"

I mutter, striding into the forest. It's very dark with only a little moonlight creeping through the branches to light the way. But I've never been afraid of the dark. And on Glorandal Night, no fae I meet will bring me harm. They can't. None would dare break the sacred trust of Glorandal for fear of the gods' swift retribution.

So I stride along as swiftly as I can, my skirts gathered up out of the way of my feet. The forest feels unusually large tonight. It's always large, always enigmatic, of course. But there's something about the magic in the air that makes me more aware than ever of the many layers contained within this space.

Suddenly, a new sound tickles my ear.

I stop, tilt my head, listening closely. Am I mistaken? Did I only imagine—

No! There it is again.

Heavy breathing.

I turn slowly, my hunter's instincts quickening. Something is there. Something in the Wood with me. Something large and . . . close.

Something not fae.

"Dire?" I whisper. Then I clear my throat and call out a little louder. "Dire, is that you?"

A huge, bulky shape steps out from behind a tree.

A werebeast. Not Dire. This is one of Granny's other creatures, a shaggy gray-and-black beast. The other male.

I choke on a scream and leap several paces back. Idiot! Why didn't I at least bring my knife with me? But it's against the unspoken rules of Glorandal Night to bring weapons to the dancing lawn. Still, I should have brought something so I wouldn't end up totally unarmed and alone in the dark.

I grit my teeth and brace myself, hands clenched into fists. "What are you doing here?" I snarl, refusing to let even a trace of fear tinge my voice.

The werebeast is mostly animal at this hour, with only the barest traces of humanity beginning to return. He lumbers toward me, leaning heavily on his forelimbs. I take another step back and cast about for anything that might serve as a weapon. Spying a fallen branch, I snatch it up. It's useless, of course, dry as it is. It'll break to pieces the minute I strike that hulking hide. But I feel better having something in my hands.

The werebeast's eyes flash, roving over the stick. Then it shifts its gaze to me. "You can't . . . escape . . . Granny," it says, struggling to make the words fit through its warped muzzle and sharp teeth.

"Oh really?" I brandish my stick a little higher. "I've done a fairly good job of eluding her these last few days. I kind of like my chances."

The werebeast snarls, takes another heavy step. Then its eyes goggle, unnaturally large in its awful face. I bite back another scream as that already warped visage warps again, like it's formed from warm wax and invisible fingers are pushing and prying and pulling at it. The shape begins to solidify again, and I realize that what I'm seeing isn't *real* exactly—it's almost like a glamour. But a glamour only ever works on the surface layers of the reality it changes. This is deeper than that, a dark magic, an evil magic, crawling up from the inside out. The werebeast's features change, transforming into . . . into . . .

"Granny!" The name bursts from my tongue. The next instant, I turn, try to run.

"Stay where you are!" Granny's voice barks through the werebeast's muzzle.

I stop dead in my tracks, feeling all the compulsions and enchantments I've been able to ignore these last few days reasserting themselves with triple their former force. What a fool I was to even think I had the power to resist such magic!

"We have a bargain, you and I," Granny says. The werebeast stalks toward me where I stand rooted to the ground. The magic around its head swims bizarrely, giving me glimpses sometimes of the monster behind my grandmother's face. Both sights are horrible, but the sight of Granny's head stuck on top of that monstrous body is worse by far. "We have a bargain struck in blood. Don't think you can escape so easily."

She stops in front of me. Hot monster breath pants in my face, stinking of carnage. But there's also the smell of Granny— her hyacinth perfume which perpetually hovers around her in a miasma of sweetness.

My stomach knots. I might be sick.

"You are *mine*," the witch says. "Seven years of your life . . . *mine*. And you will obey me, child. You will do exactly as I say."

*No, no, no!* I shake my head. Or try to. Though I strain every muscle in my body, though I strain the whole of my will, I can't wrest any control. My muscles ache with the need to move, but they are no longer mine to command.

Only my thoughts are my own. For the present at least.

*No!* The thought reverberates through my head and bursts from my glaring eyes. *I'll never be yours! You can bind me and ensorcel me all you like, but deep down, I still belong to me!*

Granny draws back as though the words were spat in her eye. For a flickering instant, the werebeast head comes back into view. I stare into that gruesome, snarling face, expecting it to lunge at me, expecting those massive jaws to tear into my throat. One word, one mere thought from Granny is all it would take.

But then the head of my grandmother swims back into visibility. Her smile is hard as iron.

"No more of these games, Brielle." She holds up one of the werebeast's hands, clenching it into a fist just in front of my nose. "Obey me. *Obey me.*"

Gods above, help! I try to fight, but the spell coils deeper and deeper, down under my skin, down to the very marrow of my bones.

"You have one job, little girl," Granny's voice says, creeping into my head and throbbing in time with my pulse. "One job to fulfill. Then we can overlook this flight of rebellion. All will be as it should be."

The werebeast lifts its hand and grabs me by the head. Its hot palm presses into my brow. I scream, writhe, but cannot fight.

Granny's voice pierces like a knife straight through my skull:

"Kill Dire. Bring back his head."

Suddenly I'm on my hands and knees, gasping for breath. I seem to be lying at the base of a tree, very cold. The world around me is dark and still. No sign of any werebeast. I crane my head, peer up through the branches overhead and see just the faintest hint of gray in the sky.

Dawn is coming. Which means . . .

I close my eyes, let out a long breath. The compulsion is there, knotted inside of me. Funny how I'd thought I could resist it. Funny how I'd imagined I could hide. Hide? Here in Granny's own domain? What a simpleton I was!

I should have taken Dire's advice and fled into Faerieland while I had the chance. I wouldn't have survived long, but at least I would've died knowing I wasn't Granny's tool.

Too late now.

Everything is too late now.

I pick myself up. All around me there is movement. When I turn to look, I can't quite see anything, but I know what it is—the fae folk returning from Glorandal Night. They must make their way through Whispering Wood and find the gates back into their own worlds before sunrise. If not, they'll be held accountable for Pledge-breaking, and Granny will not be lenient in her judgements against those fae who dare trespass in her wardship.

I close my eyes, breathing deeply. Once more, I feel the stirring magic in my bones. Funny how simple everything has become. But then, it was always simple really. I may have tried to make it more complicated, but that was nothing more than an illusion. The reality was always there underneath. I am Granny's creature. Her huntress. Her justice. And now . . .

I turn and face toward Phaendar Hall. My lips tilt in a faint half smile.

"Now he must die," I whisper.

## 22

## DIRE

I wake in the early dawn glow, lying on my face, naked and cold. Leaves and twigs and bits of forest debris cling to my beard and loose hair. I lift my head, give it a shake, and stare down at my man hands planted beneath me.

A pit of loathing opens in my gut—loathing of those hands, loathing of the lie they represent. Because I know the truth only too well. The truth is the monster that I was last night. The monster which had dared take Brielle in its arms. The monster which had frightened her, which had nearly torn her to pieces in a storm of lust and hunger.

I close my eyes, cursing softly. Even then, I can't forget the taste of her lips against mine. That one, perfect, stolen kiss.

How I ache for her! Ache with a need that will surely destroy me from the inside out. I can only pray she'll be wise. Perhaps she succeeded where I had not and found some word of her sister. Perhaps she is even now on her way to a gate and another world entirely.

A growl like a sob swells in my throat. I choke it back and push onto my knees, then to my feet. Morning chill ekes through my bare flesh into my bones. I look down at my naked body, at the little bit of remnant clothing still clinging in places. Not enough to make any difference. I'm almost entirely human now as the sun begins to rise. A few tufts of gray fur still cling to my elbows and shoulders, but they'll soon be gone.

Gods above, how exhausted I am! I don't know what I did after the beast overtook me so suddenly at midnight. Some form of mindless, nocturnal rampaging. Something bloody, something horrible.

Now I turn and make my way back home. I'm not sure why I do this. I'm like a dog, having wandered all night, returning at last to familiar surroundings. But I shouldn't have stayed at Phaendar Hall as long as I have. It's not safe for me to stay put. If it weren't for Brielle and her need for recovery, I would have left it long ago.

But left for where? I'm still trapped within the boundaries of Elorata's world. There's only one escape for me now . . .

It doesn't matter. Too tired to fight my own basic needs, I stagger through the trees until I reach the hall, push open the front door, and stare dully into the foyer. It looks even more overgrown than it did when I left last evening. I make my way to the stair, climb it step by heavy step, then proceed down the hall to my own former bedroom. I stop at the door, however, and look over my shoulder to a different door further down the hall.

I pause, consider.

Then, stumbling like a drunkard, I enter Brielle's room. I open the door, stand on the threshold, and breathe in the scent of her—the scent of pine and leather and honey which is so intoxicating to my senses. When I open my eyes again, I see her boots stashed in one corner of the chamber, her bow and knife where I left them in a pile that first night I brought her here. Signs of her are everywhere.

*Brielle . . . oh, Brielle . . .*

Guilt stabs my heart. It's been twenty years since Misery's death. Twenty years that I've mourned her. And I mourn her still. I always will. Though her true name has been taken from me, I'll never forget her; she's a vital part of my heart, my soul, until the day I die.

But now there is Brielle.

Brielle who is so different from that sweet, gentle creature who once held my heart so completely. Where *she* was soft, Brielle is hard. Where *she* was mild, Brielle is prickly, aggressive. Where *she* was sunshine and light, Brielle is like a wild and exhilarating storm.

Why does the very scent of her call to me so? Why does my spirit yearn for hers, why do my very bones ache for her?

I know why. Because I've changed. I'm not the young man I once was, either the tender lover, or the callow youth. I've become *this*. More monster than man, full of animal drives and ferocity, sometimes so powerful they overwhelm every good thought or feeling inside me. I could not love that gentle, shy little creature now. I would only frighten her, break her.

But not Brielle. She is my equal. No, not my equal—my superior. Fierce and fearless, strong and true. Like a heroine from some old legend sprung suddenly to life.

Heavy on my feet, I cross the room and fall on the bed. The pillow smells of her, and I bury my face in it, breathing in the memories it calls to mind. However long or short my life may be from this moment on, at least I'll have those memories. And one in particular—the memory of her arms around my neck, of her lips pressed against mine. That little slice of stolen joy.

The door creaks open.

My muscles tense. Every nerve comes alive, waiting. A strange sort of expectation that wasn't there before hums in the atmosphere.

I hear a soft step. An even softer breath.

I lie still in the bed, feigning sleep. I won't look. I won't let myself hope that it's her . . . Brielle, returned after the long night to join me. I keep my eyes firmly closed and don't move a muscle.

Footsteps cross the room. There's a sound like fabric rustling. Then the covers lift, and a weight gently lowers the side of the bed.

Warmth. Sudden warmth pressed against my naked flesh.

Growling, I roll over. Dream or not, disappointment or not, I have to see. I must know. So I turn, and I look and . . . and . . .

She's there.

Impossibly, she's there. Lying beside me.

She's removed the outer blue gown, which lies in a pile on the floor. Now she wears only the corset and snowy chemise. Her hair flows free, framing her face with such vibrant color as she gazes at me from those incredible eyes of hers.

Slowly, she blinks.

We don't speak. There are no words.

I ought to rise, slip from the bed. Flee this room. Flee this moment. But she's here. I thought I'd never see her again . . . but she's here.

With a harsh exhalation of breath, I roll my body on top of hers, pressing her beneath me. Her breath is hot and fast against my face in the instant before my lips cover hers.

At first, she lies very still. I kiss her hungrily, desperately, but she does not respond. Am I wrong? Have I misunderstood something? I draw back, gazing down at her, gazing into those dangerous green eyes. She meets my gaze. So solemn, so serious. I don't understand. There's something . . . something almost *lost* about her. Something sad.

"I'm sorry!" I growl, shaking my head at my own foolishness as I start to pull away. "I'm sorry, I shouldn't have—"

Her hands dart out, catch the back of my head. She pulls me down to her, and her lips meet mine in a vicious crash of connection that's almost painful. My body explodes in response, every inch of me ignited, burning, ready to consume.

I kiss her and kiss her again. I kiss her until she's out of breath, gasping and arching her back, lifting her jaw so that she can draw air into her lungs. But I can't wait, not now. My lips, having felt hers beneath them, are too greedy. I continue kissing along her jaw to her ear, my teeth toying with her lobe. I breathe in the honey and pine scent of her hair, and it makes me dizzy, delirious. With one hand, I support my body so that I do not crush her. With the other, I trace the line of her cheek down to her neck, to her shoulder, sliding the delicate chemise out of my way as I go. The swell of her breast is warm against my fingertips, but the corset boning stops me.

I sit upright, shaking hair out of my eyes. She props up onto her elbows, her eyes wide, her chest swelling with each fast breath she takes. She seems to understand my dilemma and, a shy smile curving her lips, begins to undo the front laces of her corset.

She's not fast enough.

I push her hands aside, rip the laces apart and toss the little bit of fabric and boning to the floor. Now she lies beneath me, clad only in her thin chemise, already slipped down from one shoulder. I draw her to me, kissing that shoulder and the sweet dent of her collarbone. A moan escapes her lips, and my senses thrill at the sound. I twine my fingers through her long hair, pulling her head back until her throat is exposed to my mouth. I can hear the pulse of blood in her veins, and the throb nearly drives me mad.

Then she plants her hands on my chest, pressing hard. I withdraw immediately, but she's not through with me yet. She catches hold of my shoulders, wraps herself around me and pushes me down on the bed. The next moment, she's on top of me, her legs straddling my waist, the chemise half fallen from her bosom, exposing far more than it hides.

She plants her lips against my throat, my jaw, the shell of my ear. I pull apart the laces of the chemise and run my palms down her back, drinking in the feel of her skin. I breathe in deeply . . .

But this time, it's not the perfume of pine and honey I smell.

It's hyacinth.

My eyes widen. I grip her shoulders, yank her away from me, staring into Brielle's face. She looks straight into my eyes and smiles.

It's not Brielle's smile.

"Elorata!" I gasp.

"Good morning, pretty boy," the witch says through Brielle's kiss-swollen lips. "Having a good time?"

Before I can react, she whips a knife out from under the pillow beside me. The blade flashes in the dawn light pouring through the nearest window as she plunges it straight for my eye.

# 23

## BRIELLE

I feel it all.

I'm there. I'm present.

But I'm totally helpless. Helpless as my body does and acts against my will and reason. Helpless as all those myriad sensations burst upon my senses.

Helpless as my fingers close upon the hilt of the knife, as I draw back my arm.

He's just fast enough. With animal-quick reflexes, he sees what I'm about to do, rolls to one side, and escapes the deadly blow. I merely cut off a few locks of hair as the blade sinks into his pillow. The next moment, he tosses me from the bed. I sprawl where I land, my chemise askew, my body exposed.

But I have no time for modesty, not while the curse inside is driving me to act. I spring up, the knife still in my grip, angled to slash.

"Perhaps I shouldn't have indulged." The voice purring from my throat sounds like mine, but these are not my words. I want to scream, to rage, to beat my head against the wall. "You are such a tempting hunk of manhood," the voice continues, "I simply couldn't resist! Ah well. I always was a fool for a pretty face and manly form."

Dire stares at me like I've transformed into some hideous demon. He's naked, but the fur of his wolf form is starting to return, along with his animal strength.

I lunge. I don't want to. But I can't stop. My arm lashes out, the big hunting knife cutting the flesh of his upper arm as he turns to escape. He dives, putting the bed between us. "Brielle!" he cries, and the sound of my name on his lips hurts like a blow. "Brielle, fight it! This isn't you!"

But I can't fight, I can't resist.

Maybe I could before. Not anymore.

I hurl myself at him, springing onto the bed and slashing wildly. He raises an arm, blocks my blow, then catches hold of me and yanks me from the bed. The next moment, he spins me around and slams my back up against the wall.

I'm at his mercy. He presses hard against my chest, and I feel the great strength in his arm, how easily he could squeeze the life out of me. But his eyes stare into mine. His weakness shines in his dilated pupils.

*Me.*

*I* am his weakness.

*I* will be his undoing.

I wrench a hand free and claw at his face. He yelps and leaps back, not quite fast enough to ward off another swipe of my knife. The serrated blade whisks across his ribcage, and a bright red line appears, blood pouring down his skin.

I don't wait for him to recover. I lunge again, the compulsion completely overwhelming everything else now. I must end this. I must end him. That's all I know, all I am capable of knowing. I aim my next blow for his throat, intending to plunge the blade deep, to sever the artery.

But Dire is quick. He pivots at the last moment, avoiding the strike, and without a second's hesitation darts for the open window. For a moment, I see him silhouetted there in the morning light, his arms extended, his hands gripping the frame on either side. Then he leaps.

My breath catches in my throat.

With a vicious shake of my head, I force my feet into motion, stumble for the window. Leaning heavily against the sill, I look out and down.

He lies on the ground below. Did he break every bone in his body?

But no. He rises slowly, staggers, catches his feet, then straightens his spine. I see now just how much of the animal form has already reasserted itself. One arm wrapped around his ribs where I cut him, he tilts back his head, looking up at me. Feral fire flashes in his eyes.

I spring back from the window and rush across the room. My bow and quiver lie near the door. It's but the work of a few moments for me to snatch them up, to string the bow, nock an arrow, and return to the window again.

I'm already too late. Dire is gone.

I stand there, breathing hard, gazing into that empty space where he was. My heart thuds painfully against my breastbone, and I can feel Granny's wrath humming along the spell that binds me to her.

Despite that spell, despite that control, I manage a small smile.

Then I lower my weapons and let my chin sink to my breast. My brow puckers as I take in my disheveled appearance, the gaping chemise, all that exposed skin. A flood of shame rushes through me, and a sob swells in my throat.

Dire had wanted me. But it wasn't *me*.

Gods on high, I never so much as kissed a man before last night! To go from that to . . . to everything I just felt, everything I just experienced . . . and none of it my own choice . . . I grimace, cursing bitterly. I feel used, violated.

But not by Dire.

"I should never have given that wish away," I whisper. Shuddering, I drop my bow and unused arrow on the floor. My fingers are shaking too hard to be of much use, but I try to force them to tie up the front laces of my chemise, to reclaim some sense of modesty.

Then I feel it—the pull on my spirit.

Granny is summoning me home.

I pull myself together using bits and pieces of clothing I find around the house. My own clothes have been disposed of, but I manage to scrounge up a simple riding habit from Lady Phaendar's wardrobe. After I've torn away a few superfluous flounces, it will serve me well enough. Thank the gods, my boots are still in good shape.

I don't actually know the way back to Granny's house from here. But the moment I step out of the house, I find my face turning northeast and feel the tug of the spell. Granny knows, and she is pulling me along, like I'm some stray dog caught on her leash.

I shrug my quiver onto my shoulders and set out walking. Granny hasn't made me pursue Dire's trail right away. That's got to count for something. Not that he'll be able to get far. The boundaries of Granny's wardship will contain him, and eventually, like it or not, I will find him again.

Oh, why didn't he just kill me when he had the chance?

The journey home is shorter than I like. I come upon a holly bush and use the Hinter Path to cover many miles in a few seconds. As I walk through the shadowy otherworld, I toy with the idea of simply leaping off to one side or the other, falling into the Hinter. I'd like to see Granny try to pull me back from that!

In the end, I'm not brave enough. The Hinter is too strange, too terrible. And I don't even have the certainty of death to look forward to.

So I continue, following the path to its end. When I step back into the natural forest, I see Granny's iron gate through the trees. My heart sinks like a stone to my gut. Over the last week, I foolishly let myself believe I'd never have to return this way. Granny's control seemed so weak, weak enough to allow for the escape Dire and I dared to discuss.

I should have known it was too good to be true.

Now the gate looms before me, silent, menacing. Like the jaws of a great beast waiting to open wide and swallow me whole. I have no choice but to march straight up to them and stand at attention.

At first nothing happens. Then, as though suddenly realizing I'm there, the gate swings open.

The nothingness of Granny's garden spreads before me once more. I feel a bit like nothingness myself—an ensorcelled creation, conjured into being by Granny's malicious imagination, only given substance and life when Granny herself requires my services. Otherwise, I'm like this garden—indistinct, murky. Nothing.

Cold to the bone, I drift on through the garden until I reach the house itself. The front door stands open, so I step inside, passing through equally indistinct passages until I come to the Hall of Heads.

I stop.

All those heads hanging from their mounts, still and lifeless . . . they suddenly seem to turn and fix their dead, glassy eyes on me. I cannot look away. One by one, I meet those gazes. All those young women and young men, former apprentices who had come to my grandmother expecting training. Bitterly betrayed. Transformed, used, and discarded.

The compulsion yanks on my spirit. I stumble forward, progressing between those solemn trophies. As I pass each one, I make myself look up and see the face, see the humanity behind the animal.

I pause a little longer before Misery, fighting Granny's pull.

I pause again before Dreg.

I want to salute them somehow. Want to let them know that I know. That I understand. That I *see* them for who they were. But it doesn't matter now. They're gone. Dead.

And soon Dire will join them.

"I'm sorry," I whisper. Tears spill over onto my cheeks and race down my face in two streaks. "I'm . . . I'm so sorry . . ."

"Brielle?" A melodic voice calls from the open doorway at the end of the hall. "Brielle, my darling, is that you at last?"

Sickness ripples through my gut. I pull my gaze away from Dreg and march on to the end of the passage, stepping into the doorway. The room is the same one in which I last saw my grandmother, complete with its cheery fire and large, tall-backed, throne-like chair. But this time, the chamber has been warped into a much larger space than before. Large enough to contain the two monstrous werebeasts standing in front of the fire. A female, not unlike Dreg but slenderer, almost foxlike; and the big black-and-gray beast I met last night, with his savage face and inflamed red eyes. They are both halfway through their transformation from human to animal.

They hold a young girl standing between them.

She can't be more than fifteen years old at the most. Round faced, rosy cheeked, with curly brown hair tumbling about her shoulders. She wears a simple gown and soft-soled shoes. Some farmer's daughter, I would guess, no one exalted or important. Her face is doll-like, utterly without expression. Well, no . . . when I look a little closer, I can just detect a faint sheen of fear glinting in the depths of her eyes. But she is too deeply entranced to act on that fear.

I can almost smell the stink of magic surrounding her.

On the far side of the room, Granny stands by a table full of various odds and ends, which I cannot see clearly. She turns and smiles graciously at me. How beautiful she is this morning! After several days away from her, the power of her glamour is almost overwhelming. Firelight catches in her lustrous hair, turning the strands to molten hues. Her gown is of saffron silk, richly embroidered in gold and fitted to perfection.

"Do have a seat, my dear," she says, waving a hand toward a small wooden chair by the wall. "I'll be with you momentarily."

I have no choice. I walk to the chair and perch there, every muscle tense and straining. I want to resist, to stand my ground. But her power is too strong. I watch her narrowly as she continues fiddling with the strange objects on the table. At one point, I see her hold up something that looks like . . . no, I must be mistaken. Is it an apple core?

My stomach plunges. I know what it is: the same golden apple I fetched from the Quisandoral's garden all those months ago. The apple Dire begged me not to give her, begged me to throw away.

One by one, Granny flicks the black seeds into a little bowl. Then, taking up a pestle, she begins grinding them to powder. A strong stink of magic rises like a cloud in the room, overwhelming my senses. My heart leaps to my throat, pounding hard. I glance from Granny to the girl standing between those two monsters. I know what's about to happen. Is there nothing I can do?

Her grinding complete, Granny sets aside the pestle then pours the contents of the mortar into a crystal decanter. It looks as though the decanter is filled with pure water, but as the seed powder mixes in, the liquid turns a sickly greenish color.

"It's been some time since I last took an apprentice," Granny says mildly, lifting the decanter and giving the contents a gentle swirl. She glances my way. "The last one was positively bursting with magic potential, so I didn't think I'd need to take another for many more years. But the coven has insisted. And I'm nothing if not obliging."

My stomach churns. I look at the girl and the two werebeasts again. Am I going to just sit here and watch Granny take this girl's magic? Watch her transform her right before my eyes, stealing her future, her potential, her life?

I should have listened to Dire and destroyed that apple. I should have tried to, at least. Why did I give in so easily? I can resist, I've proven that!

If only . . . if only . . .

I stare at that decanter in Granny's hand, at the brew within, reeking of evil. Black Magic, Mother Ulla said. My grandmother is delving into Black Magic. But that apple she made me fetch, it was a holy thing, grown from a tree planted by a goddess. Which makes the evil purpose for which it's being used so much worse.

Granny glides across the room, holding the brew high and swirling it again. Her face is serene, but I can feel the simmering rage inside her. Rage that I had dared thwart her, had failed her.

But there's more here as well. Behind that rage lurks another emotion, something I can *almost* detect. I study her face, leaning into the spell connecting us, pushing back against that one-way flow of power. It's like standing in the middle of a river and trying to catch it in a bucket. The futility will soon exhaust me, but for the moment I hold my ground, push a little harder and . . .

There it is. I feel it. I feel what she's trying to hide from me.

*Fear.*

But that's ridiculous! Why should Granny be afraid? She holds all the power here.

Unless . . .

I don't know if Granny can feel what I'm doing or not. If she does, she gives no sign as she approaches the girl standing between the werebeasts. Extending one elegant hand, she tilts the girl's chin up so she can smile into her eyes.

"Ah, yes!" Granny sighs. "Such a lovely young thing. So full of potential. Is there anything in this world more beautiful than potential? More delicious?" She licks her lips slowly, hungrily. "Young people never know what to *do* with this gift. It's entirely wasted on them."

She pours a drop of her evil brew onto her finger then dabs it across the girl's forehead. Closing her eyes, she begins to speak in a low, rhythmic cadence: *"Sakhous hadaic mor likous sidarha. Ul me rahtu solac sakhousa . . ."*

The words pour from her mouth in a dark stream that I can *feel*, if not see. That darkness spirals in wicked tentacles straight for the girl, wrapping around her, permeating her skin, plunging inside her.

I clench my jaw, my breath tight in my chest. But when I push again at Granny's hold on me, I sense a faint *give* that wasn't there a moment before. Granny is distracted, caught up in the spell she's creating. For the moment at least, her hold on me is weakened. Not by much, but enough?

I reach inside myself, reach down to where my heart pounds, pulsing blood through my body. Closing my eyes, I feel for the connection between me and my grandmother. Not the connection of magic, but the other, deeper, more profound connection of blood.

I've resisted her before. I can do it again.

Think of Dreg.

Think of Misery.

Think of . . . *him*. The man I love, whose true name has been taken, leaving him with a false identity, a warped body. But he himself is still true, down underneath the curses. He is true and noble and brave.

He needs me.

They need me.

This girl standing there so helpless, wreathed in black magic, needs me.

*I can do this.*

I move one foot, sliding it along the floor. Then I move my arm, just a fraction, bracing myself to rise. Granny doesn't react. She's fully concentrated on her spell, the incantation flowing from her tongue, swelling with darkness that fills the whole chamber. I push up from my chair, stand. Sway. I'm so dizzy, I fear I'll collapse. My chest rises and falls with each panting breath, and sweat beads my forehead. But I stand. I don't fall. I don't sit back down.

The girl's body is starting to warp. I can still see the real girl beneath the whirling darkness, but that darkness becomes more solid by the moment. I don't have much time. I must decide. Now. If I break Granny's hold on me one more time, surely the bargain between us will be compromised. And what will the forfeit be? My life?

It doesn't matter. I'm going to stop this. Come what may.

"*Holrad worlorda, ir resta norlorda . . .*" Granny chants, her head thrown back, her arms outstretched, one hand still gripping the crystal decanter. The darkness pours out of her in thick, wafting ribbons. She does not see me approach from behind.

The two werebeasts do, however. They watch me, their eyes

hooded and intent. But they don't alert their mistress. Do they know what I'm about to do? Perhaps . . . and perhaps they want it to happen. They may have no will to resist their mistress, but in their hearts, resistance is all they crave.

I take another step. Another. Each step feels like a whole journey in and of itself. Gritting my teeth, I stretch out my hand . . .

And snatch the decanter from Granny's grasp.

A bestial roar bursts from the witch's throat, shaking that whole room. The magic, the glamours, all of it cracks. The world around me suddenly twists into strange, nightmarish shapes that don't fit within my realm of understanding. I feel madness threatening to break through and catch me in its clutches. But I hold on, drawing back several steps, the decanter pressed against my chest.

Granny whirls and faces me. Even as she does so, the dark cloud surrounding the girl disperses. She sags where she stands, fainting in the werebeasts' arms. Granny shrieks as her spell falls to pieces around her, and for the space of a single breath, I see the truth of the witch—the ugly hag beneath the beauty glamours. Dark magic teems beneath her pasty white skin, alive with its own malicious purpose.

"On your knees, girl!" she roars, pointing straight at me. I feel the power of compulsion going out from her. "On your knees and grovel! Beg for my mercy!"

I look her in the eye.

Then I lift the decanter over my head and, just as she screams, "*No!*" I dash it into the ground.

Glass shatters. Liquid spatters.

Darkness whorls into my eyes, blinding me, filling the whole of that strange, twisted chamber. I can't see anything, can't feel anything. There's only blackness and a stink like sulfur pouring into my eyes, my nostrils, the pores of my skin.

Then the darkness parts. Granny's face, distorted with age and evil, manifests before me.

"You little wretch!" she snarls. "You and your petty rebellions! You're nothing, *nothing*, do you hear me? Unworthy of my daughter's blood. You are no true granddaughter of mine."

I don't know how. I don't know why. But suddenly a laugh ripples up my throat and emerges in a burst. "No granddaughter of yours?" I cry. "Face it, Granny—none of us get to choose our family. I might not be magically gifted, but I'm still half Dorrel, like it or not!"

"Never." Granny moves toward me. I can see nothing but her head, like an apparition floating toward me, disembodied. "I could have made you something, but you had to go and ruin it. Ruin everything. You're no Dorrel. I reject you; I reject everything about you!"

As she speaks, the darkness around her seems to condense, becoming something solid. I see the vague impression of her haggish hands rolling, turning, spinning. She's making something, shaping a spell.

My stomach drops. I turn and try to run. Within two paces, I slam into a wall I cannot see. I pound it with my fists, trying to find a way through. I can't. I'm trapped.

I turn, look back over my shoulder . . . just as Granny flings the gathered magic straight at me. It hits me full in the face, and I scream, fall, crumple to my knees.

    That's when the pain begins.

    The breaking of bones.

    The tearing of claws.

    The rending of flesh.

    Pain, pain, so much pain, and then . . .

    I see red.

## 24

### DIRE

I flee through the woods. Mindless. Ravening. Furious without understanding.

I need blood. Fresh, hot, flowing blood.

As I run, a single name throbs in my brain, over and over again: *Elorata! Elorata!*

Sometimes, however, it morphs and becomes something else: *Brielle . . . Brielle . . .*

But these names, these thoughts, they don't belong to me. They are human thoughts, and I am not human. I am animal, I am beast. I want to tear and rend and break and shred. I want to sink my teeth into flesh and feel bones break between my jaws.

*Elorata . . . Brielle . . .*

I come to a stop, my forepaws digging into the soil, my head hanging low, foam dripping from my jaws. Every instinct tells me to turn around now, to find her scent, to track her down. She might kill me with a well-placed arrow, but I can't think of that. I can't bring myself to care. I just want . . . I want . . .

*It's not her fault.*

I snarl, shaking my head roughly. But that small part of me still clinging to humanity holds on fast.

*It wasn't her fault. She didn't mean to do it.*

*It was the witch, only the witch.*

With a roar, I plunge on through the trees, running as fast as I can, trying to escape that voice. I don't know if the huntress is on my trail or not. I haven't smelled her in miles. But instinct tells me I need to go deeper, put more distance between us. By the time the sun has reached the apex of the sky, I'm fully animal once more. All names, all rage, all accusations or defenses fade and disappear. I simply cannot hold onto such thoughts. I'm nothing but *hungry*. I sink into that feeling, revel in the joy of the animal unleashed.

It's time to hunt.

When I come to at last, I'm crouched over the carcass of a young deer. There's blood and bone and bits of fur everywhere, and my mouth is full of warm flesh. At first, I try not to be aware, try to make my mind sink back into the safety of the animal. But my man-self relentlessly pushes further and further to the forefront of my awareness until I can no longer ignore what I am and what I am doing.

I sit back on my hairy haunches, staring at the carnage before me. At least it's only a deer. A brutal death for such a gentle creature, but a swift one. I know my own prowess as a hunter.

Sighing, I look down at my fur-covered form, already beginning to show signs of humanity again. I'm smeared all over with gore. I could try to lick my coat clean but can't bring myself to do so. Other days I wouldn't hesitate. Twenty years of living like this has dulled my sense of propriety.

But after last night—after tasting the sweetness of what humanity can mean—I can't bear to let myself fully sink back into the beast I am. Not while I have any choice about it.

"Gods help me!" I growl, rising and turning from the mutilated deer. The scent of running water tickles my nose, and I follow it to a swift-flowing creek. The icy water cannot penetrate my fur coat, but it serves well enough to wash away most of the gore and blood. By the time I climb out, I'm a little more human again, almost able to stand upright. I take a moment to inspect the two cuts from Brielle's knife. They're not deep, which is a mercy, for I have nothing with which to bind them. They'll have to heal on their own, and I can only hope they won't become infected.

Sitting heavily on the edge of the stream, I gaze down at my rippling reflection in the water, taking in the half man that I am. Then I close my eyes . . .

And I see Brielle. Lying beside me in that bed. Her body warm, her lips parted. Her eyes full of desire.

What a fool I was! To think she would come to me like that, to let myself fall for such an easy seduction! I knew better. Even in the moment I knew better. Because Brielle isn't like that. The kiss we shared the night before . . . it was so different. *Innocent* in a way, though no less passionate for its innocence. It was a kiss that gave and made me want to give. It wasn't that grasping desperation, that groping need. That possession.

I should have smelled Elorata's influence right away. If I hadn't fallen prey to my own cravings, my own weakness.

Growling again, I open my eyes and stare again into the water. I long ago gave up any real hope for myself. But I'd honestly believed I might be able to save Brielle. Now even that small hope is gone. Unless the witch herself can be brought down. But who would be foolish enough to try? Elorata is the most powerful ward witch in centuries. I remember only too clearly how the coven of witches and warlocks at her table cowered before her. Even Mother Ulla, stubborn and defiant though she was, ultimately would not cross her.

So Granny Dorrel will continue to rule this wardship for generations to come, sustained by her own dark magic.

My shoulders slump and my head sags heavily from my neck. I stare down at my hands planted on the earth before me—still mostly animal, but my fingers are beginning to lengthen and emerge once more. I clench them tight, squeezing hard, as though I can somehow squeeze out my own frailty.

Suddenly, my ears twitch. I frown, lifting my head, angling a little to one side. What is that sound? Am I imagining it? No, for there it goes again.

Screaming. *Human* screaming.

I rise to all fours, muscles tense, hair bristling down my spine. Instinct tells me to run. Screaming can mean nothing good, after all. I shouldn't let myself get involved. Not with humans.

But what if . . . what if I could . . .

"Gods damn!" I snarl and turn toward the sound, springing into a lumbering stride. As I go, I realize I'm not as deep into Whispering Wood as I thought I was. Unless I'm much mistaken, my mindless wanderings took me in circles, and I'm no more than a mile or two away from Phaendar Hall. A disturbing thought. And where is this screaming coming from? Multiple voices, men, women, and children. Distant still, but I'm closing that distance swiftly.

I reach the edge of the forest, emerge on the rise above the dancing green. The rooftops of Gilhorn are outlined against the sky up ahead. That's where the screaming is coming from.

I hesitate. I've never ventured into town while in this monstrous state. The very idea makes me recoil. But the screaming continues, tearing the air, full of terror, and beneath that screaming there's something else. Something I can't quite hear or sense, but which I recognize, nonetheless.

*Elorata.*

Gathering my limbs, I spring into motion, loping out from the shelter of the trees and across the dancing green, picking up speed as I go. People flee into the countryside all around me—men with their arms around their wives, women carrying their children. At the sight of me, their terror redoubles. The men try to fling themselves in front of their families, the women clutch their small ones close to their bosoms. Pitchforks, spades, and scythes flash before my eyes.

I ignore this rustic weaponry and plunge on into the town itself. Dodging terrified townsfolk, I make my way through the streets, head for the town square where the bulk of the noise seems to be coming from. I emerge from a narrow street and skid to a halt, swiftly taking in the scene before me. Two big oxen lie on the ground, still trapped in their traces. One of them is dead, the other dying. Blood spatters the paving stones, and the air stinks of death and carnage.

And in the midst of it all . . . the beast.

It's a werebeast. I recognize the magic and the warping at once. But it's not one I've met before, a big catlike thing with golden-red fur and stripes around its eyes and hindquarters. Despite the lateness of the day, it is wholly animal, huge and monstrous, with only the very faintest traces of humanity in its features. This is a recent transformation.

Elorata has taken a new apprentice.

Men rush into the square—three speckle-faced youths who pass for the Gilhorn town watchmen. Clad in humble leather armor, carrying rusty old swords handed down from their great-grandfathers, they surround the monster. But they stink of fear, and I know the beast can smell it too.

The werecat lunges at the first of them, knocking his sword to one side and sending him sprawling flat on his back. One huge paw plants on his chest, claws digging straight into the leather. The young man screams. One of his fellow watchmen stands in place, shocked, staring. The other, however charges the cat from behind. The werecat's sensitive ears hear his approach, and it whips around, avoiding the slice of his old blade. The steel hits the stones like a ringing bell, and the watchman stumbles. A sideswipe from a great paw sends him flying. I would be tempted to laugh the scene wasn't so grim.

The werecat turns again to the pinned man. Throwing back its head, it lets out a wild roar, then lunges as though to tear out the young fellow's throat. But I'm already on the move.

I hurtle into the monster from the side, throwing all the force of my body into that blow. The beast sprawls on the paving stones but scrambles back to its feet much faster than I would have expected. Spitting foam, it locks its gaze on me, fire dancing in its green eyes. If it's surprised to see another werebeast, it doesn't show it.

"Easy there, kittycat," I say, forcing the words through my half-animal muzzle. "You don't really want to do this. I know it's frightening just now, but soon you will—"

The cat throws back its head and yowls. The next instant, it hurtles straight at me. I'm neither as fast nor as nimble as the werecat, impeded by my own slowly returning humanity. But I'm bigger and bulkier by far. I use that bulk now, rising to meet the beast's attack. It launches into me, but I catch it by its outstretched forelimbs. We struggle, both braced on our hind legs, eye to eye. And as I stare into those eyes, I see . . . I see . . .

"Brielle?" I gasp.

The werecat blinks.

Then it lunges again, using all the force in its powerful haunches. I'm too startled, and the force of her lunge knocks me from my feet. I land hard, the breath knocked out of me, and have no time to recover before she's on top of me, jaws tearing at my throat. The thick fur of my ruff offers some protection. I catch hold of her with my clawed hands, wrenching her head back. She tears at my shoulders, my chest, her claws seeking to dig into my flesh.

Some distant part of me is aware of the watchmen regathering. Someone is shouting something about crossbows.

The next instant, a bolt hits the ground right next to my ear and *pings* off the stone. I whip my head about, looking for the source of that bolt. The werecat takes the opportunity to spring away from me. A second bolt whistles just over her head. She flinches, crouching to all fours.

"Get out of here!" I cry, turning to her desperately. "Get out of here before they kill us both!"

But she's too wild. She doesn't understand.

She snarls at the archers positioned in the upper windows of the nearest building. Her sights set on them with predatory bloodlust, she lunges straight for the building, heedless of my cries.

A single flying leap takes her most of the way to the windowsill, and her claws dig into wood and plaster. She climbs, impossibly, even as more crossbow bolts fly at her. But the angle is wrong; the marksmen cannot land a hit. She reaches the window, catches one man by the front of his tunic, flings him out over her shoulder.

I'm on my feet and diving already. I catch the fellow and roll across the ground with him in my arms. I don't have time to set him down gently, but simply drop him where we land.

Then I'm running toward the building myself, leaping, flying through the air. I hit the werecat, wrap my arms around her, drag her back down. We land hard with her on top. Shocked by the impact, I lie stunned, the breath knocked from my lungs.

The werecat rolls off me, her lips pulled back in a terrible snarl. She's about to lunge at me again when a bolt strikes her in the haunch. She screams and spins in place, trying to knock the thing out. Another bolt hits her shoulder.

"Brielle!" I shout. "Brielle, *run!*"

Does she understand me? Her gaze, frenzied with pain, meets mine for an instant. Is there a flash of comprehension there?

Then, moving fast despite the bolts bristling from her body, she springs away from the village square and disappears among the houses. I can only hope she'll make it out to the green and, beyond that, to the Wood.

I rise, chest heaving. Watchmen surround me, both the three on foot in the square and the archers in the windows above. They're reloading their crossbows. I cast a glance at the fellow I'd caught and saved, who's just pulling himself up, shaking his head blearily. We lock gazes for an instant. His eyes widen.

Then I turn and gallop away, leap over the carcass of the dead ox, and race back through the streets of Gilhorn in pursuit of the werecat.

## BRIELLE

I'm lost.

Lost in this darkness. Lost in this curse.

Deep down inside, I can feel something stirring, moving. Screaming.

I shake my head and run faster and faster. Pain burns in my shoulder and haunch. I need to escape, need to get away from the stink of humans. Those vicious creatures that hacked at me with their blades and shot at me with their bolts. But underneath the fear, I still hear that voice. That vicious voice that shakes me to my core:

"*It's time to root out my precious Dire once and for all. Go to his village and slaughter everything in sight. He won't be able to resist playing bold protector. He'll appear soon enough. And then you must kill him."*

Kill him . . . kill him . . . kill him . . .

I roar, desperate to drown out that voice. There's too much pain, too much confusion. My haunch and shoulder throb. Soon I can't run anymore. I stop and try to pull the bolts out with my teeth, but they're out of reach. I twist and gyrate my body, but that only makes the pain worse. Panting with exhaustion, mewling with frustration, I stagger on through the sheltering green of the forest.

The sound of water attracts me, and I steer my limping paws that way. The sight and smell of the stream brings a rush of relief. I bend my head, lapping water with my tongue, relieved as the cooling water slides down my throat. I'm so hot, so tired. More than tired . . . ready to drop from sheer exhaustion.

I lift my head, look down at the murky reflection in the moving water below me. For an instant, I see not an animal, but . . . me.

*No!*

I shy away, sitting down hard. Pain from the bolt in my haunch radiates through my body, driving out all other thoughts. With a moan, I fall on one side, my ribcage expanding and contracting with short, gasping breaths. My mind spins in and out. Sometimes it's fully animal, and I feel only the agony and the fear and the exhaustion, all waves of sensation without clear thought.

Sometimes, however, when the pain is greatest, *I* claw back to the surface of my mind. Back into awareness.

*What have I done?*

*What have I become?*

I try to think back, try to remember. Did I kill anyone? Did Granny's compulsion truly drive me to slaughter? I remember seeing a child and feeling the thrum of predatory impulse in my veins. Had I acted on that impulse? Had I obeyed Granny's command?

No. No, I turned to the oxen instead, tore into their flesh. Blood, blood, so much blood! Hot and gushing and exhilarating, spilling over my nose, my face, my fur.

It was glorious.

It was terrible.

I wanted more, more, *more* . . .

Then those two-legged creatures had attacked me. Those *men*. With their sorry weapons and their soft hides. I'd wanted to rend them, break them, devour them. I'd wanted to . . .

No! That's not what I wanted! I wanted to stop, to flee, to hide! And the conflict inside me had nearly ripped me in two.

I lift my head, looking at my wounds again. Wounds I can do nothing about. Blood flows freely through the striped fur. Maybe I'll die soon. Oh, gods on high, please let me die!

I close my eyes and lie back on the grass, my nose pointed toward the stream. My mind is still foggy, still mostly animal, but I think I feel my body starting to revert from beast to human form. I hope I die before I transform entirely. I don't want to have to face what I've become while in my right mind.

The sound of footsteps, light and nimble, just catches my

sensitive ears. I don't fully comprehend what I'm hearing, not this close to unconsciousness. Then I sniff, inhaling the barest breath of a familiar scent. The scent of a wolf.

*Dire . . . Dire . . .*

Suddenly gentle hands are on my body, running over my bare, shivering, pain-ridden flesh. An equally gentle voice says, "Brielle! Brielle, my darling, what has she done to you?"

Something deep inside me, down underneath the pain, thrills at the tenderness in those words. Thrills that he could speak like that. To *me*.

With an effort, I pry my eyes open. I'm too dizzy to discern anything more than a faint outline against the light of the setting sun. But I know it's him. And if this is the last sight I'll ever see, so be it. I can thank the gods and die peacefully now.

"Dire," I whisper, the name forming on my lips but not quite able to escape.

Then I close my eyes and slip into oblivion.

## 26

## DIRE

She left a clear trail into the wood. I can be grateful for that, at least. I scarcely need my wolf senses to guide me; I simply follow the blood and broken branches, an obvious path even for an inexpert tracker.

She makes it farther than I thought possible. With those wounds, I would have expected her to collapse long before now. But Brielle always surprises me with her strength of spirit. And with this new monstrous form Elorata has given her, she now has bodily strength to match. Maybe she'll even survive those wounds. Maybe . . .

I hasten on. The sun is falling faster now, and I'm losing my wolf form, becoming nothing more than a man. But I push on. I have no way of knowing what I'll find at the end of the trail. A dead girl? A savage monster? When I was first transformed, it was days before my human form returned. But then, I wasn't Elorata's blood kin. I had nothing with which to fight her magic, while Brielle is much more resistant than she realizes.

The bloody trail seems a little fresher now. I'm getting close, I'm sure of it. The gurgle of running water plays in my ears. I redouble my pace. She'll make for water. If her animal senses are guiding her, she'll be drawn that way.

I push through foliage and low branches, which lash at my bare skin, leaving small cuts. But I emerge in a clear space by the stream and, turning my gaze upstream, I spy her at last. Not the great golden cat that she was, but *her*. Brielle. She lies outstretched beside the water, one hand and long snarls of her hair trailing in the flow. Naked. Small. Vulnerable.

My heart thuds painfully at the sight.

At first, I'm almost afraid to approach, afraid to discover that she's dead. But no! She's breathing. I can see her ribcage rising and falling. I step to her side, kneel, my hands hesitant to reach out and touch her. She looks so small, so frail in her nakedness. And, though I hate to admit it, my gaze longs to drink in the sight of her like this, to take in her well-formed, muscular limbs, her soft, feminine curves . . .

I shake this unwholesome desire away, concentrating instead on her injuries. Neither of the crossbow bolts penetrated deeply, thank the gods. They lie nearby; I guess they fell out when her body reverted to human shape. But she's still bleeding badly, and

I have nothing with which to stop the blood. I don't even have clothes of my own to tear and turn into makeshift bandages.

I make do with what I can find, grabbing leaves from a nearby sycamore and pressing them against her shoulder and thigh. The bolt to her shoulder struck not far from the scar left by Conrad's knife, but at least this wound is not so deep. I manage to get the blood stopped, then pack more leaves against the wounds and tie them in place with a bit of tough vine pulled from a nearby tree. It'll have to do.

And now . . . what?

I sit back, gazing down at the girl. Fur is starting to creep back in along her shoulders and arms. My human form won't last much longer either, for the sun is already mostly set, and darkness closes in. Do I dare pick her up and carry her back to Phaendar Hall? But Elorata knows that's where I took her before. Once she realizes Brielle is missing again, she'll send her two werebeasts directly there to sniff us out. I've got to think of something else.

A memory stirs in the back of my mind: an image of Brielle standing on the edge of Elorata's northernmost border, talking to a fat witch on the other side.

Mother Ulla.

Mother Ulla, who had, at least to a certain degree, stood up to Elorata.

Mother Ulla, who had even dared leave a rune mark on one of Granny's trees.

Would she help us? Is there even a chance?

Desperation churning my gut, I scoop Brielle into my arms, shivering at the sensation of her bare flesh pressed against mine. But our animal bodies will return soon, and with them the barrier of fur between us. Meanwhile, I can't wait for propriety's sake. I've got to get moving.

Cradling her close to my pounding heart, I stride into the forest, setting a determined pace.

It is many hours past sunset by the time I reach the border. My wolf form is dominant, which is good. I need those animal senses to help me navigate through the night shadows.

Struggling a little to walk upright and carry Brielle in my forelimbs, I creep up to a certain tree, sniffing at recent knife cuts. I think I smell the residue of the rune mark the witch left. This is definitely the place where Brielle confronted that fat little ward witch.

I look down at my burden. She's much more animal than human now. I no longer feel the feverish warmth of her skin, for velvety fur covers most of her body. She's very still in my arms, but I feel the pulse of life in her, thready but present.

"I spend much too much of my life carrying your wounded hide around the Wood," I growl softly.

Did she stir at the sound of my voice? Did her brows pucker slightly? It might be a trick of the light and my own imagination.

Turning my gaze to the forest on the far side of the invisible boundary, I draw a deep breath into my lungs. Then I throw back my head and howl, *"Mother Ulla!"* My voice rings through the trees, echoing and reechoing until it is lost.

Only silence answers.

But then, what did I expect? The ward witch probably retired to her bed long ago. Why would she *happen* to be out at such a late hour, patrolling this particular part of her wardship? It was foolish of me to hope. But I can't give up now.

I howl again, throwing my voice even further. *"Mother Ulla! Help us! Please!"*

I sound more animal than human, my words almost inarticulate. But the emotion and the need are there. I want to howl and howl and keep on howling until I've made enough noise to bring the old witch running. But it won't do Brielle any good if the racket I make draws Elorata's two other werebeasts to us. No doubt they're out hunting even now.

Growling, I pace up and down the border, scanning the far side for any sign of movement. Several times I step too near the invisible boundary and leap back as searing pain rips across my senses. I know well enough what will happen if I try to cross over. Will it be the same for Brielle? Have I brought her out here for nothing?

Shaking these thoughts from my head, I lift my voice, crying out one last time, *"Mother Ulla, I beg of you! Hear me!"*

"All right, all right, enough of that racket."

I spring back from the boundary, blinking hard. Even with my wolf senses, I struggle to discern anything on the far side. There's just an *impression*. A shape, a silhouette that I smell rather than see. It smells of mothballs and basil and good, clean dirt.

"Mother Ulla?" I ask.

The next moment, the impression clarifies. The silhouette becomes a fat old lady in a patchwork gown, her broad-brimmed hat pulled low over one eye, both gnarled hands gripping a long, twisted witch's staff. Her one visible eye snaps at me like a glinting hot coal in the night.

"Well now. Ain't you looking a bit different from how I last saw you? I knew you was wearin' glamours when you served at table that night, but . . . gods above love me, I had no idea them glamours were *that* strong."

"They weren't," I answer. "At that hour, I'm mostly human anyway. The glamours simply maintained the appearance a little longer than usual."

"Eh?" The witch snorts. "You sayin' *this* ain't your natural self? You goes back and forth?"

I nod. "Indeed, good Mother." My tone is respectful, if a bit rumbling in my animal throat. "I'm a werewolf. I spend my life between two states of existence, sometimes more of one, sometimes more of the other."

Mother Ulla lets out a long, wheezing breath that ends with a curse. "A werewolf!" She shakes her head, the bent peak of her tall hat flapping. "I've heard rumors here and there, but . . . you know how it is. None of us likes to cross Granny now, does we? Sometimes it's easiest to turn a blind eye or a deaf ear. Not proud of it, but it's the truth. Still, I knew in my bones all weren't well."

She nods then at the bundle in my arms. "And what's that there? The girl? Granny's girl?"

I take a half step closer to the boundary, holding Brielle up so that a stray beam of moonlight falls on her face, illuminating the catlike features. Mother Ulla inhales a sharp hiss. "Gods save us, did that old crone go and use Black Magic on her own flesh and blood?"

I nod again. "She's wounded," I add. "Marksmen from Gilhorn. She was out of the wood, rampaging through town like a rabid creature. They shot her."

"*Rampaging* you say?" Mother Ulla grunts. "I ain't never heard tell of a werebeast being that careless. Granny must have sent her there. Must have *wanted* her to get shot."

Bile rises in my throat. I've wondered as much myself, however. After all, in the twenty years of my enslavement, I've never once stepped foot out of Whispering Wood. Granny doesn't like her creatures being seen.

"Please," I say, "can you help her?"

Mother Ulla's lips twitch to one side then the other, her visible eye glimmering as she studies the creature Brielle has become. "Granny put a compulsion on her, didn't she? I ain't often known Granny Dorrel to put a foot wrong, but she's made a mistake here all right. Compulsion magic is wicked stuff at the best of times, but putting it on your own kin? That's downright stupid, that is! No wonder the girl revolted. And this!" She lifts a hand from her staff and waves it vaguely to indicate Brielle's transformed body. "A curse like that on top of a compulsion is just too much. If Granny ain't broken some of her own spells along the way, she's certainly compromised them."

"What does that mean?" I don't know whether to be hopeful, frustrated, or fearful. "Can you help her or not?"

"Ain't sure. But I might. Under ordinary circumstances, no way. But in this case . . ." The witch sucks on one tooth thoughtfully for some moments. Then she nods. "Put her down on the ground there, easy-like. I'm going to try something."

I obey, laying Brielle as close to the borderline as I dare. Even then, the proximity makes my fur prickle uncomfortably. I hope it doesn't add to Brielle's pain. I arrange her body to put as little pressure on the wounds as possible. My awkward leaf and vine bandages are falling apart, but I can smell that no fresh blood is flowing. That's a good sign at least.

Mother Ulla, meanwhile, mutters to herself and digs the end of her staff in the dirt. I don't have much affinity for magic, but I feel a tension in the air that tells me magic is stirring. Are those runes the witch is drawing in the earth?

Finally, Mother Ulla comes to the end of her spell. She crouches, groaning as she does so, her back and knees clicking audibly. But once she's close to the ground, she lays out her staff so that the twisted, rootlike head points toward Elorata's boundary. To my surprise, the roots begin to grow and twist, shooting out from the end of the staff. A greenish glow surrounds them, a glow I'm not quite certain I see but might be *smelling* instead. It's a sharp scent, not altogether unpleasant.

The roots stretch further and further until they creep across the boundary line into Granny's wardship. Once across, they sprout more little branching arms that wrap around Brielle, covering her from head to foot. I growl sharply, but stop myself from lunging at it, no matter how much I want to. I came to Mother Ulla for help, after all. I'd better not interfere now.

Slowly, cautiously, the staff branches pull Brielle to the boundary. Every nerve in my body spikes, every hair stands on end. Will she survive? Or will Elorata's curse kill her for trying to escape?

There's a moment of resistance . . . a moment when I feel Elorata's magic pushing back. Mother Ulla grunts and mutters something, scratching in the dirt next to the staff with one hand. Another rune, another flare of magic. The resistance gives way. The branches pull Brielle to the other side of the boundary, all the way to where the witch crouches.

Mother Ulla puts a finger to Brielle's pulse.

"Is she all right?" I ask, leaning heavily on my forelegs. "Is she alive?"

"Yup. Still breathing." Mother Ulla shoots me a wry look. "Gone and lost your heart to this fool girl, didn't you? Well, I guess a body can't blame you, brute that you are. Like calls to like, so they say."

While I'm still puzzling out whether I've just been insulted, Mother Ulla gets to her feet and picks up her staff. To my shock, she lifts Brielle right along with it—the girl suspended in the air above the witch's head in a network of tiny branches, like a bizarre parasol.

"Sorry I can't get you over," Mother Ulla says, tossing me a look over her shoulder. "That curse Granny's got on you . . . it's a bad'un. Not something I can break. But it *can* be broken; did you know?"

"Yes," I answer.

"But you ain't gots the guts to go through with it?"

I shake my head slowly. "I would rather die."

Mother Ulla cackles. "Typical! You sound a bit like this one here."

"What will happen to her?" I ask, taking a tentative step nearer the boundary. I try to see Brielle's face through the snarl of branches containing her, but they're too densely grown. "Can you help her?"

"I should think so. And then I'm gonna try to convince her to put as much distance between herself and her grandmother as she possibly can. Something tells me she ain't going to like what I've got to say, however." The witch raises a bristling eyebrow, giving me a significant look. "Something tells me she'll be hightailing it back here as soon as she rightly can."

"You can't let her."

"Don't think I gots much say in the matter." She shrugs. "But I'll do my best. Off with you now, wolf boy! You done what you can for the girl. I'll do what I can now."

With that, she turns away from the boundary line and totters off into the night-darkened forest, leaning heavily on her staff for support. Her staff, which continues to *smell* of glowing magic, and which holds Brielle wrapped in its branchy grip over the witch's head. It's the strangest sight I've ever seen.

I watch until they vanish into the underbrush. Then I stand there a while longer, breathing deep, inhaling the last traces of Brielle's scent.

She's gone.

Gone.

Gods willing, she won't be back.

My lips curled back in an ugly snarl, I turn my back to the boundary line. Then, tossing back my head, I howl to the moon overhead before racing off into the trees.

## 27

## BRIELLE

My shoulder hurts. Again.

Gods above, now my thigh hurts as well! Can't I manage to keep myself whole for even one week?

I don't want to open my eyes. Despite the pain in my shoulder and hip, I'm relatively comfortable. More comfortable than I remember being for a long time. Warm, but not too warm. Just kind of fuzzy.

*Fuzzy . . .*

I draw a sharp breath. Memories start creeping back, slowly at first. Then a little faster, a little fiercer. Memories of tearing into ox hide and hot blood spurting in my face. Memories of men with weapons surrounding me, harrying me. Memories of a monster, huge and grey and terrible, knocking me to the ground.

No, not a monster.

*Dire.*

"Oh!" The sound shudders through my lips. Now consciousness returns in full force. But I still won't open my eyes. I just lie there, feeling the pain, both of my wounds and of those recent memories.

Dire. I fought with Dire. I was supposed to kill him. Yet again. But it hadn't worked. Somehow, miraculously . . . the compulsion had broken down.

My lips curve in a small smile. And I realize then that I'm *able* to smile. I have a mouth, a human-shaped mouth. Am I properly human again? Are those memories of monsterhood not memories at all, but rather some sort of dark dream?

"I know you's awake, girlie," a creaking old voice says. "Come on, no use pretending otherwise. Get those eyes of yours open."

I know that voice. Shivering, I force one eyelid up and peer into a face like a withered apple grinning down at me with three white teeth. "Mother Ulla?" I groan.

"Here. Drink this."

I find my head lifted, supported, and something pushed against my lips. I could fight, but I don't really have the energy. Instead, I let myself be bullied into drinking a strong, bitter brew. I nearly choke on the first sip, but there is something undeniably soothing about it. So I take another sip, then another. Then I down the whole cupful in a few big gulps.

This task accomplished, I lie back on the pillow and gaze blearily up into that old face again. My vision is clearer now.

Mother Ulla might be the ugliest woman I've ever seen, but just now, surrounded by the golden glow off her hearth, she seems like some sort of squat, funny-looking angel.

"That's better," the witch says and sets the cup down somewhere out of my range of sight. Then she hitches up her skirts and settles herself down on the edge of my bed, her wide bottom nearly flattening my hand under the blankets. "You should be all right soon enough now. Those crossbow bolts didn't do much damage, just made you bleed a bunch. But I gots that taken care of, and for the most part, you'll just be a bit stiff the next few days."

I frown. Then, moving gingerly, I wriggle, squirm, and manage to sit upright in the bed and lean heavily against the headboard. I turn my head slightly, letting my gaze rove around the cottage, which ripples with glamours. Nowhere near as strong or overwhelming as those at Granny's house, these glamours simply make Mother Ulla's cottage a little snugger and cozier than it probably is in reality. The mattress under me is no doubt stuffed with straw, but it *feels* like I'm lying on downy feathers. The walls are probably just old boards, but they *look* whitewashed and cheerful in the firelight.

Dawn glow flows through the easternmost window. Dawn . . . now why does that matter to me so much? I look down at my hands. Real, human hands. Not claw tipped or covered in fur.

Mother Ulla grunts. "Sorry, girl," she says, patting my knee in an almost but not quite maternal gesture. "You's still cursed, I'm afraid. I can't break another witch's curses, you know. Dawn is giving you a little grace, it seems, but you'll be sprouting fur again in another hour or so." She gives me a once-over, and there's an unsettling gleam of admiration in her gaze. "I gots to say, I knew your grandmother was gifted with a bigger helping of talent than most folks ever see. But I ain't never seen magic quite like this! Black magic, to be sure . . . but impressive stuff."

"She steals it," I say.

Mother Ulla blinks and tilts her head to one side. "Come again?"

"Her magic. She steals it. She takes it from the apprentices sent her way and turns them into monsters while she's at it."

The old witch stares at me, her eyes dangerously bright. "I see," she says at last. "I think . . . yes, I think I see." Shaking her head, she grunts, then continues, "And that friend of yours? The big handsome wolf fellow? Did she take magic from him too?"

"I don't think so. He never had magic, really. She did that to him as part of a bargain."

"*Pshaw!* Granny and her *bargains!*" Mother Ulla spits on the floor and makes a sign with one hand, as though warding off impending evil. "She did quite a number on that poor boy, I can tell you that."

I nod. "She hates him. Because . . . because I think she loves him."

"Granny Dorrel never did quite know how to separate them two feelings. She was the same with her own daughter, your mother. Loved her to the point of hatred. But then, you knows that well enough, don't you?"

I close my eyes, bow my head. It hurts to think of the mother I never met. I try not to most of the time. Try not to think of what her life must have been, raised by someone like Granny.

"Well," Mother Ulla continues, crossing her arms across her ample stomach, "you's out of her wardship now. Out of her reach."

At this, I raise my head. "How did that happen? I thought I *couldn't* leave Granny's wardship while under her spell."

"Well, that would be true under normal circumstances. Granny's compulsions are powerful. But they're Black Magic, just as I suspected all along. And Black Magic shouldn't *ever* be used on one's own blood. Granny's an arrogant old biddy to think she can get away with it. And, to give her credit, she very nearly did!

"But when she used another Black Magic spell on her own kin, that was one bad spell too many. The curse was good and solid to start with, but it's fraying around the edges already. Plenty of leeway to work with, including leeway to get you through her borders."

I look down at my hands resting in my lap. What Mother Ulla says makes sense, of course. How else could I have defied Granny's command to wreak carnage on the folk at Gilhorn? Though I had set out on her orders readily enough, when the critical moment came, it had been almost too easy to resist.

"It's the blood connection," Mother Ulla continues, breaking into my thoughts. "It makes the curse more chaotic, less controlled. Not even a witch like your Granny can handle it now."

"Does that mean I can break it?" I ask, lifting a hopeful gaze.

"Well . . ." Mother Ulla shrugs her shoulders up to her ears. "Undoing a transformation ain't so easy as all that. Her *control* over you might be broken, but the rest of the curse is solid, blood ties notwithstanding. I'm afraid you'll stay as you are until your Granny dies. If she ever does."

My heart sinks. But it's not like I'm surprised. "And what about Dire?"

"What about him?"

"Is he also cursed until Granny's death?"

The old witch heaves a sigh and grimaces, showing a lot of red gums. "I'm afraid his curse is much worse than that. Granny mixed his spell with something extra malicious. She used *heartsblood*."

I shake my head, frowning. "What does that mean?"

Instead of answering, Mother Ulla slides from the bed and bustles about, making another cup of strong herbal tea. She brings it back to the bed and makes me take several sips before I can persuade her to talk again. "What is heartsblood?" I persist, setting the half-finished cup down in its saucer.

Her face is grim, unsettling. She settles back on the edge of the bed and once more folds her arms. "I'm afraid your Granny's death won't be enough to liberate Dire. Not like it would the other werebeasts in her thrall. He can only be liberated when his heartsblood mingles with hers."

"But what does that *mean?*"

"Oh, it can mean several things, of course. Most curses have a little wiggle room in their breaking. But what your *Granny* had in mind . . . well, I'll let you figure that out for yourself."

I stare down at the cup in my lap, run my finger around the rim. I think I know what Mother Ulla is implying. Granny wanted Dire. She desired him. I know that better than I care to after the events of yesterday's dawn! And mingled heartsblood? That could mean . . . a child, perhaps. A way for their blood to mingle as one. It made sense in a sick, twisted sort of way. Granny felt as though she lost her only child, my mother, when she ran away to marry my father. Did Granny want another child to replace the one she'd lost?

If she had set her heart on Dire being the father, well . . .

I close my eyes. I don't want to think of it, but memories of that seductive encounter flood back into my brain. I acted in ways I'd never thought I could, inexperienced as I was in such matters. And all the while, Granny drove me. So eager. So vile. Taking what should have been mine, what should have been precious and sweet, and turning it into something sordid.

I shudder, the tea in my stomach churning uncomfortably. How had everything gotten so complicated, so . . . disgusting?

"Careful there. You's going to break my teacup, and I only gots three left." Mother Ulla takes the cup and saucer from my hands where I'd been unconsciously twisting them around. She waddles across the room and carelessly dumps them both in a pile of other dirty dishes. Then she turns and faces me again, her eyes narrow and cunning.

"You know, the wolf boy wants you to run away. While you still can."

"Run away? Like this?" I hold up my hands, which are just beginning to show traces of returning fur. "Where could I go?"

Mother Ulla shrugs dismissively. "There's plenty of places you could hide in the Wood. If you run deep enough and stay away from Granny's wardship, you should do all right. You was always more of a wild thing anyway."

I smile grimly at that. After all, wasn't that always my childhood dream? To run off and live in Whispering Wood, throwing myself into adventure after adventure? Granted, I'd never imagined being turned into a monster like this, but a monster has certain advantages. Even the fae would hesitate to cross me in this awful new shape.

But how can I bear to run now? Knowing what I know, knowing what my grandmother will continue doing after I've gone? There might not be any real hope for Dire, but maybe ... just maybe ... I could stop Granny myself.

"You say I have leeway. Within the restrictions of this bargain with Granny. How much leeway do you mean?"

Mother Ulla looks thoughtful. "There was always a goodly amount. Now she's gone and cursed you, I should think you could break her control over you pretty easily if you tried. In fact, I wouldn't be surprised if you'd already done it."

"Really?" I'm not convinced. After all, Granny's hold had seemed absolute when the transformation first came over me. But how much of that was simply the curse itself overwhelming every part of me? It may have *felt* like control, while in reality it was much more chaotic.

I look at my hands again, studying the way the golden fur lies as it slowly emerges. My nails are lengthening as well and will soon harden into claws. What a ferocious thing I've become! Ferocious and monstrous.

Monstrous enough to kill my own grandmother?

"If you's thinking of facing off with your Granny," Mother Ulla says, drawing my attention back to her, "I'd recommend you gets to it sooner rather than later. Best not to put off unpleasant tasks, I always say."

My brow wrinkles. "Do you think . . . is there a chance I could do it? A chance I could stop her once and for all?"

"There's always a chance. But . . ." Mother Ulla shrugs again. "It's hard to kill one's own kinfolk. Even when they're as bad to the core as that grandmother of yours. She's still your kin."

I nod, dropping my gaze. I don't like to think about it, not the actual reality of causing Granny's death. But when I consider the horrors she's perpetrated . . . when I think about that Hall of Heads displayed so proudly in her own home . . . how can I retreat from this moment?

Slowly I move my shoulder, then my hip, testing the places where the crossbow bolts had pierced. To my surprise, I feel little more than a twinge. I'm still sore from the older knife wound, but these newer injuries are much further along in their recovery. I shoot Mother Ulla another sharp look.

The ward witch smiles, showing all three teeth. "I knows a thing or two about healing magic. And something told me you was going to be up and at 'em sooner rather than later."

Mother Ulla gives me a set of loose garments to wear that should survive my inevitable transition from human to cat to human again. They're not exactly comfortable, but I'm grateful, nonetheless.

My body is already mostly covered in fur by the time I step out the cottage door and face the forest. When I tentatively explore my face with my fingertips, I find it altered as well, my features beginning to warp, a muzzle slowly becoming more pronounced. But at least this change is not so abrupt as the excruciating first transformation when Granny flung her curse at me.

I turn to the old witch standing in the doorway behind me, watching me with that stoic indifference I've always found so infuriating. I wonder if I should thank her for her help. The idea galls. How many years have I *hated* this woman for her callous refusal to help me rescue Valera? That feeling hasn't fully faded.

But she took me in last night, risking Granny Dorrel's wrath. She healed me, sheltered me. Maybe she cares more than she lets on. More than she needs to, even.

"Thank you," I manage, my voice a little hoarse. The words feel lame, insufficient, but I don't have any more.

Mother Ulla holds my gaze. I see a gleam of understanding in those little eyes half hidden behind wrinkles. She nods. "You wants to head thataway," she says, jutting her chin. "That'll take you back to the boundary where you crossed over. You'll be able to pick up the wolf boy's scent from there."

I flush and duck my head. I hadn't told her my intention to search for Dire before returning to Granny's house. Am I so transparent?

Reading my mind yet again, the old witch chuckles. "Good luck, girlie. May the gods bring you success in all your endeavors."

I offer a short nod. Then, without another word, I turn and set out into Whispering Wood.

# 28

## DIRE

I lift my muzzle, sniff the air.

There's a werebeast on my trail. I'm sure of it.

Throughout the day and into the night, I fled deeper and deeper into the wilder parts of Granny's ward, where the Wood grows thick and dense and not even the fae would dare venture without utmost caution. Here, the shadows themselves seem infused with predatory purpose.

But nothing in this place is more deadly than I.

By now, Elorata must know her newest creation has failed to take me down. What's more, Brielle is gone, beyond her boundaries, no longer subject to her will. If she wants to make a final end of me, she'll need to use other means, and if her two remaining werebeasts can't do it, she'll hire another Monster Hunter. One way or another, I can't be allowed to live.

My lip ripples back in a snarling grin. I don't intend to go down quietly. I'll make as much trouble for her as I can.

Kill...

The instinct is there. To stalk the witch, to break through her defenses, to savage her, end her. But something in me recoils from that bloodthirsty urging... that part of me which, even at this time of night, is still somewhat human. I *must* hold onto that humanity right up until the end. If I let myself go, if I let the beast fully take over, then Elorata will win. Even as I rip her to shreds, she'll win.

I shake my heavy head and trot on through the trees. A full day has passed, and night has returned to Whispering Wood. I've survived again. A little longer at least. But now that telltale scent tickles my nose. I dare not ignore it.

Turning my head, I peer back over my hunched shoulder, my ears cupped, my nostrils quivering. There's a werebeast out there. And it's getting closer.

I am more wolf than man by now, and it's easy enough for me to blend into the shadows, becoming like a shadow myself as I begin the careful, predatory dance of circling my pursuer. It takes a little time, a little caution, a great deal of precision... but soon I am downwind of the creature. Which means I am now the predator, not the prey.

My nose guides me through the trees and underbrush. I glide soft footed, taking care to make no sound despite the bulk of my transforming body. The other werebeast, by contrast, is clumsy in its movements. When at last I spy it creeping through a patch of moonlight, its head is down, too intent upon the trail it follows, too intent upon its immediate surroundings. Unaware of the shift in dynamic.

I smile.

Then I lunge from hiding, using the muscled power in my hind legs to send me flying across the distance. I slam into that other monster and knock it clean off its feet. We roll, snarling, and I feel claws trying to tear through my thick coat. When the rolling stops, I'm on top, my foe pinned beneath me.

And I look down into the face of a green-eyed werecat.

All the animal instincts in me vanish in a sudden flood of humanity. My mouth moves, my awful jaws, teeth, and tongue trying to speak her name. It comes out a barking growl. Frustrated, I shake my head and back off, my ears pinned back, a whine vibrating in my throat.

She picks herself up with great dignity, shaking out her coat. Her forelimbs are still overlong for her body, and a trace of her curved, womanly torso remains. Her long tail twitches with a life of its own, fur standing up along her spine.

Then she looks at me, half closes her eyes, and begins to purr. It's such a loud, rumbling sound, I almost mistake it for a growl at first. But when she approaches me, there is no menace in her stance. She stretches out her face, rubs her cheek against mine. A completely catlike and possessive gesture.

Startled, I cringe away. But she continues purring and rubbing, pressing her warm body up against me. Her tail flicks under my nose as she loops around me, then she pads alongside me and sticks her head under my chin.

Oh, Brielle! Brielle! Why did you not flee when you had the chance? If I had a voice, I would urge you even now to go, to escape.

But I don't have a voice. And . . . I'm glad.

Whining again, I lick her face. It's such a ridiculous animal gesture. But it's the most I can give. She shakes her head, surprised, and puts her ears back irritably. The next moment, a little yowl burbles in her throat, and she springs into motion, darting away into the trees.

I don't stop to think, to consider. I simply rush after her, chasing her at first, then running alongside her. Our long limbs tear up the ground beneath us, and the trees seem almost to part and make room for our passing. We glory in the freedom of movement, in the power of our strange forms. I'm faster, but she is far nimbler, sometimes leaping up into tree branches and springing to the tops of jutting boulders.

We run through the night. We run until we are fully animal with no trace of humanity remaining. We run until the animal begins to recede, and our human selves slowly creep back. As our limbs lengthen and become more awkward, we slow our pace and eventually begin to walk upright. We don't speak. Even now that our voices have returned, we hold our silence.

At some point, our hands clasp. Our fingers intwine.

Dawn finds us on the edge of a cliff, high above a rushing river.

Not far from the place where Conrad fell, I suspect, though I can't say for sure. We sit there and watch the moon fade and the sun begin to rise. When at last I turn to look at her, there's very little cat remaining in her features. The pink dawn light falls on Brielle's face, so fierce, so strong.

My gaze drifts downward, despite my best efforts. She's wearing next to nothing—just a loose garment that serves to cover some of her nakedness, but not much. Just enough to make what is visible all the more enticing.

I, by contrast, am completely naked. I should be embarrassed, but strangely, I am not. After our wild run together, after the night shared as animals, modesty simply doesn't matter as it once did.

She's aware of my gaze on her. I can see by the way her jaw tightens and her intense concentration on the view before us. She's aware, but she's afraid of breaking this silence between us, of breaking this tentative connection we share.

But I'm not afraid. Not anymore.

I reach out and gently tuck a strand of tangled red hair behind her ear. She shivers at the brush of my fingertips and closes her eyes.

"I love you," I say.

It's funny how simple it is to speak the words now. For some reason, I'd thought it would be more difficult. But here they come, lightly spilling from my lips. Simple though they are, there is nothing frail about them, however. They are the strongest words I've ever spoken.

Brielle opens her eyes, her gaze still directed at the rising sun rather than at me. But I'm in no rush. I wait, watching her, drinking in the loveliness of her face in the glow of the new day.

Finally, she says, "I . . . I think I might love you too."

My lips quirk. "You *think* so?" I chuckle and shake my head. "Well, I suppose I'll be satisfied with that."

She turns then, facing me. And there's so much feeling in her eyes, her human eyes. Things I can't even fully comprehend. I realize all over again how complicated this girl is. Loving her won't be a simple matter.

As though responding to an impulse, she reaches out, catches me by the back of my head, and pulls me into a kiss. A smile breaks across my lips, making it difficult to kiss her back, despite my best efforts. She pulls away, stares into my eyes, and gasps, "You know I love you. You know I do."

"Maybe," I admit, still smiling. "But it's nice to hear you say it."

Then I wrap my arms around her, drawing her close for another kiss and another. And suddenly it both matters and doesn't matter that we are so naked. In some ways, it's a bit embarrassing . . . but also undeniably convenient.

## 29

## BRIELLE

I lie in the crook of Dire's arm, resting my head on his shoulder. My fingers trail along the lines of his chest, feeling the pattern of fur as it begins to return. I frown softly, regretting the loss of his bare skin under my hand. Our stolen dawn moments were just that—stolen.

Soon, we will both be monsters again.

I tilt my head, gazing up at his face. He lies in complete repose, his eyes closed, his head resting on his other arm. I never thought it possible, but his expression is almost *serene*. And happy. That thought gives me a flush of pleasure. I've made him happy. Perhaps only for a short while . . . but I've done it. Amid all the terror and turmoil that assaults us from every side, we gave each other something beautiful.

I close my eyes and nuzzle my face under his chin, bristling both with beard and incoming wolf fur. How much this last hour contained! All those new, tentative, joyful discoveries made in the light of the new day and the new love declared. If only we could go on like this, discovering more and more about each other, day after day. If only we had a lifetime ahead of us. Even a year. Even a few days . . .

A frown knots my brow, and my soaring heart suddenly sinks like lead. There's no more *if only* for us. The last hour was a lovely dream. But it's time to wake up and face the reality ahead.

Drawing a deep breath, I sit upright, pushing against his chest for support, then adjusting my body so that I need not touch him. I shove tangles of hair out of my face, and in doing so, am startled by the sensation of claws on the ends of my fingertips, raking through the long red strands. I'll never get used to that.

"Dire," I say. Already my voice sounds more animal than before. "Dire, are you awake?"

He cracks his eyes open and looks lazily up at me. At the sight of my face, however, his expression grows more serious. He props up onto his elbows and turns his head to one side in an unconsciously doglike manner. "What's wrong? Tell me, Brielle. Should I not have—"

I quickly put out a hand, pressing two fingers against his lips. "No, it's not that. Not at all. You were—you *are*—everything I want. I'm glad, so glad we could be together for a little while. I wish . . . I wish . . ."

I wish we could run away. Animal or human, it hardly matters to me. I wish we could simply find a place where we could exist. But the boundaries of Granny's wardship are too small. We're living on borrowed time as it is.

I bow my head, breaking his gaze. "There's something I must do. I'm . . . I'm going back to Granny's house."

He sits upright then, taking hold of my hand and clutching it tight. For a long while, we are silent, sitting there in the morning light. I wonder what he'll say, if he'll say anything.

Finally, he reaches out and tilts my chin, lifting my gaze to his. His eyes are yellow again now. Wolf's eyes. Not the gray, human eyes which had burned into mine so short a time ago.

"What are you going to do?" he asks, his voice a soft rumble.

"I'm going to kill her." The words fall from my lips like stones. So heavy. Too heavy. "At least, I'm going to try."

His nostrils flare as he takes a deep breath. "And what if she reasserts her command over you? She's done it before."

"Yes, but . . ." I shrug. "Mother Ulla says she made a mistake when she cursed me. She weakened her hold on me rather than strengthening it. Mother Ulla believes I could break Granny's control entirely now. I may have done so already."

"Mother Ulla . . ." Dire's voice trails off, and he gazes out over the cliffside again. For a long moment, silence stretches between us, underscored by the not-so-distant roar of the river. "I hoped Mother Ulla would talk you into running away."

"Yes, well, I had different ideas." I run a hand over my head, noting that my long hair is already noticeably shorter, blending in with the fur running down my back and spine. "I'm not asking you to come with me."

"I know."

"This is something *I* need to do. She's my grandmother. And she's been . . . the things she's done . . ." I close my eyes, seeing again the images of those heads in the hall. Misery. Dreg. The empty plaque reserved for Dire. I also see the round-cheeked young girl held between the two looming werebeasts. "She must be stopped," I finish firmly.

"I know that too."

There's something in his tone, something I don't quite understand. Something to make me look up and catch his wolfish gaze again. But the expression in his eyes is not that of a wolf. I see nothing but very human love shining in those depths.

"You are by far the bravest creature I've ever known," he says.

I flush and duck my head. "Well, you're the hairiest creature *I've* ever known. So I suppose we're even."

He tosses back his head and barks a great laugh. Then, standing, he offers his hand. His awful, warped, fur-covered, claw-tipped hand. I take it and let him help me to my feet. "Come on then," he says, flashing sharp fangs in something resembling a smile. "Let's go witch hunting."

We don't take the holly paths back to Granny's house. I suspect she'll be watching them closely; we'll walk into a trap if we try. Instead, Dire guides us through the Wood, navigating by nose. I'm surprised at how well my own animal senses pick out the intricacies of detail in the forest. I *might* even be able to make my way back to Granny's house by smell alone if I had to. But I'm nowhere near as experienced as Dire, so I let him take the lead.

As we proceed, we become more beastlike. By noon, we're both completely animal . . . but that hour passes, and we slowly revert to humanity. I'm still not used to this transformation and find it uncomfortable. Like the stabbing pains I used to get as a child that Valera called "growing pains." Only much worse.

The whole day feels surreal. Now and then I make myself stop and consider what it is I'm about to attempt, that I am on my way to commit a murder. Or at least, to attempt murder. Without weapons either—no bow, no arrows, no knife. Just my own strange new body, complete with powerful jaws and claws.

Will it be enough?

It'll have to be.

Abruptly, Dire stops. I step up beside him, our shoulders almost brushing. "What is it?"

"Do you smell that?" He sniffs the air, his eyes flashing. "It's . . . it's not . . ."

I take a delicate sniff. My whiskers tingle, and my lips curl in a hiss. "Conrad!" I snarl.

It's the Monster Hunter, all right. He's here. Quite close. My blood runs cold. I'd assumed he was dead after that fall. Then again, part of me always knew that a mere fall and a little rushing water wouldn't be enough to take down the mountainous man. He's too much of a force of nature himself.

There's another scent, however. Conrad is not alone. "The other two werebeasts. They're here too," I say.

Dire nods grimly. "She's called in her defenses. She must know we're close. We need to stay together and—"

"No!" I shake my head. "No, we split up. Separate our enemies, make them come after us."

He looks worried. It's late afternoon by now, and his human features are starting to come back. Even his eyes are human already. "I don't want you to face Conrad on your own. Or the werebeasts for that matter. You're still so . . . so *new* at this."

"I'll be fine," I answer with more confidence than I feel. "I'm not afraid. When we split, we divide their attention. Once they're taken care of, we meet again at the gates."

For a moment, I fear he's going to protest more. But he merely sighs and reaches out, cupping my cheek with his clawed hand. "Be careful," he says. And in those words I hear the unspoken: *I love you.*

I smile back, showing my pointed teeth. "And you."

I wish I could kiss him again but can't imagine it would be pleasant with our mouths in their current shapes. Instead, I simply turn away and lumber into the trees, heading south. I think he watches me until I disappear into the greenery, but I don't look back to be sure.

Moving as silently as I can on my warped cat feet, I draw closer to Granny's house. This part of the Wood is familiar to me at least. I could navigate it even without my new cat senses. Soon enough I come within sight of the moss-grown stone wall. There's no gate on this side, but I wonder if I might simply leap to the top of the wall and over into the gardens. It would be simpler, after all, to avoid meeting the Monster Hunter or werebeasts altogether, to cut straight through and face Granny head-on.

I'm still considering this possibility when movement on my right catches my eye. I turn my head seconds before a massive gray-and-black form surges from the foliage, roaring. We tumble into the dirt, and I have just enough awareness to get my hindlegs up and use the claws on my back feet to tear at his soft underbelly. A few good scrapes, and he pushes away from me. But he doesn't allow me to get to my feet. As I try to rise, he cuffs me with one huge paw, knocking me flat on my back.

He's on me again then, his twisted, half-human face revealing only a hint of the man he used to be. Slavering jaws snap in my face. I wrap my hands around his throat, holding him back by inches.

"I'm here to help you!" I shout, desperate to be heard over his snarling. "I'm here to kill Granny!"

That gets through to him. He pauses, his eyes widening, and draws back. His heavy hands are pressed into my shoulders, pinning me to the ground, but I can see the desire in him to let me go. For a few moments, he resists Granny's compulsion.

But he can't resist long.

With another vicious roar, he lunges at my face again. This time, I'm ready for him. My searching hand found a large rock, and I bring it up and crack him on the side of the head. It's a very human maneuver, not at all what he expected from me in this current shape. He yipes and his eyes roll back. Then he slumps on his side.

I gasp for breath as the weight of his body falls from me. Perhaps there's some advantage to being the newest of Granny's creations . . . I've not yet grown so dependent on my animal senses and abilities. I pick myself up, glancing at the fallen creature. I hope he's not dead. If I can succeed today, he and the other werebeast will be free of Granny's curse. There may not be much hope for Dire or me, but at least—

Before I can finish the thought, something solid hits me from behind. Slender but strong arms, covered in red fur, wrap around my middle, and teeth tear into my ear. I yowl with pain, double over, and hurl my attacker over my head onto the ground in front of me. She lies stunned for a moment, giving me a chance to leap on top of her and catch her by the throat. Thank the gods, she's neither as big nor as strong as the other one.

"Stand down!" I snarl into her face. "I'm here to help you!"

"There . . . is no help . . . for us!" she chokes out, her huge eyes bulging from her twisted face. Unlike the other beast, she seems to remember that she's part human now. She sticks her free hand in my face, trying to drive her fingers into my eye. I turn away and keep on squeezing, squeezing, cutting off her breath.

"I'm going to kill Granny Dorrel," I say, hoping she can hear me even as darkness closes in. "I'm going to save you. And I won't let you stop me!"

Her swiping blows are weaker now, her arms trembling, shivering. Finally, they drop to the ground. Her goggling eyes half close. She lies still beneath me.

Hastily, I press my head to her chest. There's a heartbeat there, I'm almost sure of it. I sit up again, stare down at her.

Something whistles past my ear.

I turn and see an arrow plant in the ground beyond me. Snarling, I whip about, following the path of the arrow back to its source. Conrad! He's standing not twenty yards away. His one good eye burns beneath his heavy brow.

He's already nocking another arrow.

I freeze. I know I need to lunge either left or right. The wall is behind me; I cannot retreat. But if I make a move too soon, it'll be easy for him to follow and shoot. I force myself to remain where I'm crouched, to take a breath, to wait for the last possible instant.

My gaze locks with his. I feel the burn of predatory fire even from this distance. I smell the stink that emanates from every pore of the Monster Hunter, all the blood he's shed over many years.

"Conrad!" I call out, his name snarling through my teeth. "Conrad Torosson, you don't have to do this!"

He blinks, startled. For an instant, the fire in his eye flickers out. "How do you know my na—"

Before he can finish the question, Dire is upon him. Though

more man than wolf by now, he hurtles into the Monster Hunter, knocking him into a tree so hard, he drops his bow and arrow. Conrad turns, throwing punches, but Dire eludes them and lands two hits of his own, one to Conrad's jaw, another to his gut.

The big man doubles over, and Dire kicks him to the ground. Once there, however, the hunter grabs Dire by the ankles and pulls him off his feet. He lands hard on his back, the air knocked out of him. Conrad lunges, trying to get the upper hand, but Dire reacts too quickly, rolls out of reach, and comes up in a crouch. He snarls, his wolf teeth flecked with foam. With a ripple of muscle from his hind quarters, he throws himself at the Monster Hunter, snapping at his face, his throat.

I'm up and in motion by then. "Wait!" I cry and hurl myself into the fray. I catch hold of Dire, pulling him back. He tries to throw me off before realizing that it's me. Then he calms under my touch, allowing me to yank him to his feet and push him a pace or two behind me.

I turn and face Conrad. "We're not here for you." I catch and hold his gaze. "We're *not* monsters."

The big man picks himself up off the ground. His hands are bleeding from where he gripped Dire's jaw, trying to hold off the werewolf's bites. When he shakes his head, his long hair flies about his face so that he looks almost animal himself. His eye flicks back and forth between me and Dire. At last his gaze lands on me and stays there for several silent moments.

Finally, he says, "I know you."

I nod. "You do."

"You're . . . you're that girl. The witch's girl. The huntress."

I nod again.

He blinks slowly, his expression mystified. "But . . . how?"

"I told you. We're not monsters. None of us are. Granny made us like this."

"She *made* you?" The horror in the big man's voice is almost comical. He turns his gaze from us to the two unconscious werebeasts nearby. "She *made* you and then she . . . she ordered your deaths."

I shudder. Even though I've known the truth for a while, hearing it spoken out loud still makes my skin crawl. "It's Black Magic. Goes against the laws of the coven. She can't hold any of us enthralled forever, but when she lets us go, she can't risk us telling anyone what she's up to here in her wardship."

Conrad's face is grim and hard. He looks again from me to Dire. Dire, whom he had so recently hunted. Just as he hunted Dreg.

At last, he bows his head. His dark hair hangs in a curtain, covering most of his brutal face. "I didn't know."

I sigh. "You're not the only one."

"I don't hunt cursed folk," he continues. "Only monsters. If I'd realized . . ."

If he'd realized, would Dreg still be alive? Probably not. Granny would have found someone else to do the deed for her. But it would be useless to try to say as much to Conrad. It wouldn't comfort him.

"We're going to put a stop to this," I say instead, more boldly perhaps than I feel.

Conrad's dark brow rises above his eyepatch. "I'm no witch-hunter. I cannot help you. But neither will I hinder your efforts."

"Thank you." It sounds lame, but I'm not sure what else to say under the circumstances. So I simply repeat, "Thank you."

Conrad nods once. Then, limping a little, he gathers his scattered weapons and arrow. Without another word or look for either me or Dire, he puts his back to Granny's house and marches into Whispering Wood, vanishing as silently as a wraith.

I let out a long sigh. Only then do I realize I'm holding Dire's hand. I look down, noting how very human our fingers are now, entwined together. Which isn't good. If we wait much longer, we'll be confronting Granny as our naked human selves, helpless as babes.

"We've got to hurry," I say, meeting Dire's eye.

For a moment, I fear he's going to try to talk me out of it. But he only nods. We turn together and hasten along the wall until we come to the iron gate. To my dismay, it opens silently at our approach. Welcoming us in.

It's a trap. I know it is.

But we have no choice. We must walk straight in.

# 30

## DIRE

In the twenty years of my enslavement, I've never seen the gardens like this.

Always before they've been featureless shadows of nothing unless Elorata herself was present, concentrating her efforts to transform the landscape into formal topiaries, flowering shrubs, and stone-edged beds of bright blossoms.

Now, for the first time, I see what has been beneath those glamours all along—a huge, sprawling garden, not unlike those in her illusions. Only this one is entirely lost to ruin and decay. The few standing trees are gnarled with tumors, and the rest lie rotten from the inside out. Dead black petals cling to the once bountiful flowering shrubs, and the beds crawl with maggots. Everything stinks of death.

Brielle's fingers squeeze my hand a little tighter. "She's drawing in her power," she says softly, speaking aloud what had already occurred to me. "She's consolidating her magic. To use on us."

I nod. But she already knows we're here. We must keep going.

The house looms before us. As with the gardens, this is the first time I've ever seen it un-glamourized. I'm surprised by how huge it is. Or rather, *was*. An entire castle with turreted towers, all since crumbled to rubble. Only one small portion remains intact, what might once have been a secondary keep. Elorata has built all her illusions around the memory of grandeur.

"I wonder who lived here," I murmur. "Back before, I mean."

Brielle grunts. "I don't like it." She stops suddenly and pulls on my hand. "I don't like just marching up to the door like this."

I don't either. We don't have a plan. We never did, beyond simply getting through the gates. I don't think either of us expected to make it this far. Now that we have, however, it seems a pity to waste the opportunity. But what can we do now, unarmed and un-magicked as we are?

"Our best bet is boldness," I say. "That, and Elorata's arrogance."

Brielle nods. We continue forward, our footsteps steady, our heads high. We are a good many yards still from the front door of the little building when it opens.

Elorata Dorrel steps through, ducking her head under the lintel, then stands tall before us. Extremely tall—taller than I've ever seen her before. She towers like a giantess of old, a good eight feet or more. Now I know where all those glamours have gone.

They wrap around her, creating a profound illusion of a strong, beautiful, terrible being, like an avenging angel. Her hair flows free about her shoulders, moving on its own like a living fire. Pure power simmers in the air around her and sparks from the depths of her eyes.

Eyes which fix solely on me.

"So, my love," she says, her voice both crooning and cruel. "So, you betray me one last time. And the bitterest betrayal of all . . . with my own flesh and blood."

I pull back my shoulders. "It's over, Elorata," I snarl. "This ends here, today."

"Oh, is that what you think? The two of you, united in love, will here and now make your final stand against me?" She laughs, a silvery laugh that flits through the air like a song. "Have you any idea, children, how long I've been mistress of this wardship? How many foes have tried to wrest my power from me, how many have fallen beneath my hand? I am stronger than you can possibly imagine!"

Her words pierce me like arrows, knocking me back a step. But when I look at her again, it's as though I can see through the glamours, through the image she projects, down to the frail old woman at her core. Too frail for what she's attempting now. If she tries to keep all her magic contained inside her much longer, she'll break to pieces.

I hope Brielle can see this too, can recognize our foe's vulnerability.

Brielle . . . where is she? I turn, realizing that she's slipped free of my hand and is carefully putting distance between us. A wise precaution, no doubt, though I feel the lack of her beside me. At least now if Elorata lashes out, she won't take us both down at once. And maybe I can keep the witch distracted.

"It's all well and good to posture, old woman," I say, letting the malice in my heart pour into my words. "But what are you really? Just a series of paper masks. Pretty enough, to be sure, but flimsy."

Her beautiful face twists with rage. She lifts one hand and begins tracing a sign in the air, creating burning lines of red light out of nothing. Runes. She's preparing a spell.

I must stop her.

I take three lunging strides forward but hit a barrier I could not see and rebound off it, landing hard on my back. Stunned.

"Dire!" Brielle cries, and takes a step or two my way before realizing her mistake. She's drawn her grandmother's gaze.

"Darling granddaughter," Elorata says with another bell-like laugh, "are you so faithless that you would break our bargain? A solemn oath sworn by your own sister's blood?"

"Our bargain was broken the moment you cursed me," Brielle responds, turning on the witch, her eyes burning, her fists clenched. "If only I'd realized it sooner! You have no power over me. It was all just an illusion, but I see through it now!"

Granny's teeth flash between her too-red lips. "Young people these days. Entirely without respect for their elders!"

She draws her arm back and hurls the magic she's accumulated.

It manifests as a flaming spear, burning crimson as it streaks straight at Brielle. But Brielle still has some of her catlike reflexes. She springs to one side, and the spear strikes the ground where she stood with a crack like thunder, leaving a smoking hole behind.

Brielle lands hard but is up and running the next instant, darting in among the ruinous walls of the fallen castle. Elorata's attention is still on her. Which means I have a chance to get in close. Now, before she draws up another rune.

I rush at the witch, summoning all the remaining animal strength I possess. I leap straight at her, arms outstretched . . . but a sudden burst of raw magic knocks me back. Like a kite rising on a swelling breeze, Elorata rides the magic up into the air above us. A radiant red glow permeates her skin, making her glow like a star.

She looks down at me as I struggle to recover my bearings. Her eyes spark with red light. "Pitiful," she sneers. "And here I once thought you so strong, so desirable!"

Her hand moves, tracing another burning rune in the air. The next instant, a second spear hurtles for my heart. I turn, but it catches me by the shoulder, piercing through flesh and bone. I cry out and fall to the ground, pain radiating through my body. There's magic as well, burning magic, pulsing from the spearhead like poison into my veins.

Out of the corner of my eye, I see Brielle spring to the top of a pile of rubble. With a savage cry, she leaps. Somehow, she penetrates the storm of magic surrounding Elorata, and her arms wrap around the witch's waist from behind. She looks like a child compared to this swollen, magically enlarged apparition, but she struggles fiercely, trying to climb up her grandmother's torso, to reach her neck.

Laughing, Elorata twists and flings the girl off like a limp ragdoll. Brielle lands hard and lies stunned, staring up at the red-glowing witch.

"Foolish creature!" Elorata's voice billows like fire from her lungs. "You are nothing. Nothing! A mere dilution of my blood. The true power is all mine. No one dares stand up to me, not the coven, not even your precious Mother Ulla. One day soon, I'll take them all, crush them, turn them to my will. Then I will become the great Black Witch of the Wood, queen of all I survey!" Her smile flashes, full of devouring hatred. "But first things first . . ."

Her hand is already in motion. The rune is drawn; the spear manifests in her grip.

She draws her arm back, aiming at Brielle.

"*No!*" I cry and wrench the spear from my shoulder. With all the strength I have left to me, I leap to my feet and try to run. But the burning of her curse magic is too much. It brings me crashing to my face in the dirt.

I can't fail Brielle. I can't watch her die. I pull myself up onto my knees, summon all my will, and get to my feet. The world spins around me. I can't run. I can only stand where I am, using everything I've got to stay upright.

Elorata turns, observing my feeble struggles. "Poor little monster." She clucks and shakes her head sadly. "Still trying to play the hero? I'm afraid that's not how your story ends, my sweet."

She brandishes the spear. Then lets it go.

It speeds through the air, pierces my chest, strikes the ground behind me.

I stare down at the glowing shaft protruding through my ribcage. And I feel my shattered heart slow . . . slow . . . stop . . .

## 31

## BRIELLE

I watch it happen. I'm helpless to stop it.

I watch the spear fly from Granny's hand.

I watch it enter Dire's chest. Emerge through his back. Pierce the ground, shaft quivering. While he's still half upright, his back bent, his eyes wide, staring down in horror at what has just happened to him.

His hand comes up, tries to grasp the shaft, to pull it free. Then his eyes roll back, and his body sags. Still upright, held suspended on that spear.

This can't be real. I must have hit my head when I fell, must have fallen into a dream, a nightmare. Otherwise, wouldn't I be screaming? Wouldn't I be sobbing, cursing, pleading with the gods to undo what has just happened? Wouldn't I feel something more than this cold numbness overtaking my body and soul?

Then suddenly, it's all there—all the horror, all the sorrow. It hits me at once. And I realize that I already am screaming, howling like a beast. Crawling across the space between me and Dire as tears pour down my face. I reach him and pull myself upright, struggling to breathe through my sobs. With a single kick, I break the spear shaft underneath him, catch his body and lower him to the ground. The rest of the shaft still protrudes from his chest.

His eyelids flutter. He's still alive.

"Dire!" I cry. "Dire, Dire!" I hate in that moment that I don't know any other name for him. I hate that even if he hears me, all he'll hear is the monster name given him by my grandmother.

A shadow passes over me. The heat of raw, red magic burns the back of my head. I twist, gazing up at the terrible image of Granny hovering overhead.

"Weep and sob, little girl." She spits the words cruelly. "It'll do him no good. Ultimately, this is the best end for him. He would never break his own curse, even when he knew how it could be broken." She draws her chin up, her lovely face rippling with red magic beneath the skin. "He chose this fate. He deserves it."

I stare at her, stare at that apparition. The glamours are strong, but she's losing her hold on them. I can see through the cracks to the old, haggard creature underneath. A shriveled husk, its outer shell of glory swiftly rotting away.

Granny meets my gaze. Hatred flares in her eye, and she begins to form another rune in the air. A third and final spear. This one intended for me.

Shuddering, I turn away from her. I'm too tired to run, too tired to play this game of cat and mouse. I gaze into Dire's face, drained of all color, framed by his long gray hair.

We're going to die. Together. In just another moment now. It will all be over.

"He can only be liberated when his heartsblood mingles with hers."

I frown. Why is that voice suddenly there in my head? That old voice, grumpy and uncaring and yet . . .

"Mingles with hers," I whisper.

An idea takes hold. But it's mad. Totally mad, ridiculous, insane. If I were in my right mind, I'd never think such a thing. But what does that matter now? There's no time left for anything other than madness.

Gritting my teeth, I grip the spear shaft and wrench it out of Dire's chest. Blood spurts from the wound, but I lay down across him, pressing my heart against that broken place where his once beat, wrapping my arms around him.

"I love you," I whisper in his ear. "I love—"

I don't get to finish.

Granny's spear pierces between my shoulder blades. Perfectly aimed, sharp and true, it slides through me, through Dire, and embeds in the ground beneath us.

The pain is more than I could ever have imagined. My body spasms. But somehow, even as a ragged scream tears from my throat, I manage to tighten my hold on Dire, to keep my face pressed into his neck and shoulder.

Darkness overwhelms me, full of endless agony. No, not endless . . . surely death will come soon! And in death, there must be some relief. The gods are too merciful to let this moment go on and on and on.

My heartsblood flows free. Flows from my chest into Dire's gaping wound. And even through the pain, I feel it, that moment of pure connection.

Then . . .

*Light.*

The world around me tears into tiny shreds, letting in another world full of pure, perfect light, brilliant with myriad colors for which I have no name. Magic rushes over me, floods into my body, my blood, my soul. Layer after layer of reality rips, and I fall, holding onto Dire, deeper and deeper.

No, wait. I'm not falling.

*I'm rising.*

Rising and whirling in a vortex full of inexplicable explosions of energy, color, and song. My senses are not enough to take it in, to comprehend any of this experience. Is this what dying is? Like a new birth, like coming out of closed darkness into sudden light and air? I'm terrified and exhilarated.

Somewhere, far away in another world, I hear a scream. Granny's scream.

A ripple of darkness rolls through the light and strikes me in an icy blast. I throw back my head, crying out at the pain. But I don't fall. I'm still held in that vortex. And now the light is sinking under my skin, burning. It's painful, but a glorious sort of pain that I could never begin to describe. It pours into me and then out again, through my mouth and eyes and nostrils.

Some small part of me is aware that I still cling to Dire's shoulders. That he is full of heat and burning as well. We are fusing together, becoming one. I'm breaking to pieces so that I can be remade whole. With him.

A final burst of light radiates through and around me. I'm sure I've broken into a million particles of stardust. But if that's true, how can I feel this sense of falling? Because I *am* falling now. Faster and faster, shooting back through all the layers of reality through which I've traveled. Then . . .

All is still. Calm. Quiet.

I open my eyes.

I lie in a world of whirling dust, broken stone, dead trees. Something warm and solid moves rhythmically under my ear. There's a dull *thud, thud, thud* that strikes me as the most beautiful sound I've ever heard, though in that moment, I couldn't say why.

Then I realize: it's a heartbeat.

"Dire?" I try to speak through cracked and blistered lips. "Dire, is that . . . are you . . . ?" I can't get the words out. I don't have the strength just yet. But it doesn't matter.

Nothing matters except the sudden feel of strong arms wrapping around me, holding me close.

## 32

## DIRE

I'm fairly certain I'm dead.

I must be. That spear pierced right through my heart, skewered me like a piece of meat. I passed through every level of agony imaginable, then on through a veil of light and darkness unlike anything I can describe. So, I must be dead. Right?

And this is . . . heaven?

I breathe in deep, inhaling that bouquet of pine and leather and honey that I always associate with Brielle. Brielle's arms are around me too, and I can feel her heartbeat thudding in rhythm with mine. But that's impossible. Because my heart was torn in two. I felt it tear.

I keep my eyes closed, my arms wrapped tightly around her thin, warm body. If this is heaven, I might as well enjoy it. No more curses. No more witches. No more hunts and blood and pain. Gods above, I'd be happy to simply lie here forever!

*Eadmund.*

I frown. Where did that thought come from?

*Eadmund.*

There it is again. A name. A strange name. A name I didn't know I knew until this moment.

*My name?*

I search deeper into my mind, down under that thought. There's another name as well, another name I'd thought lost forever—*Omylia.* The moment I think it, I see her face. That gentle smooth brow, those warm eyes, and that slow, shy smile which had once set my heart dancing.

*Omylia.* My first love.

I smile. The sorrow of her loss is still there. But it doesn't hurt like it once did. She's no longer lost so completely as she had been. I can see her now, not as the beast she became, but as the girl I once knew. And her name is sweet and pure and true. But . . .

She is no longer the one for whom my heart longs. Not now. Not in this time, this place. I may love her still. But it's a love of memory.

The love of *now* is here. In my arms.

It's in that moment that I realize I can't be dead. In fact, I am unexpectedly very much alive.

I open my eyes and am met by the sight of snarled red hair. There's a face snuggled up to my neck, tucked under my ear. "Brielle," I breathe.

She tenses. Then suddenly, she pushes upright, tossing hair back from her eyes, and stares down at me. For a long, long moment, we simply look at each other.

Then, with a little "Oh!" she catches my face with both hands and kisses me. A short, quick little peck, but I'm not ready to leave it at that. I pull her back down for another, deeper kiss. It's like a collision of hearts, an explosion of tremendous force that could shatter us both to our core. But in the wake of that shattering, we are made new. Whole.

She lifts her face at last, and I'm surprised to see tears spilling through her lashes. Funny . . . I'd never quite been able to imagine that fierce little face of hers with tears on her cheeks. I wipe them away gently with my thumb. She turns into the touch of my palm, and more tears fall on my hand, my face, my chest.

Then she looks down at me again. "I . . . I don't know . . . What is your name?"

I smile up at her, my heart soaring like a bird up into the clear blue sky. "I'm Eadmund."

She swallows hard, nods, and blinks out a last few stray tears. "Pleased to meet you, Eadmund," she says.

Then she kisses me again.

Sadly, we can't lie there forever. We're eventually obliged to get up and try to figure out what in the world has happened. Elorata

Dorrel's garden, which was already in shambles, is now blasted beyond recognition. The few remaining trees are flattened, the dead and dying shrubs turned to ash. Even the outer wall has been decimated, as though from an explosion.

An explosion that seems to have come from . . . us.

We stand at the epicenter of dark, scorched earth. Yet we are entirely unharmed.

Of Granny, there is no sign whatsoever. She seems to have been burned up with the rest of this place, evaporated. I remember hearing a final scream, but I'm not sure if it's a real memory or merely imagination.

"She's gone," Brielle says in answer to my unspoken question. She takes my hand and gives it a firm, confident squeeze. "Mother Ulla said Granny tied up too much of her power in your curse. She used her own heartsblood to make it, but when the curse was broken *not* in the way she intended, it broke her as well."

I'm not sure I understand this completely. I'm not even sure I want to. All I care about is that the curse is done for. And Brielle is beside me.

I look down at her. It's hard to see her in this light, for I no longer have my wolf senses to rely on, and the night is deepening fast. All that I can see for certain is that she's . . . well, naked. As am I. Breaking Granny's curse did not miraculously generate clothing for either of us.

I reach out and gently brush my fingertip across the scar I can just perceive on her pale chest. "Your blood," I whisper. "The blood you shared with her . . ."

Brielle nods slowly. "Mingled with yours," she answers softly.

Then she grips my hand and presses it harder against her beating heart. Her eyes seek mine, full of promise, full of need.

The distance between us closes easily. Our arms are meant to be around each other, our bodies, pressed together. Right there, right in the center of all that destruction. We have nothing anymore save each other. But that's more than enough for now. For always.

We can't very well go tromping through Whispering Wood unclothed as we are. When dawn arrives, we pick our way through the castle ruins, searching for anything that might serve as a covering. Brielle manages to scrounge up a ragged chemise and gown. I am less lucky. I find an old tablecloth and wrap it around my midsection. It'll have to do.

"First, we'll go back to Phaendar," I say, offering Brielle my hand as we climb out from among the ruins again. "It'll be a bit of a hike, but at least there we should be able to find proper clothing."

"Let's hope so!" Brielle mutters. She's somehow unearthed her bow and arrows and wears them slung over her shoulder. Regardless of whatever else she's wearing, she looks more complete with her weapons on hand. "And after that? What next?"

I smile and pull her toward me, dropping a quick kiss on her lips. "Well, if it's all the same with you . . . as soon as we're both decent, I think we ought to make our way back to Gilhorn and find ourselves a priest."

"A priest?" Brow furrowed, she shoots me a quick look. "Why a priest?"

"Because, to my understanding, when a man feels about a woman the way I feel about you, they get married."

She stares at me. Then her brow clears and her face breaks into a smile. "Married? After all that's just happened, I'm not sure a few vows spoken in front of a priest will make us any more, um, *bonded*."

"Perhaps not." I shrug. "But I'm old fashioned like that."

She tucks her body under my shoulder and wraps an arm around my waist. "You're very sure of yourself, Eadmund Phaendar. So, tell me, once we're married, what do you think will happen next?"

"I think," I say, resting my cheek against the top of her head, "that's when the real adventure begins."

## 33

### BRIELLE

I face the shadows of Whispering Wood, adjusting the strap of my quiver across my breast. Eadmund stands beside me. My husband.

My husband...

I still can't quite get over that idea.

We spent most of the day making our way back to Phaendar Hall. Even though it's been less than a day since Granny's death, the Wood has already gone wild and tangled without someone to guard it. I hope the witch coven will appoint a replacement soon, or there may be problems for Virra County.

As we travelled, we searched for some sign of the other two werebeasts but found nothing. I trust they were both liberated from their curses too. Even more, I hope they'll manage to make their way safely home.

I also kept my eyes peeled for some sign of the new apprentice, the one I kept from being cursed. But she's not here. Maybe Granny dismissed her after I destroyed her spell. She wouldn't have any use for the girl anymore, after all. Either way, I'll be certain to send a message to Mother Ulla, asking her to look into the matter.

Eventually, we found our way to Eadmund's old family home. It was already much more ruinous than when we last saw it, but we managed to find more suitable clothing. I even found a tunic that's only a *little* too big for me, and a pair of trousers I can belt comfortably enough. Not exactly bridal wear. But when I emerged in my new costume, Eadmund gave me an appraising once-over and smiled.

"No bride ever looked lovelier," he said.

At which I laughed outright.

We proceeded to Gilhorn from there and interrupted a priest just as he was sitting down to his dinner. With a little persuasion— and more than a little gold coin taken from the Phaendar vaults— we convinced him to perform a simple wedding ceremony. A local pig keeper and goose girl were brought in to bear witness.

It's funny, but when Eadmund took me in his arms at the end of the ceremony and kissed me, there was something a bit . . . different. Something sweeter. Deeper. I hadn't believed we could be more connected by a few simple vows, but apparently I was wrong.

There is nothing in this world quite like kissing *my husband*.

Now we stand together, facing the Wood. I turn a wry smile up at him, catching his eye. "Are you sure about this?"

"Very sure," he responds without hesitation.

"But you . . . you could have a life here. Now that Granny's gone, you might be able to get the other ward witches to help you reclaim Phaendar Hall. You could find your family, reestablish your place in the county."

He shakes his head. Though he tries to hide it, I see a gleam of sorrow in his eyes. But only a gleam. "That life is over," he says firmly. "Over and done. Twenty years done! Wherever my family is, they've moved on. There's no going back. Not for them, not for me." He lifts my hand to his lips and kisses my knuckles. "There's only going forward."

I purse my dry lips, then offer a smile in return before turning my gaze back to the Wood. All those deep, dark secrets that had once beckoned me so keenly beckon once more. I feel the same stirring in my blood that I knew as a child, urging me to plunge in over my head and take whatever adventure the gods deemed fit to send me.

"Lunulyr. Is that right?" Eadmund says. "That's what the fae woman told you—a Lord of Lunulyr has taken a Moonfire Bride?"

I nod. "It might be Valera. It *must* be."

He places a finger under my chin, turns my face to his. "Whether it's her or not, we'll find her. Together."

I couldn't stop the smile spreading across my face even if I tried. It doesn't matter how many perils stand between me and my sister now. I can't begin to guess the strange and wonderful worlds through which we'll have to pass, the paths we'll have to walk, the beings we'll have to face. Whatever comes, I'll face it all with Eadmund. My heart is bound to his, our heartsblood mingled.

Eyes dancing, I grip his hand hard. "Come on then!" I say and break into a run.

Together we plunge into the shadows of Whispering Wood, leaving behind the mortal world forever.

## ALSO BY SYLVIA MERCEDES

This arranged marriage romance about a human princess forced to wed a dark and desperate Shadow King is sure to entice!

Though she is the oldest daughter, Princess Faraine lives in the background, shunned from court and kept out of sight. Her chronic illness makes her a liability to the crown, and she has learned to give place to her beautiful, favored younger sister in all things.

When the handsome and enigmatic Shadow King comes seeking a bride, Faraine is not surprised that her sister is his choice.

Though not eager to take a human bride, King Vor is willing to do what is necessary for the sake of his people. When he meets the lively Princess Ilsevel, he agrees to a marriage.

So why can't he get the haunting eyes of her older sister out of his head?

The first book in a new fantasy romance series, this sweeping tale of love and betrayal is perfect for readers looking for a touch of spice to go with the sweet in their next swoony, slow-burn romance.

A CLEVER THIEF. A DISFIGURED MAGE.
A KISS OF POISON.

# THE SCARRED MAGE OF ROSEWARD

For fifteen years, Soran Silveri has fought to suppress the nightmarish monster stalking Roseward. His weapons are few and running low, and the curse placed upon him cripples his once unmatched power. Isolation has driven him to the brink of madness, and he knows he won't be able to hold on much longer.

When a sharp-tongued, uncouth, and undeniably beautiful young woman shows up on his shore, Soran resolves to drive her away. He won't be responsible for another death.

But Nelle is equally determined not to be frightened off by the hideously scarred mage. Not until she gets what she came for . . . .

Can two outcasts thrown together in a tangle of lies discover they are each other's only hope? Or will the haunted darkness of Roseward tear them apart?

*This romantic series about a mortal librarian and her dealings with a roguish fae prince will keep you turning pages late into the night!*

# ENTRANCED

## PRINCE OF THE DOOMED CITY:

### BOOK 1

Clara is an Obligate—an indentured servant of the fae. Serving out a fifteen-year sentence for a crime she doesn't remember committing, she spends her days working in the king's glorious library. Her only hope is to keep her head down, attract no attention, and survive to the end of her Obligation. Only then can she get home to her beloved brother.

But when the conniving Prince of the Doomed City arrives at court, all Clara's hopes are dashed. He is determined to buy her Obligation for his own dark purpose. And he doesn't care who gets in his way.

The only problem? He hates her. More than anyone else in all the worlds. But his hatred just might be the key to discovering why she was bound to this fate in the first place.

Can Clara recover her forgotten memories before the nightmares of her past return to claim her? Or will she be swallowed up by the darkness of the Doomed City and lost forever?

# ABOUT THE AUTHOR

SYLVIA MERCEDES makes her home in the idyllic North Carolina countryside with her handsome husband, numerous small children, and the feline duo affectionately known as the Fluffy Brothers. When she's not writing she's . . . okay, let's be honest. When she's not writing, she's running around after her kids, cleaning up glitter, trying to plan healthy-ish meals, and wondering where she left her phone. In between, she reads a steady diet of fantasy novels.

But mostly she's writing.

After a short career in Traditional Publishing (under a different name), Sylvia decided to take the plunge into the Indie Publishing World and is enjoying every minute of it. She's the author of the acclaimed Venatrix Chronicles, as well as The Scarred Mage of Roseward trilogy, and the fantasy romance, Bride of the Shadow King.

Made in United States
Troutdale, OR
03/01/2025